Praise for *Odessa, Odessa*

"The vivid events and rich details of the intricate story are compelling and important—immigrants like the Kolopskys helped make America into the land readers recognize today (Israel, too). Readers should understand more of their world at the end of this engrossing novel than they did when they began it . . . A complex but rewarding epic of family ties, fading memories, and immigrants who—through hard work and luck—better the lives of their progeny."

—*Kirkus Reviews*

"Grounded in meticulous reconstruction of time and place and rich with memorable characters—a story with an evocative echo of biblical sibling rivalry—we enjoy decades of an immigrant family and a revelation when American sisters travel to Israel to meet a distant cousin and share histories that propelled their long-estranged kinfolk through time and tumult."

—Belle Elving, Writer, Development at National Public Radio

"Artson's mastery over the details and nuances of the lives she creates, and her sense of the history that surrounds them, show her to be a writer of depth and sensitivity."

—Melanie Sperling, Professor Emerita,
University of California, Riverside

"*Odessa, Odessa* is a vivid immigrant journey of tragedy and triumphs that keeps us engaged until the unexpected and tearful, but optimistic and poignant, ending."

—Dr. Linda Tucker, best-selling author of
At a Crossroads: Finding the Right Psychotherapist
and host of the podcast *Challenge Your Thinking*

"As Artson lovingly shakes the family tree, easily-relatable relatives fall out that readers will fall in love with. A visual writer, she creates scenes worthy of a movie adaptation. Steven Spielberg, are you listening?"

—Ruthe Stein, *San Francisco Chronicle*
Senior Movie Correspondent

"This story of family exodus into the wider world illuminates both the cultural and political freedoms and constraints that shape and re-shape the quiet dignity of ordinary and striving lives."

—Sandra Butler, co-author of *It Never Ends:
Mothering Middle-Aged Daughters*

"Barbara Artson's novel speaks to the human spirit, and to its resilience and courage under oppression....A story from 100 years ago, *Odessa, Odessa* is a haunting reminder of the struggles endured by refugees--even in the twenty-first century."

—Rabbi Michael Lerner, editor of Tikkun, chair of the Network of Spiritual Progressive, and author of *Revolutionary*

"This far-reaching novel of epic proportions chronicles three generations of a Jewish family: from the shtetl near Odessa in Western Russia, to an immigrant community in New York, and finally on a journey to Israel in 1996 to meet long-lost cousins and solve an enduring family mystery. Artson vividly evokes the immigrant experience of coming through Ellis island and trying to create a new life in the United States in the early years of the 20th century. A poignant story, full of unforgettable characters and rich historical details."

—Barbara Ridley, author of *When It's Over*

"This passionately and artfully told tale reminds us of the courage of people who leave their past, their families, their culture and their lives behind for the hope and promise of a new world, the America that was, and remains, a beacon of freedom, opportunity and hope to dreamers world-wide."

—Frederick R. Levick, CEO, Ramah Darom

"This well researched novel brings alive a century of time from the world of Jews in a small village in eastern Europe, to the teeming streets of Brooklyn, to the bedroom communities of New Jersey and finally to modern day Israel. *Odessa, Odessa* is a moving testimony to the complicated legacy of trauma born of genocidal persecution, skillfully told through the interweaving lives of a very human, relatable family."

—Barbara Stark-Nemon, author of *Even in Darkness*

"A beautifully written story which takes the reader on an emotional journey filled with insights into the experiences of all who have endured hardship and persecution."

—J. L. Witterick, International Best Selling Author
of *My Mother's Secret*

"Barbara Artson's debut novel, *Odessa, Odessa*, is a beautifully written tale of a Russian Jewish family's immigration and assimilation into American culture. Artson seamlessly weaves various storylines of the Kolopsky family back and forth in time to create a rich tapestry of historical detail and authentic dialogue that leaves the reader craving more. A stunning achievement!"

—Michelle Cox, Acclaimed author of
the Henrietta and Inspector Howard series

ODESSA,
ODESSA

ODESSA, ODESSA

A NOVEL

BARBARA ARTSON

She Writes Press, a BookSparks imprint
A Division of SparkPointStudio, LLC.

Published 2018
Printed in the United States of America

ISBN: 978-1-63152-443-1 pbk
ISBN: 978-1-63152-444-8 ebk
Library of Congress Control Number: 2018939231

For information, address:
She Writes Press
1563 Solano Ave #546
Berkeley, CA 94707

She Writes Press is a division of SparkPoint Studio, LLC.

This is a work of fiction. All incidents, characters, and dialogue, with the exception of some well-known historical events, are products of the author's imagination and are not to be construed as real. In all other respects, any resemblance to persons living or dead is entirely coincidental.

Immigrants Arriving in New York City, 1987 Engraving

They gave so much to their new country in music,
literature, the sciences, and the arts—the immigrants.

I dedicate this book to immigrants of all races and
creeds, and to my children, Tracy and Bradley Artson,
the offspring of those audacious people and
the most precious of my creative accomplishments.
We are all immigrants.

Emma Goldman's exposition on variants of patriotism excerpted from her 1917 trial for challenging mandatory conscription during the First World War.
(Source: The Emma Goldman Papers)

We love America, we love her beauty, we love her riches, we love her mountains and her forests, and . . . we love the dreamers and the philosophers and the thinkers who are giving America liberty. But that must not make us blind to the social faults of America. That cannot make us deaf to the discords of America.

—*Emma Goldman*

CONTENTS

III: BACK TO THE BEGINNING

CAST OF CHARACTERS

FIRST GENERATION:

Rabbi Yonkel Israel and Adina Kolopsky	Mendel's father and mother
Mendel Kolopsky	1865 Rebbe, and husband of Henya
Henya Chanah	1867 Wife of Mendel, a rebbetzin
Shimson Kolopsky (Samson, Samuel, Shmuel Keter)	1862 Eldest brother of Mendel
Moishe Kolopsky	1863 Middle brother of Mendel, moves to Boston

SECOND GENERATION: MENDEL & HENYA'S CHILDREN

Faigel (Faye)	1891 Eldest child, a daughter
Yosef Bifson (Joseph/Joe)	Faigel's husband
Levi (Leon)	1893 Second child
Shmuel (Stewart)	1896 Third child
Yonkel	1899 Child, a son, who lives one week
Avram (Abe)	1900 Fourth child
Dora (Disha)	1904 Fifth child, mother of Hannah and Roberta
Saul Sussman	Dora's husband, father of Hannah and Roberta
Sadie	Saul's aunt, Dora's coworker
Hannah Sussman	Saul's mother
Freddy Cohen	Dora's first boyfriend
Minnie	Dora's girlfriend

Leib (Lenny)	1906 Sixth child
Marya	1909 Youngest child, a daughter
Bessie Geisman	Henya's shipboard friend and Dora's friend
Max Baline	Bessie's husband

THIRD GENERATION:

Hannah Sussman (Hindel Hyah)	Dora and Saul's oldest daughter
Bert Zimmerman	Hannah's husband
Roberta Sussman (Beulkah)	Dora and Saul's youngest child
Jerome Schwartz	Roberta's first husband
Richard Boswell	Roberta's second husband

THIRD GENERATION IN ISRAEL:

Reuben and Rivka Keter	Roberta and Hannah's cousins, Shimshon's grandchildren
Shoshanna	Reuben and Rivka's children
Hadar	
Zechariah	
Tamir	
Nehemia	
Batya	
Da'oud	Reuben's Palestinian friend

FOURTH GENERATION IN ISRAEL:

Yaa'kov	Shimshon's (Samuel Keter's) great-grandson

ARRIVAL IN THE UNITED STATES:

1910: Faigel arrives in the United States; she is almost nineteen.

1913: Mendel, forty-seven, arrives in January with Levi, nineteen, and Shmuel, sixteen.

1914: Henya, forty-six, arrives in November with Avram, thirteen; Dora, ten; Leib, seven; and Marya, five.

I. THE BEGINNING

Chapter 1

HENYA CHANAH: KILL THE YIDS

October 1908/1909

Henya Chanah is a woman who no longer bleeds, so she puzzles over how this could have happened. Try as she might, she can't remember the last time she and Mendel were together. *We must have been,* she thinks, *otherwise how could this be?* She smiles, thinking of how he touched her when they were younger, but now?

The results of his touching were Faigel and Levi, followed by Shmuel and Avram, all born by her thirty-third year. There was a respite of four years—not counting the one who died a week after his birth—followed by Disha and, two years later, by Leib. Henya can't recall a time when there wasn't a babe sucking at her breast and one, two, or three toddlers tugging at the hemline of her skirt, all pleading for attention. God knows, there was little enough to go around. And now, thinking another might be on its way, her heartbeat races, knowing full well the pressing burden of yet another mouth to feed.

Without room enough for the children already born, she frets about where she will put this one. She frets about her languishing strength. She frets about whether—not whether but when—the

1

Cossacks will make another unwelcome visit. The violence against Jews since the czar's murder in 1881 leaves the community's nerves raw. And the peasant horde, encouraged by the authorities eager to reassign blame for the country's abominable conditions, even for the pogroms, points the finger at the Yids. Always the Yids. There is nothing Henya can do about her fears, so, as the practical woman she is, she turns to those concerns she can do something about. "It's God's will; I'll put the baby in our room," she determines.

With barely enough to keep her family dressed and with food in their stomachs, she worries whether her milk will last. "It was plenty before," she reassures herself, "but now, at my age?" She worries, too, about whether she can survive another labor, recalling the last, when she almost died.

One day in November of the previous year, as she folded laundry, stiff and damp from the blistering winter weather, Henya caught sight of her hazy image in the mottled mirror that hangs above the threadbare couch, a hand-me-down from Mendel's family, and startled when she saw what looked to be the very likeness of her mother.

"Mama?" she murmured in disbelief. "Can that be you?"

But when the question remained unanswered, she asked herself, "Who is that old lady staring back at me? I look just like Mama before she died." She shook her head from side to side as if to drive the reflection out of her rattled brain and then withdrew her gaze and vowed to take better care of herself, knowing full well that she wouldn't. And couldn't.

"What difference does it make? I never was a beauty anyway, and Mendel loved me then. So stop already with your fussing," she whispered, not wanting to awaken her sleeping husband.

Henya has little time to preen in the morning. Her day begins before the cock crows and the sun rises. Today, she haphazardly arranges her thinning, dappled salt-and-pepper hair into a bun at the nape of her neck, held together with oversized hairpins. Then, she dons her sheitel, the wig for married Orthodox women, and tucks a strand of stray hair behind her ear. She hastily steps into the dark muslin duster she routinely places on the chair before falling, exhausted, into bed and hurries to the kitchen to set water on the stove to boil in time for the children's wakening.

She is a short, large-featured woman with heavy eyebrows that frame her large brown eyes, and although passably attractive in her youth, she has been worn down by a life of devotion to others' needs. Everyone's demands, stated and unstated, she places before her own. Henya is the first one that neighbors turn to when sick or in need of extra oats or barley or wood or coal, or counsel, or water when winter limits their sparing supply. After all, she is the Rebbe Mendel's wife, and that's what a rebbetzin must do.

She loves and respects Mendel, a good but difficult man, who, as the wise man of the shtetl and teacher of young boys, totally devoted to the study of Torah, has little time to help with the children or the daily round of domestic chores. Nor should he, she feels. He has more important things to do. It's not that she feels her role insignificant; it's just not for a rebbe to do what she does. She was raised to know that the life of a rebbe is one of contemplation, meditation, study, and prayer and to know it is a woman's place to attend to her husband's needs.

Growing up, she witnessed her mother performing the same routine. And at fourteen, when her mother died, Henya stepped in to fill the void. She cooked and cleaned and attended to the vegetable garden and cared for her father and younger siblings. No one had to ask; she knew her duty then, and she knows it now.

She gets little help from her three older children, who are seldom around when she needs them. Faigel, the oldest of the brood, spends most of the day with Yosef, her boyfriend, when she could be home helping Henya. For the most part, Henya accepts her lot in life without complaint, but at times she wonders what it would have been like if she had been allowed to study Torah, or at least learned how to read. She recalls how she would sit outside of her father's crowded study, littered with books, listening enraptured as he attempted to enlighten her brothers or the eager young scholars who came to their home to learn.

It's October. Henya's thoughts drift to the approaching Russian winter and to the wind that rips across the Pale of Settlement, to the pogroms, and to the cramped quarters in which they live. She ponders the lack of water that will come with the hoarfrost. Then, the water in the well that serves the shtetl is a frozen, glacier-like mass and leaves the residents without enough of that precious liquid. No water for bathing, little for cooking, and none to wet one's cracking lips. She sighs as she thinks of springtime, when the water carrier delivers fresh water daily from home to home, which she scoops from a large wooden pail that hangs precariously from a slender pole resting on his broad, muscular shoulders. *A nice but simple man*, she thinks.

In November, when the river freezes over, Henya will daily direct one of the older boys to cut a square of ice that she will place in a cooking vessel over the stove to melt but will supply barely enough water for cooking. The shortage of wood and coal makes it hard to get out of bed in the morning, especially for the younger children. At times, in the middle of the day, she will put them to bed to keep their lips from chattering and their limbs from turning blue. This, she reminds herself, is her life and her mother's life and, before that, her grandmother's life.

Is it any wonder, she thinks, *that the little ones wet the bed at night? Who wants to go outside to pish in the hut when it's warm under the blankets, their little bodies huddled together? I'm used to it, but they shouldn't know of such tsuris.*

Their home is confined. The older boys, Levi, Shmuel, and Avram, sleep on one side of the larger bedroom, while the girls, Faigel and Disha and little Leib, sleep on the other side, partitioned by a worn-out sheet. There is a second bedroom, smaller by half, shared by Mendel and Henya, its cardboard-thin wall separating them from the children's bedroom. Aside from a kitchen—if one could call the closet-sized alcove located in the living room a kitchen—with its diminutive window facing the porch, there is a tiny sitting room. There, a couch and several chairs rest on a once-colorful rug covering the irregular, planked wooden floor.

Faigel, at eighteen, is thirteen years older than Disha and fifteen years older than Leib. She vehemently and frequently vents her resentment at having to share a room with the *kinder* and at being her mother's slave, as she calls it. She hates it that the older boys get away with avoiding most chores. She hates their privileged position based solely on being a boy. Often, she threatens to move in with Yosef and his parents, who live a mile or two away, or marry and move to America. Although desperate to escape the degradation she experiences in such constrained quarters, not to speak of the constant bedlam of her home, her outbursts mostly serve to irritate her father and to rid herself of the pent-up rage toward her oppressive life. "All he wants are future rabbis to bear his name," she protests to her mother.

Mendel, out of helplessness, retaliates with threats of his own; he calls her a *nafka,* a whore.

"If it's privacy you want," he rants, "I'll show you privacy, your high and mighty czarina. You bring shame upon my head with your big mouth. Move in with Yosef? Over my dead body you'll move in with Yosef. You think it's better at his place with their nine kids? Better you should be helping your mother."

Only to himself does Mendel acknowledge that this is no life for a girl of marriageable age. He knows it isn't good for her to sleep with the younger children, but she certainly can't sleep in the same room with the older boys. At times he notices Avram looking at Faigel in a way that makes his skin shiver. *She should have her own room*, he thinks, but then quickly reverses himself mid-thought to eradicate the pain of knowing there is nothing to be done.

Mendel grows increasingly aggravated when his ruminations turn to whispered rumors that young men—even Jews—are being conscripted into the Russian Army for twenty-five years. His own sons will go, and even Yosef, so who can blame her for wanting to go to America? *Wouldn't I go myself if I had the money?* His obstinacy keeps him from apologizing to Faigel after his heated outbursts, so when next he sees her, his remorse comes as a pat on her head.

He determines, once again, to write to his two-years-older brother, Moishe, in America, to ask for money to make the crossing. Yes, it would mean leaving Henya and the younger children behind, but he thinks it would be better than being here, and besides, with the gelt you make in the new country, it would take a short time for him to send for the rest of his family and to repay his brother. The older children could work, and he could get a job as a teacher, and then as a rabbi in a small synagogue, they could start their life anew.

Faigel never fulfills her oft-declared threat to live with Yosef, but she will leave for the new world in little over a year, where she and Yosef will claim their new American identities as Mr. and Mrs. Joseph and Faye Bifson. From their tiny apartment on the Lower East Side, they will work conscientiously with the cast-off sewing machine Joseph at first borrows and then buys from his boss—a landsman from Odessa—and then two, three, and four more, stitching elastic to the waistbands of ladies' bloomers. Joseph will work at his boss's factory during the day and return home to toil well into the night with his wife by his side. No one will imagine that this small venture, begun with the labor of Faigel and Yosef's needle-pricked fingers, will grow into a thriving enterprise that eventually will employ more than thirty people, one of whom will be little Disha.

For the first several months, Henya refuses to admit that she might be pregnant. She goes to great lengths to avoid accepting that possibility. She attributes her lethargy and weight gain to getting old. By this age, she reminds herself, most of her friends had stopped bleeding, and some had even passed on. One of her sisters has already died from cholera and a brother from tuberculosis, both before their fiftieth birthday. And her dear mother, blessed be her name, was forty-four when she died from a growth that ravished her guts.

In early January, when the bump begins to show, she dwells on the likelihood a tumor might be growing and that she, like her mother, will die from it, leaving her young children to fend for themselves. She tries to convince herself that, should it occur—*nisht duggehdacht*, may it never happen—Faigel is old enough to take care of them. She finds it hard to admit that, of all her children, Faigel is the least likely to sacrifice herself for anything or anyone. It is also hard to admit that, although she admires her resolve, she also dislikes this child. She only thinks of herself, Yosef, and how she looks. On the other hand, who can blame her? She is young, strong, and ambitious. Who wouldn't want a better life?

At times, Henya thinks that Faigel, with her mulish determination to succeed, her keen intelligence, her way with words, should have been a man. *She thinks she is tougher than Shmuel— or Levi, for that matter. Or me.* It's no wonder Faigel and Disha, as young as she is, don't get along—sisters, but already so different.

When Henya begins to feel the familiar stretching movements that ripple across her belly like the sands gusting effortlessly across the desert, she can no longer attribute it to her mother's deadly disease or to the flagging flesh of aging. The reality sinks in with both relief and dread. She is forced to accept what she had been trying not to know, pushing the thought away whenever it crept in, that she is with child. Or, as Mendel would say, "in a delicate condition." Yes, another mouth to feed. She puts off telling Mendel for fear he might blame her for being careless, but when she finally gets up the nerve to reveal her situation, he takes delight in the disclosure.

"Mazel tov!" he proclaims, exhilarated by his prowess in being able to impregnate his wife. He chuckles as he imagines announcing the news to the ten men in his minyan.

"It's a blessing from God, you know. Besides, for every Jew they kill, those murderers, we must make two or three," he tells his wife. "Like the Maccabees, we must fight until our dying breath. We should name him Yehudah, after our brave leader. What do you think?"

Privately, he worries for his wife and the burden she faces; he tries to appear hopeful about the inevitable event to ease her mind. His real concern is for her strength and what another long labor might do to her health. *She could die*, he thinks, recalling the last near-death one. *Or the child could die. Not another death, dear God Almighty. I couldn't take it.* He shudders and then shakes his head, as if to purge the dreadful thoughts from his mind.

When his wife's fears or the racket from the younger children's encounters intensify or his own despair is too much for him to endure, he puts on his heavy overcoat and ventures outside to return to the respite of the shul, where, in spite of the cracks in the walls and fractured window panes, he finds solace. There, he experiences the comforting embrace of God. There, his head ceases to throb with his own anguish about his family's future or making it through yet another winter season or when, or whether, they will get to America.

Of course he'd say he's happy, Henya notes silently. *What else could he say? And with his head always in the books, studying and praying and making up lessons for his students, it's more work for me.* She was released from her apprehension, however, when his reaction was one of pride rather than the expected disapproval.

Fate robs Mendel of a future Talmud scholar or a Maccabean namesake to destroy Jewish enemies. Instead, the child is a girl, born in May, a month prematurely, and weighing a mere four pounds—a frail but beautiful and healthy child with starry blue eyes and pale, lucent skin. She easily slips out of her mother's womb, moments after Henya's contractions begin. This child, unlike her brothers and sisters with their dense, dark, curly hair, wears a wispy cap of wheat-colored silk. She is a mellow child who rarely cries unless hungry or sleepy or wet, but even when she does, her protests are plaintive, catlike mewls, not the demanding wail of her older siblings.

Henya is forty-two in May, when Maryusa Freide is born. They fall into calling her Marya shortly after her birth, to go with her diminutive size. The midwife who delivered all of Henya and Mendel's children—even Yonkel, the boy who died—calls Marya a change-of-life baby.

"It's not so unusual. I've seen it time and again," she explains, "even though you've stopped bleeding. Who knows how? All I know is it happens. But look, this one seems different from the others. I'm not exactly superstitious," she says, taking a pinch of salt and throwing it over her shoulder, "but there is something different about her. Her eyes, so blue and sad and piercing and expressive. Look."

Henya looks deeply into her child's eyes—the bluest of blues, like the cobalt waters of the Black Sea—but all she sees is blind trust and unrelenting demands.

"I predict," the midwife continues, "that she will bring great happiness and, sorry to say, great sorrow into your life. So vulnerable, so innocent, so beautiful."

Henya sees the inexplicable quality of which the midwife speaks, and she also knows in her *kishkas* that she is the one to nurse and nourish and keep her warm. And safe. She is the one to bear the bittersweet joy and burden that comes with maternal love.

Marya is quick to laugh but only when Disha or Leib gather around her worn straw sleeping basket waving colorful rags fashioned into dolls, or when they make funny faces or whirl her round and round in their arms. The older children, bored with yet another dependent infant that curtails their activities, pay her scant attention. Rather, they mostly express disgust with their parents' behavior as they gossip among themselves.

"Pick up the baby! Change her diapers! Give her some fresh air! How many times must I go through this," badgers Faigel. "Imagine," she bitterly protests to Levi. "First she walks around with a belly the size of a mountain, and now she sits nursing her baby with her shriveled breasts hanging down to her *pupik* like deflated balloons. It's so disgusting. Better it should be me."

In time, Mendel shows his disenchantment with "yet another girl" by simply ignoring her, which is easy for him to do. But Henya, of course, cannot. After the first month or so, she senses that something is not quite right. Marya seems much too placid, too unengaged with her surroundings, unless one of the children entertains her. She doesn't turn her head when a loud noise sounds, nor does she respond to the *toomel* in their crowded home or to the constant clank of street noise. Nothing disturbs her sleep.

When Henya finally confides her concern to Mendel, he tries to allay her qualms with stern words of advice and a dismissive flourish of his hand.

"Don't trouble your head. She eats. She sleeps. She's a good baby. What do you expect, she should be reciting Torah? Be glad we don't have another Faigel to talk our ears off with her nagging and dreams of going to America."

He reassures her that God will take care of their little Marya. And then he turns back to his prayers or to his books or to his lesson plans. But when he puts aside those diversions, he too is uneasy. He catches himself thinking that God didn't watch over his Yonkel, so how can he be so sure he will protect Marya? He has bigger concerns to take care of, doesn't he?

Marya begins to walk at thirteen months of age. She never crawls, except, for a while, backward. One day, to everyone's astonishment, she just pulls herself up, tentatively takes a step or two, then, with outstretched arms, she toddles toward her father, shrieking with joy in her newfound ability.

"There. You see?" Mendel chides Henya as he watches his baby's accomplishment. "Nothing to worry about. Come to Papa, my *shayna meydeleh*!" She falls just short of her destination, but Mendel swoops her up in his arms and dances her around the room. Henya experiences a warm contentment creeping to her extremities; her previous doubts about Mendel's love for his daughter disappear like the melting snow when spring arrives.

Several weeks later, a new worry appears. "Yes, it's late for her to talk," Faigel says to her mother, "but didn't some of the others talk late? First, it's crawling, and now you're carrying on that she's not talking. Mama, what will you find to worry about next? Leib talked late and Avram didn't make a sound until he was two and a half. And he should only shut his mouth now." She pauses and then continues, "So tell me, Mama, do you remember how old I was when I talked or walked? Probably not. Who pays attention to me anyway? I'm just the old doormat who's been here forever."

Henya's agitation has increased with each passing month without the words she longs to hear from Marya's mouth. Once again, she voices her concern to Faigel. "She doesn't talk, not a word. No ma-ma, no pa-pa. Only those sounds, like she is gargling."

"Mama, this is the way I think about it. Everyone talks for her, so she doesn't have to say *bubkis* to get what she wants. With the rest of us, we had to talk or go without. She whines and you're there with your breast or food or a clean rag when she goes *kaki*. Do you ever worry about me? So let me tell you right now that before winter begins, this time for real, I'm going to America with Yosef, and Papa had better start making plans too. He keeps delaying, but every day there's another death or beating or rape. Can't you see there are warning signs all around us? Please, Mama, for once, listen to me. And with Easter coming, you know what happens. The goyim's favorite time for pogroms."

"Faygela, Faygela," Henya cajoles, employing the Yiddish diminutive for *little bird*.

When she feels compassion for her oldest child, she reverts to Faigel's childhood name, although she is anything but a little bird. More like a raucous crow. *Who does she take after? Not me,* she thinks, *or her father. Maybe Mendel's brother, Shimshon, who was disowned by his father. Dead, gone, never heard from again, like he never lived.* What she is thankful for is knowing that no matter what— sparrow, crow, or eagle—her little bird will survive and thrive.

Left alone, Henya tries to convince herself that Faigel is right. She reasons that she is smart, maybe too smart for her own good. Almost nineteen, and she's already making plans. *But she has a good head on her shoulders. And she's right—I do dwell on things too much.*

When her apprehension about Marya comes back—and it always does— she confides in Shmuel, the most sensitive of her children. Unlike Faigel, who scolds, or sullen Avram, who rattles the delicate walls when he slams the door on his way out, or Levi, who, like his father, reassures her and then returns to his books, Shmuel takes her in his arms and dances her around the small boundaries of the front room until they are both dizzy and bumping into the walls. Whether he is making somersaults on the floor and crashing into furniture or doubling the size of his kinky mass of black curls, running his fingers through his hair as he leaps up and down—arms flailing, whooping, monkey-like—his antics always lighten her mood. With him, she forgets her anguish and remembers how to laugh.

"What would I do without my Shmuel?" Henya muses.

On Easter Sunday, after supper, as Henya is bathing Marya in the tin tub, the Cossacks turn up without warning. The neighing of horses announces their arrival. In their bedroom, Mendel had wrapped himself in his tallit in preparation for his nightly prayer. Henya stands petrified, like a statue, barely breathing, so to translate the commotion coming from the streets. She hears the shouting of gruff male voices speaking Russian, the screams of women, the menace of barking dogs. She hears the blast of a musket. She hears doors being smashed. She commands her paralyzed body to move. She lifts Marya from the pan of hot, soapy water and wraps her in a towel. She gives her a sugar stick to suck.

"*Sha. Sha* still, my little one. Mendel! Mendel, come quick. God almighty, there's trouble! Bolt the door." She shouts orders like a general. Mendel obeys and then pushes the couch in front of the door.

When she hears the shrieks coming closer, she hollers, "Get Disha and Leib out of bed! Hide them under the floorboards. Where is Faigel? *Gottenyu*, another pogrom."

The thump of heavy-booted footsteps, the cries of terror, the thunder of horses' hooves close in. She shushes Marya again despite her silence.

"We're going to play a little game, *mamaleh*. Mama is going to play peek-a-boo, and you must be very, very quiet. Quiet, *mein kinde*," she gestures, putting her finger to her mouth.

Outside, the Cossacks drunkenly shatter windows and furniture and send kerosene lamps, with their scalding liquid, airborne; they set dwellings on fire with the toss of a match. Homes turn into gray, powdery rubble in minutes. They drag men, mostly the old and feeble, barefooted and in nightshirts, out of their homes. They tug at the young men's beards and side locks; they snigger as they rip yarmulkes off the heads of their victims, who try in vain to cover their bare skulls with their hands. They fire their muskets in the air for fun. They laugh as old ladies cower in the corners of their dwellings.

They throttle anyone bold enough to protest or anyone who dares to try to protect their families. With their knives, they butcher the few castaway dogs that wander in the neighborhood. They rape young girls and old women alike, toss children to the ground, and burn siddurs, all the while chanting their mantra, "Kill the Goddamn kikes! Kill the Yids! They killed our Savior."

Shmuel and Avram escape detection by hiding in a potato bin, but the soldiers pummel Levi as he walks home from cheder, head in the holy book. They heave Mendel to the floor and kick him in the ribs when he bars their way into his home. He holds them off long enough for Henya to hide sleeping Marya under a pile of dirty laundry and then collapses to the floor in agony, holding his bruised ribs. He tries to retrieve the yarmulke that has fallen from his head. A Cossack steps on Mendel's wrist with his heavy boots.

"My God, my God, why have you forsaken me?" he moans.

The screams and cries of terror, the stench of smoke and the burning of sacred prayer books, the river of blood, the barricaded doors and windows caving in to the invader's powerful fists and clubs bring confusion and dread to all but Marya, who sleeps peacefully in her little wicker basket, concealed beneath a pile of dirty laundry and still sucking her sugar stick.

Henya knows now, without a doubt, that her baby girl is deaf.

Chapter 2

MENDEL: I AM NOT MY BROTHER'S KEEPER

February 1909

Mendel's footsteps crunch as he blindly battles his way, shoulders hunched, against the gale-force winds slapping his face with hardened snow crystals. Escaping tears turn quickly into pendants of ice strung from his beard, like toy icicles suspended from the eaves of a dollhouse.

Winters in the Pale of Settlement are savage, especially in Odessa, where temperatures plummet to well below zero. Odessa is in the southernmost region of the Pale, a vast expanse established by Catherine the Great in 1791 to geographically restrict the hundreds of thousands of Jews brought to Russia after the partition of Poland.

Residents lack firewood, coal, water, and, for some, the protective covering of an intact roof. Deaths of the elderly and infants occur daily, at times without notice or remark. People learn to harden their hearts when tragedy strikes. And it does. What else can they do but bear it?

With gloved hands tucked into the pockets of his black frock coat, Mendel passes a small circle of mourners, men and women, struggling to dig a hole in the frozen ground to bury the small pine box containing the still-warm remains of their dear one.

"Ahhh, a child," he whispers to himself, observing the miniature casket, "another child. Dear God, when does it end? And yet . . . and yet it could have been my Leib. Or Disha. So I should feel lucky." He pauses. "I say lucky? How many years since I lost my Yonkel. Ten years he's been in the ground. Who knows, maybe he's better off. For us, we watch our children go hungry, go to bed with cold feet, teeth chattering, no books to read, brutality and fear all around. So maybe it's a blessing to die before we know such heartache."

On the canvas of his mind, Mendel envisions his infant son, who died in 1899, a year before Avram's birth. He named him Yonkel Israel after his beloved father, Rabbi Yonkel Israel Kolopsky. Little Yonkel's fragile life lasted a mere week. He died cradled in his father's arms, his wife still recovering from the arduous birth, her womb ripped open like a tattered purse. No matter how much time passes, Mendel will never rid himself of that memory—a memory etched in stone on his soul. Nor will the sorrow that permeates his heart abate.

Henya endured an unsparing labor of seventy-two never-ending hours. With each passing day, her moans diminished in intensity until she lay pale and depleted, with hardly the strength to open her eyes, much less push the child out into the world. The midwife, like the hand of God, reached into Henya's ineffectual womb to rescue him from the dark abyss of certain death. A reprieve of seven days.

Mendel remained by his wife's side. Sleepless. He prayed night and day, swaying to and fro, holding Yonkel to his chest as he would a sacred Torah scroll. Despite his petition and promises to God, one week to the day after his entry into the world, with just enough time for the village carpenter to construct the diminutive burial box, they laid their infant son to rest as the shadows that heralded Shabbos shrouded them.

The sound of scraping earth jolts Mendel from his painful reminiscence to the reality of the present. Although halting to help the mourners will make him late for Shabbos service, Mendel pries a shovel from an elderly man's palsied fingers and joins the grieving relatives as they race the setting sun. He ruminates about why death seems to arrive just as Shabbos beckons.

Maybe, he muses, *it makes us more aware of the brevity of life. Not to take the gift of life for granted. Or reminds us that God is showing us that he is all-powerful and that we are only his servants to do his bidding. He gives us life in the blink of an eye and takes it back with another.*

Physical labor serves to ease the pain Mendel feels whenever images of his dead child crash the protective barrier of unconsciousness—just as his philosophizing keeps him from feeling the magnitude of his loss or the reality of his helplessness. He continues the sad task at the gravesite, helps the men lower the casket into the breach, and awakens from his trance when the sound of gravel striking the wooden coffin eases.

His thoughts wander to Henya. He broods about her health of late, for she seems removed and irritable, so unlike her typically sweet demeanor.

My wife is truly an aishet chayil, *a woman of valor*, he reflects. In his mind's eye, he sees the thickening of her waist but dismisses his ruminations and the thought that she might be in a delicate condition. *It's ridiculous*, he convinces himself, *the fantasy of an old man, that's all it is. Lunacy, definitely. Mendel the lunatic, that's me.* He chuckles and reminds himself of the passing time.

With his toil at an end, he plants the shovel into the ground with the sense of satisfaction he experiences after fulfilling one of God's six hundred and thirteen commandments, mitzvoth. He seldom misses an opportunity.

Mendel's faith rarely wavers, not even when he lost Yonkel Israel.

The Shabbos following his son's death, Mendel wrote an elegy that he delivered to his congregation:

Woe, woe, woe is me for my anguish

    My ruination is as vast as the earth that covers my precious son, as vast as the sky that covers the earth, as vast as the oceans that cover the world.

    My dear beloved is taken from me, never to be held in his mother's arms again.

    My small child, my little Yonkel, is no more, for the Lord has taken him.

    I am stalked by sorrow and darkness in my soul.

    Only the pain of loss and mourning remain. Desolation and thoughts of

Death haunt me.

    Woe is me for to have gazed at his sweet face, to see the face of G-d.

    From my arms to Yours, Dear G-d, please hold him there with You, in peace, forever until I join him.

He shakes his head to disrupt the dread he feels overtaking him and takes his leave of the lamenting mourners to make his way to the crushed rock path leading to the modest wooden structure that serves as a synagogue. He contemplates a time when he can worship in a suitable house of God. He often catches himself conjuring up, as a composer might hear a piece of music before it is notated, an edifice to house God's music.

"Nothing fancy," he tells himself, "but still, a sanctuary with a bimah and an ark for the Torah, one with carved doors. And an eternal lamp. A real shul with heat and a *mechitza*, to separate the women and men. A place safe from those butchers. They should only die! *Plotz!*" He recoils in horror as he hears the venom spewing from his lips.

"What am I doing, blaspheming on the Sabbath? Look what this violence turns people into. Me, a rabbi who should know better. Full of bitterness and hate on Shabbos, God forgive me." After a pause he whispers, a smile creeping to his lips, "And yet, a safe, warm shul would be very nice."

Mendel's reveries are interrupted when he glimpses, protruding from the snow-covered ground, one corner of the triangle of the six-pointed star he himself had recently nailed to the lintel, now desecrated with shit.

A murderous rage blurs his vision and clouds his mind. Feeling lightheaded, he leans against the doorjamb to regain his balance. He weeps. He weeps for his people, he weeps for the mourners, he weeps for his family, he weeps for Yonkel, and he weeps for himself. He retrieves the *Mogen David,* rubs it with unspoiled snow, and touches it with his kissed fingertips to eradicate the revilement. He places it, wrapped in his handkerchief, in the pocket of his overcoat.

A sigh escapes his cracked lips as he wipes the tears from his eyes with his snow-covered sleeve; he presses his shoulder against the warped wooden door and quietly becomes one with the small flock of men, rhythmically rocking back and forth, enveloped in the privacy of their prayers. Absorbed in the cadence of their Shabbos entreaties to Elohim, they don't notice Mendel's entrance.

When he is standing next to his companions, he removes his hat, a worn but still-functional sheepskin *ushanka* with ear flaps, an unexpected treasure found in a garbage can, to reveal his yarmulke.

Mendel's father, Rabbi Yonkel Israel Kolopsky—a descendant of a line of Kohanim, the ancient tribe of priests descended from Moses—gave it to him several months before he died. It is a black skullcap elaborately embroidered with red and gold thread. The old rabbi bestowed it upon his favorite son, his youngest, not yet knowing that with it, he was passing on his rabbinic mantle. Or did he? Mendel fingers his *tzitzit* and, like sheaves of wheat gusting gently in the autumn breeze, he merges with his swaying minyan fellows.

Not until he hears the chanting of the Shema, the affirmation of his Jewish faith, does he realize that he has missed almost half the service, and yet as he joins the chorus of bass voices, he feels at peace, the sad events of the last hour and a half slowly recede.

"*Sh'ma Yisrael Adonai Elohaynu Adonai echad . . .*" they intone. These ten men, ranging in age from forty-four to seventy-nine, pass judgment, counsel, teach the children and grandchildren of the remaining members of their ragtag community, and perform marriages and bar mitzvahs. They bury the dead and administer justice, and, like the legendary tale told in the Kabala of the Lamed Vavniks—those thirty-six just men who live, unknown to each other, in every generation to hold the world together with their good deeds—so too these men uphold the traditions of their forefathers' faith.

Mendel, at forty-four, is the youngest and yet one of the most revered members of his minyan. In spite of his relative youth, they willingly accept his wisdom, believing he may even be a tzaddik. They respect his strict devotion to tradition because, when it comes to religious observance and learning, Mendel settles for no less than total obedience to Torah. That the oldest members of the group had known and loved his esteemed father adds to their veneration of his son. Some, as children, had even known Mendel's grandfather, a cantor of some small renown.

Mendel grew up sure of his place in the world, as his father's favorite. He fervently hoped that he, not his older brother, Shimshon, was destined to follow in the footsteps of his grandfather and father. His earliest memory is of sitting at his father's side, looking at the big black leather book with strange markings written upon the worn, yellowed parchment—or so it looked to the six-year-old Mendel. He thrilled to the sound of his father's words, words his father constantly reminded him were sacred.

"You must cherish this book, boychick. And obey its every word, for it was given to us by the Almighty so many thousands of years ago; it holds all that we need to know to live a good, upright life. Always respect and protect it with all your heart and soul, Mendel. If you do this, you will lead an honorable and ethical life that you can be proud of."

Little Mendel laid his head down on his father's lap and whispered, "Yes, Papa. Just like you."

"My son, someday you will be a great rabbi, greater than your papa and even your *zaide,* of blessed memory. Like us, you will have read every word of Torah many times over. And each time you read it, you will discover new meanings and fulfillment."

"Yes, Papa," Mendel responded without truly comprehending. Nonetheless, he loved these infrequent moments of intimacy with his father.

"You will teach Torah to your sons, and they will teach it to their sons—and so on through the centuries—the way I teach it to you, the way previous generations have passed on HaShem's words."

"Yes, Papa," he murmured and shivered, basking in his winning the honor that justly belonged to his three-years-older brother, Shimshon. Often he asked his father to repeat the story of how Jacob stole his older brother Esau's birthright and how he tricked his father into getting it. He knew that what Jacob did was wrong, and yet he understood Jacob's yearning, for he, Mendel, possessed a similar longing for Shimshon's birthright. He didn't think it fair that his brother, just because he was born first, should follow in his father's footsteps, especially because he mocked his father's piety.

As he grew up, Shimshon had little use for Torah or for any

religious observance or doctrine. Always the rebel in the family and impatient with the rules and regulations their faith imposed, he refused to study or practice Jewish rituals from an early age. Unlike Mendel, he was curious about the world of ideas and events. He read anything—anything other than Torah. He hated that he was forbidden to read and write on Shabbos or to engage in activities with the group of boys who shared his interests. He read philosophy, law, and history, especially books about the Enlightenment and the Haskalah. And though he felt displaced and betrayed by his father's evident affection for his younger brother, he was also grateful to have the focus shifted from him to Mendel.

The hostility between father and son saturated the household and escalated as Shimshon neared thirteen, the age for his bar mitzvah. Shimshon resisted his father's demands to attend religious school. Whenever possible, he sneaked out of the house to meet with his friends to talk rebellion or to go to the small library to take out "forbidden books." He even belittled his father's threats to disinherit him and bestow the rabbinic mantle on Mendel.

"Disinherit me from what, Pa?" he scoffed. "Bubkes! Nothing! Your father's yarmulke? You've already made up your mind to give it to Mendel—be honest—so go ahead. It's what you've always wanted to do. A frayed prayer book? A life of blind observance and poverty, begging for handouts from the congregation? All the while the goyim are killing us?" His father's stern admonition to stop did not stem the flow of provocative words.

"Reading books written thousands of years ago that have nothing to do with our life today," Shimshon persisted. "It's all rubbish. Does not eating pig make you a better person? Does sitting in shul all day do anything to stop what's going on out there or keep the czar from passing yet another law taking yet another freedom away from Jews—what little we have?"

The old rabbi warned his son to stop. He forbade him to utter another word. He raised his hand to strike Shimshon but stopped midair, his hand close to his head as if poised to administer a military salute. Then he slowly lowered it to his side.

Shimshon insistently continued, "If you read history—real history—you'd know that first it was the Romans, then the Crusaders, then the Inquisition making us into slaves. When are you going to face reality? There's a world out there, Pa, and it's not in your books. Or your synagogue. I'm going to be part of it. I'm going to do something or die doing it. 'Remember Bar Kokhba!' is what I say. That's my motto. No more Jews being slaughtered by Romans or anyone else."

Their fights flared and abated, like logs in the hearth that smolder and ignite in the course of an evening. Three years later, they had the last battle they would wage, one in which father and son would menace each other with clenched fists and words of hate—words that, once spoken, were irrevocable.

"Shimshon? Please stop. Doesn't the Torah teach us to honor and respect our parents? Ask his forgiveness. Please, you are sinning against God. " Mendel saw where the situation was heading and turned to his father. "Papa, he's your oldest son. Don't do what you'll be sorry for the rest of your life," he pled in desperation. Moishe, the middle son, managed to stay out of these quarrels.

With years of stored up jealousy, envy, and rage for being cast in the role of the second-best son, or even third-best, Shimshon turned on Mendel. "Where was your God each time the Cossacks came to call? Did he stop those thugs when they raped my Miriam right before my eyes or when she died with her mother looking on? Killed! Only fourteen! What kind of a God abandons the youngest and oldest in their time of need? His chosen people? Doesn't that put Him on the side of our enemies? What do you say to that? Go! Go study for your bar mitzvah."

"Be careful what you say, Shimshon, before it's too late,"

implored Mendel, now trying to stifle his own anger. "I know I'm only almost thirteen, but I have been taught to respect my elders. You are my older brother. I love you, and I have always respected and looked up to you, but I have to tell you, you are wrong."

"Listen to me good, Mendel. It's all a farce—a deception to keep our minds elsewhere. There is no voice in the wilderness. There is no burning bush. No stone tablets with commandments neatly carved upon them. All I see is violence and rape and death and poverty. Is this the God you pray to?"

Mendel remained silent. Some of his brother's words reached deep within his heart. He did see the brutality of which his brother spoke. Hiding behind a tree, he'd been an eyewitness to Miriam's rape, confessed only to God. He had never forgiven himself, even though a child, for doing nothing. Often, he observed a drunken peasant or a Russian soldier or a Cossack enter the shtetl with the sole intention of mischief, which included cutting off an old man's beard or touching a woman's breast or threatening a child on his way home from Hebrew school or throwing a yarmulke to the ground. And yet, the only words that he could utter were "Please, Shimshon."

"Don't you see," Shimshon continued, his voice softening, "it will take more than prayers to halt the pogroms against the Jews? What will it take to convince you of that? Look, I gladly and willingly give you my birthright. But it would be better for you to read the other Moses—Moses Mendelssohn—and learn something about reality rather than this rubbish of the tongue-tied Moses. Like my namesake—Shimshon, the dumb, strong guy who tore down the temple—my lot is to take my enemies down even if I have to go along with them." Through eyes filled with tears, Shimshon beseeched, "Mendel, come with me. Give up these illusions."

At that moment, the old rabbi stepped up to Shimshon and slapped him hard across his face. "Get out of my house. You are no longer my son. You are dead. You are dead."

With those stinging words, Shimshon stormed out of the house, shouting, "I am not my brother's keeper." He never returned, nor was he heard from again. At least neither by his father nor his brothers.

Standing just under six feet tall and sporting a curly red beard and head of hair, Samson, as he began to call himself, was a giant of a man, taller, by far, than any man in the shtetl. After his departure, even at that young age, he used his power of persuasion and his reputation as a fearless fighter and inspiring orator to gather a small band of followers around him who would burst from the nearby woods when threats of violence menaced their community.

And there were many such occasions for him and his comrades to exhibit their strength, their bravery, and their brutality and to use their growing cache of unorthodox weapons—sticks, rocks, scythes, fists, knives, and arms—stolen from downed Cossacks and peasant farmers.

With his innate leadership skills, Samson quickly took command of his growing militia of adolescent boys. He was the first to act against the daunting edicts, evictions, and restrictions limiting the Jews' freedom.

Convinced that the restrictions were permanent, Samson warned his cohort that they would more than likely worsen. He'd read the lessons of history and knew that the past repeated itself unless action was taken to break the cycle. He knew that from medieval times and before, the Jews had been convenient scapegoats. Sitting in the library, he read of the Khmelnytsky Uprising in 1648, when Jews were murdered and kicked out of the Ukraine, then butchered by the thousands in 1654 by the Russian and Swedish armies and once again in 1768 in the Uman Massacre, when Jews were slaughtered by the thousands.

"When anything goes wrong," Samson alerted his compatriots with bitter irony, "'blame the Jews. Keep the peasants' hands and minds busy so they won't know that their stomachs are empty. Make them feel powerful when they use their fists so they won't know how powerless they really are. Not only is the government instigating these fights but they are supplying the peasants with arms. They let them do their dirty work. They let them sacrifice their blood—after all, their lives, like the Jews' lives, are worthless."

The authorities' objective, voiced by a high Russian Orthodox Church official, was to have patience: the Jews will solve the church's problem because "one-third of the Jews will convert to Christianity, one-third will flee the country, and the last third will die." Problem solved!

Several members of Samson's unit slowly advanced to Moscow, some 822 miles' distance, where, they believed, the real action was. Samson spent his time reading newspaper clippings, which he looted from the Moscow Library by posing as a soldier in a "borrowed" army uniform in order to gain entrance. Clever Samson had a way of "finding" useful items to support their cause. There he read of The Edict of Expulsion and the banishment in 1886 of Kiev's Jews. He read of the events of 1881 following the murder of Czar Alexander II, which held the Jews responsible, the result of which were the shameful 1881 pogroms in Elizavetgrad, Kiev, and Odessa and the Jews' banishment from Moscow, except for those Jews who remained useful to the functionaries—those with money to lend or with skills that were in scarce supply.

Banished too was Samson's dream of becoming a lawyer when, in 1889, the government made it difficult for Jews to enter schools of law, medicine, or, for that matter, any professional endeavor.

Step by step, edict by edict, Samson registered the removal of the few liberties that had been grudgingly granted the Jews. In 1882, Alexander III passed the May Laws banning Jews from all rural areas and towns of less than ten thousand and proscribing them from voting in local elections

He collected articles that revealed the beating and stoning and looting and burning of homes in Elizavetgrad. In 1905, he found a document invented by the regime, the *Protocols of the Elders of Zion*, a document revealing the discovery of a secret Jewish cabal plotting to overtake the world.

"It's no coincidence that they publish this lie in 1905," Meir, Samson's good friend, suggested. "Come up with a tactic so that the masses forget the real reason the revolution began. Forget their empty stomachs, forget their breaking backs, and forget their dying kids. The Jews are first-rate scapegoats."

Samson and his friends quarreled into the night about how best to stem the rising tide of repression. Some insisted that they remain hidden but close to home, at the ready for immediate reprisals when their villages were attacked. Others argued that the brutality was spreading—that it was a national problem, not just a local one.

Samson argued that they must spread out and join forces with other groups. Still others contended that the fight for equality, for liberty, for justice was not to happen in Russia and that it was time to move to the land of their forefathers. "We must return to Palestine, to tilling the soil, to farming, and to true equality—men and women alike, no rich or poor. All equal. We must return to being the people of the earth, not the book—to growing grapes for wine and olives for oil and to speaking the language of the Bible, Hebrew, not Russian, not Yiddish," he insisted.

Adding to Samson's sense of urgency was the rumor that the cantonists—a contingency of Jewish men ordered by the czar to recruit Jewish soldiers for the Russian Army—were now turning against their own people. No longer were they casting a blind eye to a neighbor's son or son-in-law, to fathers who refused to join the Russian Army. All were cannon fodder for the czar and Mother Russia.

At first the cantonists were viewed as pawns of the authorities—victims themselves. They had no choice but to serve as recruiters, reluctant to conscript the youth of the shtetl, their own sons, nephews, and cousins. But as they began to glory in the power and privilege the role yielded—with more food, better quarters, clothing, and protection for their own families—the influence they wielded perverted their sense of integrity and tribal loyalty.

When the shtetl residents learned about the payback the cantonists derived from exerting their power, and when they witnessed the fervor of their actions, their compassion for their brethren transformed into rage and the need to retaliate. Every so often a recruiter, sometimes a brother or a cousin or a father, mysteriously disappeared, to be found weeks or even months later at the bottom of a ravine, or perhaps a body bloated beyond recognition was found floating in a lake miles from home. The family silently retrieved the body and buried it, typically in the dark of the night, without fanfare or ritual.

"It's only a matter of time before our mothers and sisters will be raped," Samson raged. "It's only a matter of time before our fathers are humiliated at the hands of these dogs, or worse, maimed or murdered. It's only a matter of time before our brothers are conscripted into the enemy's army. Twenty-five years fighting for our enemies. They think that over time we'll convert to goyim. One way to get rid of the Jews—convert them to Russian Orthodox believers in Christ. Not me. I'll die first."

When Samson learned of a secular socialist labor movement forming in Vilna, he convinced the majority of his troops that the time was ripe to leave Moscow. Most joined Samson and packed what few belongings and equipment they'd collected over the months and, in the middle of the night, took their leave of the city.

When Samson wasn't heard from for over six months, Rabbi Yonkel Israel knew his son was not going to repudiate his decision to betray him, his family, and his religion, as he had hoped. He was unaware his wife had been in contact with him when he infrequently returned to Odessa. He publicly declared his son dead and began sitting *shiva,* the ritual of mourning. He placed a basin of water by the doorpost of his home for visitors to wash their hands. He covered the one mirror they owned with a cloth to keep trapped spirits from escaping and lit a large *shiva* candle. Then he and his family sat on hard wooden boxes for the required seven days of mourning and waited to receive condolence calls accompanied by gifts of food. At the end of the seventh day, Samson's father recited Kaddish, the prayer for the dead.

"*Yisgaddal v'yiskadash sh'mei rabbo B'ol'mo di v'ro khirusai* . . ."

He then removed the covering from the mirror and instructed his wife to restore order to their home, with the charge to his family never again to mention his son's name.

"Shimshon is dead! Do you hear? I have only two sons, Mendel and Moishe," he announced.

But for Mendel, Samson is never dead. Even to this day, every evening before he falls asleep, he says a prayer for his brother's safety.

Years will pass before the family learns of Samson's feats of bravery and his reputation as one of the leaders of the Jewish Bund movement. Not with the jawbone of an ass did he smite his enemies, as did his namesake, but with clubs, stones, knives, axes, shovels, bombs, oratory, and a great deal of cunning and courage.

"Never again" was Samson's constant refrain, one that will be repeated years later when six million Jews are murdered.

Chapter 3

THE NEW WORLD:
AND THERE, I WAS A SOMEBODY

1934

Stripped of his dignity and with little to occupy his once agile mind, Mendel, now sixty-nine, sits at the window of his street-level apartment on Neptune Avenue in Brighton Beach, watching the world of commerce pass: horse-drawn wagons delivering twenty-five pound blocks of ice to those with money enough to have purchased an ice box, trailed by scampering kids hoping to catch the flakes flying from the iceman's pick as he chips at his precious payload with a pickaxe; women toting beheaded, feathered chickens in their shopping bags, still warm and quivering, trailing blood—the makings of the evening meal; vendors schlepping grindstones on jerry-rigged pushcarts to sharpen household implements, repetitively imploring potential customers: "Knives! I sharpen knives. Scissors. Razors, knives. I sharpen knives."

Other aspiring capitalists carry their threadbare wares in burlap sacks secured on their backs, like downtrodden beasts of burden, wailing, "Clothes. I cash clothes. Cash for clothes."

Competition is fierce among the twenty-five thousand immigrant peddlers in Brighton Beach, pushing carts and hawking fish, "fresh" meat, fruit, vegetables, rags, shoestrings, and men's collars.

Weekly, an Italian organ grinder stops by Mendel's open apartment window to entertain with his ring-tailed monkey, paw extended to snatch pennies from the outstretched hands of the gathering crowd of delighted children. They greet each other by name in their heavily accented mélange of language.

"*Buon giorno*, rabbi."

"*Gutn morgn*, Mister Alonso."

Only early in the morning, when Mendel crosses the street to go to shul to meet with his morning minyan, is his sense of integrity, honor, intelligence, and competence restored. Momentarily. There, the humiliation of having failed at his brief and futile attempt to make a living from selling *shmatas* is stilled, as is the bitter sense of outrage that occasionally erupts like pus from a rancid boil.

There, once again, he is the scholar, respected for his knowledge of Halacha, the laws of his faith, and for the wisdom garnered from years of studying Torah, Talmud, and Mishnah. Mendel recalls his father's admonition to love and respect the holy book. He feels relieved that his papa isn't alive to see him in this diminished state. Not only is he a failed rabbi but worse, a poor husband and father who can't support his family. And takes handouts from his children. The shame is unbearable.

He also recalls what he now refers to as "my meshuga fantasy," his thought that he could get a job as a rabbi, or at least a gabbai, a rabbi's assistant. Daily, when he returns from shul to the small apartment he shares with Henya and Marya, he longs for the time when he felt passionate about his daily routine of teaching young boys their Hebrew lessons or settling arguments among his shtetl neighbors or consoling members of his small synagogue—of studying midrash and philosophy, particularly the thirteenth-century rabbinic commentary of Moses Maimonides. *Without money in America you're a nobody. No better then that organ grinder over there picking up pennies. Or his monkey. At least he doesn't take handouts from his children.* "Papa, Papa, look at your grand rabbi now," he mutters. "Look at what's become of me."

From time to time, mostly before falling asleep, his thoughts lead to Shimshon, his maverick brother. Often he dreams of him, usually wandering, forlorn and lost, like Moses in the desert. *But I'm the one who's lost,* he thinks. He recalls the Bible story of Joseph, the youngest son of the prophet Jacob. *Like me, Joseph was his father's favorite; his brothers envied him so much, they left him to die in a pit. I was to blame for getting Shimshon banished, sitting there by Papa's side for hours, saying what I knew he wanted to hear. I left Shimshon in a pit. And then I left. Mama. Papa. Cold in their graves with no one to visit them.*

Since his father's rejection of his brother, Mendel has not once mentioned his name to his children, who know nothing of their uncle's existence; nor has he ever spoken of his own past. But Mendel has never forgotten. When overcome with grief, he confides in his wife.

"It's like he disappeared from the face of the earth. I got word once or twice—someone with a message from him—asking me to join in his fight. I never answered. I was a coward. But I can understand he was mad at Papa, who sat *shiva* for him, but me? What did I do? I was a kid and he took it out on me."

"There was no other way, Mendel," Henya answers. "Maybe he got hurt. Maybe he did come back looking for you after we left. Who knows? Maybe, God forbid, he's dead."

"I think of him more now than ever as we get closer to the end. He'd be seventy-one, seventy-two. An old man, like me. I do wonder if he's alive. I wonder if he married or had children. They could be living in America, maybe next door, and we wouldn't even know them if we bumped into them on the street. No, it wasn't right."

Henya pats Mendel's shoulder in a gesture of compassion.

"Papa shouldn't have banished him. Or sat *shiva* for him or said Kaddish. I mean, should a father cut his child off forever? And he punished Mama and me too, not just . . ." He pauses. "Shimshon. I can barely say his name. But what offense could be so bad?"

"Well, you told me how he disobeyed your Papa and that he rejected God. And fought with him and used bad words. Your Papa was hurt. Nowadays, it's different. Children just do what they want, but that was the way things were done in those days."

"Okay, okay," Mendel continues, "so my brother didn't believe, but you keep telling me that good Jews drive and work on Shabbos, even our own children. And eat *traif*, like Saul. Do I reject them? No, although it hurts me plenty. Shimshon didn't steal; he didn't murder anyone. He tried to protect us, and he was just a kid himself. Sixteen. Stubborn. Like Papa. You know, I think maybe they were a lot like each other. Maybe that's why Papa couldn't stomach it. Still, I think I could have done more to get Papa to change his mind."

"Now you're blaming yourself, Mendel. Your Papa ruled the house with a giant fist, and as you said, you were only a boy," Henya whispers; then, directing her words to Mendel's bad ear, "You're a little stubborn yourself, you know."

"I know, I know, Papa wouldn't have listened. Henya, I shouldn't say this, may God cut out my tongue, but sometimes I even wonder if there is a Holy One."

"Don't even think that, Mendel!"

"Every day I think about our Marya and why she was born the way she was. What kind of a life does she have working in a laundry, cleaning rich peoples' sheets? And she couldn't have gotten that job if Shmuel weren't the boss. People making fun of her. No husband. No children to take care of her in her old age? And Marya, twenty-five with no friends even. I worry about what she'll do when we're gone. You see how our Dora takes care of us?"

Henya thinks but doesn't say, *My Disha will take care of her too. Not the rest. Well, maybe Leib or Shmuel.*

"You know, Mendel, I think about Shimshon and what you said he said about Mirium. You said he asked 'Why did she have to die? Maybe you forget that Shimshon wanted to be a lawyer, and you said he would have been good, with his mouth and mind. He spoke of the way we Jews were treated in Russia and always treated. You said he told stories about how Jews lived under the tyranny of the czars, the violence of the bigoted peasants, the pogroms, and the massacres. 'Why, I ask you?' he'd say. 'Why, if there's a God and we are his *chosen* people, why would he let that happen to us?'"

"You think he has time to think of us? But why are you bothering your head like this? We don't have enough tsuris to deal with?" whispered Henya.

A waft of smoke invades his nostrils, the residue of a passing smoker, and brings Mendel back to the present.

"Hey, *paskudnyak,* you with the cigarette! It's Shabbos. Don't you know it's forbidden to smoke on the Sabbath? Shame, shame on you."

"Oy, Mendel. You don't even know if he's a Jew," reproaches Henya. "If I've said it once, I've said it a hundred times. This is America, not Russia. It's a free country. Here, everyone smokes, even on Shabbos, even Jews. What, you think your own sons don't smoke on the Sabbath? Avram, I mean Abe, runs in, leaves his motor running out front, cigarette in his mouth. Puts it out before he comes in so you won't see. Comes in smelling of smoke. And what do you think Saul is doing when he goes for his walks when he comes with Dora and the *kinderlach*? What, you think he's sight-seeing when he walks on the boardwalk?"

"Yes, you keep telling me," he says, putting his heavily veined hand to his good ear, as if trying to block out her words.

"Look at Faigel and Joe, working so hard they can live in a mansion—eight rooms in Brooklyn. All our children work hard, take care of their families, put food on the table, and live in a nice place. And even Dora's Saul—he gives us ten dollars a month. And they don't have much themselves, what with their two girls. Mendel?" Henya's words, once again, fall on deaf ears. She thinks that maybe all his fulminating helps to diminish his frustration—to make him feel alive.

"Look at that *shtarker*," Mendel protests. "I saw him in syna-gogue this morning. Goes to shul and then, on the street, puts his yarmulke in his pocket. With that face, no beard, he thinks he looks like a goy."

He leans toward the open window, "Hey, maybe you fool some of the people, but *God* can see you, big shot!" he rants, shaking his fist. The stranger circles his ear with his index finger, calling out "meshuga" as he walks away.

"Some new world, huh, Henya? We should have stayed in Russia. So we were poor, but we knew how to honor HaShem and how to obey the commandments and celebrate the Sabbath. We knew who our enemies were— the goyim and the czar—not Jews! Here we are, again with nothing, bubkes. Nothing has changed." His voice trails off to barely a whisper. "And there . . . there I was a somebody."

Henya feels her heart breaking for her husband. He looks so old—his blue eyes dulled with cataracts, a wispy beard dappled gray and black, though his hair is still abundant. She pours him a glass of strong black tea from the blemished brass samovar, one of the few possessions she insisted on taking from the old country, a wedding gift from her Aunt Beulkah, her mother's youngest sister. She loved her Tante Beulkah, the one with yellow hair and blue eyes, like Marya.

It was her *tante* who taught her to make black bread with its thick, crusty casing and how to make borscht rich with the flavor of beets and cabbage and, when they could get it, meat. And teiglach. Her mouth waters when she recalls that childhood delicacy. She can almost taste the ginger and raisins and feel the warm honey dripping down her chin. Absentmindedly, she licks her fingers. She reminds herself to make it for the little ones. She desperately wants them to have good memories of their *bubbe*. Warm, loving memories. Sensuous memories.

Traditionally, on Friday evening, before kindling the Shabbos candles, Henya fires up the samovar by igniting a small piece of coal and pouring two quarts of water into the center cylindrical urn. She places the teapot—stuffed with Russian black tea leaves she buys at a small Russian grocery store several blocks away, whole cloves, and a pinch of cinnamon—on the crown of the samovar to keep it hot and ready to drink until Shabbos ends, marked by the lighting of the blue-and-white braided Havdalah candle.

"Better in Russia? Mendel, what do you talk? Come away from the window; have a sit by the samovar. Thank God those hoodlums on the ship didn't steal the suitcase with the samovar. Drink a *bissel* tea. I'll cut you some bread. Come, you'll feel better."

She pours herself a glass of tea, places a cube of sugar between her teeth, and drinks—her glass an empty jam jar—savoring the heat of the thick black liquid as it warms her throat. She drinks and relives the hardships she and her younger children endured after Mendel left for America in 1913 with Levi and Shmuel, leaving her to care for their youngest children and to make arrangements for their ocean passage the following year.

Henya thinks of that time, when she and her little ones boarded the teeming railroad car that took them from Odessa to Hamburg, and then on to the ship that would transport them to America. She can still feel the dread and the hope, as if it were happening today, that she experienced crossing the Atlantic to join Mendel in the New World, with all its promises.

Chapter 4

HENYA:
AN INDEPENDENT WOMAN

November 1913/1914

It is to be a golden province, its streets paved with riches—a *goldene medina*—a place where her dreams of contentment will be fulfilled; where her children will be safe and she won't have to scrimp the week long to set a festive Shabbos table; where Mendel will have noble work and a chance to study Torah undisturbed, maybe with his own synagogue and young scholars to teach; where it won't be too late for the littlest ones to go to school and get a proper education, and, who knows, maybe even college. *Jews were always people of the book*, she muses. So maybe Leib can become a doctor. And Avram a lawyer. Imagine, a doctor or a lawyer. Not like in Russia.

And Disha shall marry a nice Jewish boy, and maybe, maybe there will be a special school for Marya, her wounded bird that she loves so much. There will be no knocks on the door at midnight, unless it is the man who comes to the door to announce Shabbos on Fridays, no one beaten or killed, raped, or robbed. Whatever it offers, Henya knows it has to be better than Odessa.

In a letter, Faigel, now known as Faye, described a world Henya could not imagine. *Men driving machines—motor cars—that could take you to the next village in a matter of hours*, she wrote. Young women, some married, sewing on machines in factories, making their own money. Contributing to their family's wellbeing. Buying hats and shoes. Girls going to school to learn to read and write and become teachers. Her husband Joseph—no longer Yosef—working hard so he could own his own factory. Ice all the year round, with a metal box to store it in that keeps food fresh for days. Shops that sell kosher meat and fresh fish and vegetables. And everyone with a bathtub. And hot water. Such a pleasure, such a *mechaya*.

In 1913, with the help of Levi and Shmuel, strapping young men—who now work on the docks loading and unloading dirty laundry from steamships to delivery trucks waiting nearby to convey their contents to the Hudson Valley Laundry—and a loan from the Hebrew Benevolent Society, Mendel arranges to wire the eighty rubles required to pay for his family's journey on the *Lusitania*.

A year passes before Henya can finalize the arrangements. With no husband for emotional support and protection and without the guidance of her older children she had always relied on, she is the only one to talk to the officials, to plead and cajole and barter her way to the life of freedom she envisions in America. As though it will magically infuse her with the strength and courage she needs, she chants the name of her New World over and over, like a worshiper davening at shul. With closed eyes, she even rocks as she intones the words.

"A-*mer*-ee-ka. Amer-*ee*-ka. Amer-ee-*ka*."

The word, in spite of its jagged and foreign-sounding syllables, evokes awe and a loyal devotion to a language she will barely understand and never learn to speak. Her grandchildren will never understand her, nor she them. Documents are always missing: A nonexistent birth certificate—who ever heard of a Jew with a birth certificate in Russia? Rather, it was "she was born the year of the big fire or the flood or the blizzard or the plague." She has a letter corroborating that her husband is presently working in America and that she possesses the twenty-five American dollars required to enter her new country. The officials also demand a medical certificate affirming their good health. No one, Henya is made to understand, with diseases one could give to others, tuberculosis or cholera or trachoma, can be admitted. Nor anyone deemed mentally defective. She hears rumors circulating around the village of some turned back at Hamburg, rejected before even boarding the boat, or some hospitalized at Ellis Island because an inspector uncovered ringworm in the scalp. Rules, regulations, and more rules. Her head swims with rules.

Not enough health. Not enough money. Not enough courage. Always something. But she steadfastly pursues her dream with a resolve that grows out of love, longing, and dread of the increasingly virulent anti-Semitism in the Pale and beyond.

In the little less than a year without her family, Henya discovers a previously unknown sturdy exterior joined to a stubborn, inner resilience. When she feels frightened, and she often does, she learns to make believe—to act, as she approaches an official, at times a coquette, at times a know-nothing, whatever she feels is needed to accomplish her task. She learns that she too is clever and likes her independence.

She even picks up a few words of Russian—*spasibo,* thank you; *dasvidaniya,* good-bye; *niet,* no—a language never spoken or heard in the Pale—in order to talk to officials, since they speak little or no Yiddish, her only language. Her resolve to join her husband and older children sustains the audacity and fortitude needed to fulfill what are great feats of daring never before envisaged by her. She never knew a woman could be self-sufficient.

And so, week after week, month after month, she returns to pander to the officials' demands, always with the tacit understanding that, with each visit, she is to grease the hands of the interviewer by slipping a kopeck or two, sometimes a precious trinket, into a functionary's hand. Henya quickly learns that everyone and everything has a price. Once, the price stipulated is her body in exchange for a much-needed stamped document. She doesn't understand the words, but she understands his body language. She hides her furtive revulsion with a suggestive smile.

Unlike some of her neighbors, who aren't as wily and who impassively succumb to their demands of authority, she manages to stave off the inquisitor's appeal by bartering—now a parcel of tea and then homemade marmalade, or, in spite of the shortage of flour, one of her coveted black breads, still warm from the oven. When pushed to the brink, she relinquishes her father's precious pewter snuffbox, "the only thing I have of his," that she holds dear. But she leaves with the required document, smiling with tears of relief, satisfaction, and sadness.

Henya knows not how she overcomes the shortness of breath, the heart palpitations, the sweaty palms, the trembling legs and hands that accompany the panic she feels as she approaches each meeting.

But the time finally arrives when she and her four children board the train with three cardboard suitcases held together with twine, steamer tickets, a passport with names, ages, and port of debarkation noted—the train that will take them to their ship with a strange-sounding name, the *Lusitania*. With Marya, Leib, Disha, and Avram dressed in their best bartered finery and her American dollars secreted in a pocket she had stitched into her bloomers, they begin the journey to Hamburg and the boat that will deliver them to their new home and to Mendel and her older children. She can barely recall his face or the sound of his voice. *A year is a long time*, she thinks. *Much has changed with Marya and the children, and mostly with me.*

1914

"Phew! What a smell," howls ten-year-old Disha as she enters the railcar, holding her nose. "I want to go home." The stench of sweat combined with the smell of garlic, onions, and herring coming from the overcrowded throng of apprehensive passengers seated in the third-class compartment with their arsenal of food for the journey is overpoweringly foul. The passengers load their baskets to overflowing out of fear they will not find kosher food to eat.

Stifling tears of sadness and respite—respite from the arduous walk to the station and sorrow for the home she has known for some forty odd years, the home of her childhood and her parents' graves—Henya is in no mood to hear her daughter's protestations.

"We should thank God," Henya tells her children, "that we have the money to ride in a train. We are blessed, thanks to your Papa and the money he sent. Did you know when Papa and your brothers left for America, they didn't even have the money for that? You know what they had to do? They walked for two hundred miles. Imagine, three weeks getting to the boat that took them to America and not knowing if they could even buy a ticket when they got there. Or if they could all go together. We ride on a train. So it smells a little. I don't want to hear another word. Understand? *Fershtays?* Not another word!" Leib hunches down in his seat and pulls his hat over his eyes while Marya contentedly stares at the other passengers.

"But Mama," Disha whines, "it's not a little, it's a lot, and I don't remember Papa. I hate him. I hate this train. I just want to go home now. I don't want to go to America. I hate America too. I want to go home."

Henya, this gentle woman, for the first and only time in her life, slaps her daughter full in the face with a force that comes from too many years of numbing fright and privation. Disha's head jerks back as she receives the stunning blow. When Henya sees the crimson imprint of her hand on Disha's cheek and the look of bewilderment and terror in her daughter's eyes, she snatches the child to her bosom and joins Disha in tears. As the train whistle announces their departure, the mother weeps tears of despair, exhaustion, and release, while the daughter sobs her rage and shame. Marya and Leib unite with their sister to form a chorus of squalls.

"Oh, my God! Look what I have done. Forgive me."

Had Henya known of the trauma and misery she and her children would endure in the next several weeks, she might have listened to her daughter and returned home.

~

Anxiously adjusting her sheitel, the small, middle-aged woman, dressed in the standard black garb of immigrants, stands with her children, five-year-old Marya in her arms, a small boy and a bit older girl pressed fast to her skirt, as if attached to her sides with glue. A somewhat older boy stands stiffly, as if at military attention, a short distance away. Henya, Marya, Disha, Leib, and Avram are among the thousands of "huddled masses yearning to breathe free," awaiting entry to the ship that will carry them to their destiny.

The sight of the enormous ship temporarily erases the exhaustion and tedium of the days-long train ride from Odessa to Kowel to Dorohusk to Berlin and finally to Hamburg. Henya puts Avram in charge of overseeing the luggage, her whole life packed into three bulging, flimsy suitcases. It's all she can do to hold Marya, now asleep in her arms, and maintain her footing with Disha and Leib leaning against her. She can barely endure the smell of her own sweat and the odor of cigarette smoke and putrid food that permeates her clothing, residue of the train ride, and of Marya's vomit, which flecks her dust-laden skirt. The child's forehead burns with fever, her face a flaming archipelago of red splotches.

Henya anguishes about whether the inspectors will refuse to allow her to board the ship. What if they test Marya's hearing? What if she has a disease? She's heard they separate parents from their children. She closes her eyes to pray to God that when the inspectors come, Marya will still be asleep, her face and rash concealed beneath Henya's shawl.

"I smell like a walking herring," the immigrants' food of choice, she exclaims to Avram.

"Mama," her fourteen-year-old son asks, "what's green and hangs on a wall?"

"I don't know, what's green and hangs on a wall?" she responds.

"A herring," he answers, his dark eyes flashing.

"Avram, what do you talk? A herring is not green, and it doesn't hang on a wall."

"Mama, if you paint a herring green, it's green, and if you hang it on a wall, it hangs on a wall."

Laughing hard, Avram holds his stomach and nearly topples to the ground.

For the first time in what seems like years, Henya laughs until her belly aches, and tears of mirth, rather than misery, stream down her flushed cheeks. Henya and her four children are among the two and a half million Eastern European Jews who will arrive in America in the late-nineteenth to early-twentieth century to escape generations of penury, persecution, and peril. Outcasts from not only Russia but Moldova, Galicia, Poland, Germany, and other lands.

"Mama, look at the big boat," marvels eight-year-old Leib.

"What are those big things on the top, Mama?" asks Disha.

"They look like chimneys," Henya replies, trying to hide her own dearth of understanding. She tells them they make the boat run. "Like a train. With coal. Like what I put in my samovar to make the water boil for tea. See, there are four of them at the top because it's a very big boat. So big," she sighs. She wonders if something that big can remain afloat but reminds herself of Mendel's safe journey. She is quietly pleased with her explanation and thinks for the moment that she's not so dumb. With growing confidence, she reminds Avram, "Papa was on a big ship too, the SS *Bleucher*. Each ship has a different name. Like people. Our ship is called the *Lusitania*. Isn't this a miracle?" Disha and Leib are contentedly distracted by a finger game they are playing with each other.

"But where will we sleep? Will we have a bed? How long will it take to get to America? How long do we have to wait here? I have to make pee-pee. I'm hungry, Mama. I'm thirsty. Are there bad men on the boat? Will they hurt us? And look, there are two other big, tall things with flags waving on them. What are they for? Do they make the boat go fast?" So many questions.

"Mama," asks Avram, "if the boat sank, who would you save?"

"What kind of a question is that? The boat is not going to sink, and besides," she says, smiling and lightly cuffing her son on his head, "I can't swim, so I guess we'd all drown."

He persists, "No, Mama, just say you can swim, and just say we can't swim. Who would you save? I mean it."

"Avram, don't be a nudnik." She warmly embraces her son, aware of his greater need to be reassured of her love for him. How could he help but feel like a disappointment to his parents when his life was a replacement for Yonkel's? As the least loved and intelligent of the lot, he needed lots of reassurance.

Avram had heard his parents' whispered exchanges on each anniversary of Yonkel's death. He saw the tears falling from their eyes as they lit the yahrzeit candle each year. Try as he might, he could never live up to the illusion Henya and Mendel harbored of how their dead infant could have become a scholar and a genius and so handsome. He wondered how they could love him so much when he lived for only one week.

"He would have been six, or seven, or nine, or ten years old," was the refrain with each passing year. The flame of the candle was Avram's detested reminder that he was a flawed stand-in for the idolized brother he never knew, but hated.

The questions come from all directions, and after a time, Henya stops trying to answer them. Not because she doesn't know the answers, which she doesn't, but because she finally understands that her children don't require answers. Like the chimneys that begin to belch their black smoke from deep within their core, Disha, Leib, and Avram need to exorcise their barely containable flood of excitement and agitation.

They cannot know that one year hence, this very ship, the *HMS Lusitania*, with its four funnels and two masts, making its one-hundred-and-first round trip voyage, will be blown to bits by torpedoes fired from a German submarine, an event that will launch America's entry into World War I. They cannot know that one thousand and one of the ship's passengers will go to their black watery graves.

The snaking lines of the immigrant army begin to move. Towering Goliaths of men—or so it seems to Disha and Leib—issue orders in German, directing them into a mammoth room with two doorways, the left for men, the right for women. Avram, because he is large for his fourteen years, is forcefully parted from his mother. He looks to his mother like a frightened little boy as he is shunted into the men's queue, but not before grabbing two of the three suitcases.

"Mama!" he whimpers. "Don't let them take me, Mama."

"Dear God! *Gottenyu*! He's only a boy," she pleads to the guards, to no avail.

"Be brave, Avram," Henya yells over the cacophony of frightened voices. She is helpless to rescue her man-child and so, in default, sternly instructs Disha and Leib to hold each other's hands tightly and to hang on to her skirt no matter what, and she grabs the remaining suitcase. She puts Marya down, awakened by shouting, and instructs Disha to hold on to her sister's hand tightly.

"Macht shnell! Quick!" exclaim the uniformed men. "Men to the left. Women and children to the right."

Henya tries once again to explain that her son is a mere child, but she is silenced with a glare and a grunt.

"Move on! *Macht shnell!"*

Henya enters the women's quarters, with its scent of freshly painted walls, and inhales the distinctive odor of disinfectant fumes rising from monstrous kettles of boiling water. She and the other women and girls are herded, like cattle to the execution block, to adjacent cubicles no bigger than large closets. She and her children are instructed to remove their clothing, all but their underwear, to put it in the mesh container provided, and to give it to one of the German-speaking women dressed in white, who then place it into one of the nearby caldrons. Without any comprehension of the German language, but for those few words that resemble Yiddish, she mimics the actions of the other women and yields to the demands barked by the attendants. When she views the captured clothing thrown into the stinking brew, she takes a deep breath, relieved to know it is the clothing that will be steeped, not the people.

Bewildered and frightened, Disha and Leib, for once, submit to Henya's commands to comply with the instructions. Marya, seeing her mother and siblings nude but for their underwear, thinks the whole situation quite amusing until the white-clad woman rubs her little body with a slippery, foul-smelling substance that burns and then subjects her to a shower of cold water, which feels like a salvo of hail stones. Marya joins the refrain of other children, including Leib and Disha, who howl in protest. One guard, a small woman wearing an abundant cross on a chain around her neck, takes pity on Henya, who endured the ordeal in stony silence, and offers to hold Marya while Henya dries and dresses. She is relieved to see her familiar clothes returned, now well washed.

"Hurry, hurry," the harsh-sounding directives echo around the walls of the cavernous room.

"What is this quarantine they are warning about?" a sturdy young woman wearing a colorful babushka asks Henya.

"I'm a bit *fermisht*. I don't know quarantine?" Henya responds.

"Good, you speak Yiddish. Well, someone said that the doctors would examine us to see if we have anything catching, may God forbid it, like cholera or the Jewish disease, tuberculosis. And if we don't pass, they will keep us here or maybe even worse, send us back to Russia, *nisht duggehdacht*, may it never happen," the young woman explains. "See those people in line—over there—the ones with chalk marks and numbers pinned on their jackets? I think they are the ones who have something the matter and will be sent back," she continues. "They look so frightened. I know it's selfish, but I just hope it's not me. I have no one. So my name is Bessie. Here, I can carry your little one. Or your suitcase? You look like you have your hands full. So what's your name?"

Tentatively, Henya hands Marya over to this friendly stranger, a woman who, although more than half her years, will shortly feel as if she's been a friend for a lifetime. She trusts her open and intelligent face.

Bessie, it turns out, lived in a village not far from Henya's. She tells Henya how her parents and brothers were killed in the 1905 pogrom, leaving her an orphan at fourteen. Her neighbors took her in, and now an aunt in America—her mother's sister, who immigrated out of fear in 1905, following the failed revolution in which her uncle had participated—has sent money to cover her voyage. Bessie tells Henya that in her aunt's last letter, in which she described life in New York, she raved about her husband's successful business as a cloak maker, and although the business is housed in their apartment, they will soon be looking for larger quarters.

"I'm going to live with them. I'll sleep on the couch, and my uncle is going to give me a job," she tells Henya. Henya, proudly, and with not a little competitiveness, reveals that her daughter's husband will soon have a factory too. As they stand in line, waiting for hours to board the ship, the women exchange personal histories and quickly forge a friendship, one based on loneliness, language, fright, and old-world familiarity. It will sustain them in the wretched days to follow.

"Already I think," Henya murmurs, "what would I do without you? Look how you know things about America. And look how you help without asking. You are a mensch. *A shaynem dank.* Thank you."

Bessie replies in kind with lavish kisses on Henya's hand. "Well, you're like a mama, the one I hardly remember, Henyala. So we're lucky to find each other. Yes?"

Henya panics as she is prodded to walk the swaying gangplank to join her fellow landsman in the steerage compartment level. Distraught beyond words, she frantically searches the faces of the multitude for Avram.

"My son! Where is my son?" she screams to no one in particular. "I can't get on the boat without my son. Avram! Avram!"

In spite of her intractable unwillingness to move, the force of the crowd propels her forward. Bessie steadies her as she stumbles in her determination to resist. Shouting above the babble of voices speaking strange-sounding languages, she valiantly attempts to reassure Henya that he will show up. Then, like a miracle, Henya hears Avram's distinctively raspy outcry.

"Mama, here I am. Wait on me, I'm coming." Somehow he manages to inch his way to their side through the swarm of immigrants marching slowly along the walkway.

"Mama." Avram exclaims, breathing heavily, "Two men grabbed one of our bags and ran with them. I tried to hold on, but they hit me and I had to let go. Look, here, the bump on my head. Don't be mad at me. I couldn't help it."

"Don't worry. It doesn't matter. It's only things. I was so worried, but you found us. *Sha,* don't worry," Henya says, trying to mollify her sobbing son.

"But Mama, the doctors made me do bad things. They made me unzip my pants and pull out my pee-pee in front of everyone." He breathes deeply and continues, "And then one came and touched it and looked all over on it. Pulling it here and there. They did it to everyone, though. I had to let him touch it. Then the doctor left, and that's when the men came and tried to take the bags, those *ganefs,* but I held onto one and gave them such a big clop you know where. They ran away. Don't be mad!"

"My boy, my poor boy. Shhhhhh, it's okay now. You couldn't help it. They did something bad, not you. And I'm not mad. Shhhhhh."

Now that they were all reunited, the newly reconfigured family, Henya, Avram, Leib, Disha, Marya, and Bessie were pushed along, their hearts lighter, as they descended the narrow stairs leading to their sleeping quarters, but their carefree mood quickly paled when they saw their accommodations.

Steerage passage makes the rail ride from Odessa to Hamburg seem fit for the czar. With two tiers of wooden bunks located in the dark, dank, filthy underbelly of the ship; with the never-ceasing trembling of the ship's engines; with the lingering smell of disinfectant and urine and feces and vomit mingled with garlic, moldy bread, maggots, onions, potatoes, herring, seasickness, spoilt meat, and stale tobacco; with typhus; and with a scarcity of washrooms and water, Hell could be no worse. Ten days of roiling, rocking, pitching, stormy, stinking, airless, noisy, dehydrated, hungry Hell.

Chapter 5

FROM SHTETL TO TENEMENT

November 1914

R ising above the din of the ever-droning ship's engines, the cacophony of human voices jolts Henya awake from her dream. It sounds to her like the caterwauling of felines in heat— low, urgent, guttural yowls that rise to a chorus of wailing. She finds the tightly stacked and stained wooden bunks empty but for Marya, who remains peacefully asleep by her side, snoring lightly, thumb suspended from her half-open mouth. Gone are Avram, Disha, Leib, and Bessie. Henya is reluctant to awaken, for she is sad to forsake her dream of an Odessian Shabbos.

Too quickly, she sits up and strikes her head on the bunk above but pays little attention to the resulting swelling. More compelling is the buzz of activity she hears emanating from the upper deck: the scrambling of feet, the excited voices, the oohs, aahs, the clapping of hands.

Dressing hastily, she wraps Marya in her quilt and carefully climbs the narrow metal stairway, slippery with cold morning mist, to the rain-polished platform, where she faces hundreds of congregated immigrants. A choir of voices babbling words in the hall, Italian, Russian, Polish, Yiddish, Hungarian, Greek, and Armenian, the crowd now stands transfixed as if witnessing the face of God. It is not God they behold but the Statue of Liberty aglow in her regal copper façade.

Some are weeping, some genuflecting and making the sign of the cross, others covering their eyes with their palms, but most are exuberantly embracing, laughing, dancing, or standing silently in awe of the symbol of tolerance and freedom that stands before them. At the sighting of this miraculous vision, Henya looks at her daughter.

"Look, Marya. Maybe you don't hear the tumult, but you can see that magnificent vision. Look how tall and proud. Such a beautiful face. She's wearing a crown, not like the czar's, an American crown. She's our queen of America and you our princess."

As if she intuits the significance of her mother's words and the symbolism of the giant before her eyes, Marya emits an owl-sounding, "Hoooooo."

"We're here. We're here in America," Henya says. "No more being afraid of bad things happening and bad men. No more doors knocked down or windows smashed. And look at that beautiful castle. Oh, what a sight. *Nu,* it looks like a palace with its fancy curlicues and archways and the water all around. May I live to see the day that you will hear the sounds of your new country and learn to speak good English. Come, *bubbala*, we'll find your brothers and sister. And Bessie."

While still in the harbor, medical examiners board the ship to inspect the privileged passengers traveling in first- and second-class cabins. Most are ushered out, free to exchange their now useless money for new currency and to greet their waiting relatives at the "kissing post," then to board the ferry that will take them to Ellis Island and then to their new lives. Not for them, those with money, public humiliation. Only a few are detained and marked for further examination once they reach Ellis Island.

Not so Henya and her fellow steerage adventurers. They wait. And wait. Tagged with their names and the ship's manifest number, they are unceremoniously discharged on Ellis Island's landing slip, disoriented and deranged by the long journey and the eight days of shipboard misery and now further bewildered by the bedlam of the scene they are witnessing. They've never glimpsed so many perplexed people gathered together.

"Bessie, can you walk? It feels like the boat is still rocking and the engines still roaring under my feet," exclaims Henya as she grabs Avram's shoulder to steady herself.

"Ah, Mama! Don't shove. I can't hold myself up. Everything is moving like I'm going to fall down," Avram blurts out and then bursts into gusts of laughter. "Hooey, I'm so dizzy. Look at me, Mama, I'm walking crooked."

Jumping up and down and whooping, Disha and Leib are oblivious to the others' complaints, so thrilled are they to have escaped the dank coalmine environment of the past eight days. "*Sha!*" pleads Bessie. "Don't look shaky, Avram! And Henya, don't hang on Avram. My aunt told me people look to see if you're crippled or crazy or sick, and then they send you right back to Russia. And Avram, stop laughing like a hyena or they'll send us all to the lunatic asylum."

The next of their labors to come—labors that would have challenged the Greek warrior Odysseus, who took ten years to return to his homeland of Ithaca—quickly efface the memory of Lady Liberty and the baronial beauty of the fortress on this island of Ellis, embraced by the waters of the New York Bay that tickle its shoreline. They wait for hours before they are invited to climb the steep flight of steps leading to the inner sanctum of the great hall, unaware that the team of medical men stationed at the top of the stairs has begun the examination, carefully seeking signs of mental or physical impairment.

Who needs help as they ascend the mountain of a staircase? Check: Too old, too sick, too decrepit!

Who is breathing heavily? Check: Cardiac or lung condition!

Who is limping? Check: Lame! Cripple! Degenerate!

Who looks befuddled? Check: Mental illness or retard.

Check! Check! Check! REJECT! REJECT! REJECT!

Henya eagerly mounts the more than thirty stairs like a woman half her age, as though in a race with Bessie, who is, in fact, half her age. Even Marya, with her chubby five-year-old legs, climbs adroitly, holding on to Disha's fingers. As they reach the top of the stairs, Henya and her family, unsuspectingly, pass the first of the trials to come and escape the feared chalk marks—seventeen in all—that could expose them to a comprehensive physical and the possibility of hospitalization or, worse, a return ticket to Russia, courtesy of the shipping line. A uniformed man gestures for them to join the line on the right.

Henya gasps as she sees the cavernous great hall, with its high ceilings, painted white walls, and imposing arched windows. She glimpses two massive American flags hanging from outstretched poles, trumpeting their arrival in the United States of America. Time passes. And more time. The elderly rest on the hard floors, guarding their only remaining precious possessions, while infants nurse at their mothers' breasts. Children cavort and play games of hide and seek, concealing themselves behind stacks of luggage or their mothers' skirts. Men nervously drag on cigarettes. Couples lean on each other for mutual support. Some bicker, some eat the dregs of leftover food, and some parched souls swoon with dehydration made worse by exhaustion and apprehension.

"Oh-oh, they will definitely be marked for special medical attention," Bessie admonishes, pointing to a bedraggled family of six.

After what feels like days, large groups are divided into smaller formations and then into dozens of lines conforming to the metal railings that separate them. Doctors impatiently stand at the head of each line, eager to finish their examinations so they can return home to recover from their sixteen-hours-or-more day. They are overworked and bad-tempered.

Henya and her small assemblage finally arrive at what will prove to be the first of the three medical stations.

"What are they doing?" asks Disha, who, until now, has walked through the process as though in a trance. "Why are people taking off their shirts?"

"The doctors need to look at us. We're going to have to undress too," Bessie whispers, her voice quivering. "But it's okay, don't be frightened. I'll be right here."

"Do we *have* to?" Disha asks, beginning to whimper. Bessie directs a stern, reproving glance at Disha and says to Henya, "I think our doctor is a Jew. A Jew and a doctor. Ha! Not like in Russia."

"How," Henya presses, "do you know that?"

"By his accent," clarifies Bessie. "Listen to his Yiddish—no accent. Not like that other one. She nods toward the doctor at the head of the adjacent line. "He's like a stuttering train engine. His tongue doesn't work so good."

"Good! So maybe he'll take pity on us," returns Henya, suppressing a laugh.

Bessie winks. "Smile at him, Henya, the way you told me you used to smile at the Russian guards to get your visa. Too bad you can't make one of your breads." They exchange knowing glances, glances that only long-time friends typically share.

With stethoscopes in hand, the examining doctors listen for heart murmurs; they search for goiters and growths and abnormalities as they palpate necks and shoulders and groins; they calculate pulse beats and inspect teeth and ears and eyes, fingernails and toenails, as though the group is about to be put up on the slave block and sold to the highest bidder.

As Henya approaches the doctor, she tries to smile as Bessie instructed, but her lips stick to her teeth, her tongue cleaves to the roof of her mouth, dry as a parched riverbed.

Disregarding Henya's feeble attempt to replicate her earlier behavior with the Russian guards, the doctor turns to Avram and brusquely orders him to remove his cap. Paralyzed with fear, Avram is slow to respond. The doctor, without touching Avram, points to his head and shouts, "I told you to remove your cap." Avram understands the doctor's command but does not move.

"Off," he shouts and turns to his assistant. Without the need for further instruction, the underling closes in and sweeps Avram's cap to the ground.

Disha glares at the doctor and quickly retrieves it just as it touches the floor. Scowling, she boldly brushes off the dust and hands it to her brother with a determined flourish. Unfazed by the child's gesture, the doctor pursues his quest for ringworm, lice, or any other creature making uninvited residence in Avram's scalp. He then surveys Leib and Marya and Bessie and then scrutinizes Disha's scalp and, like the child who finds the missing half of the afikomen, holds up a specimen with tweezers, as though expecting a reward. "Aha, lice!"

Once more, at the snap of the Jewish medical man's fingers, his assistant materializes. They exchange foreign words, and Disha is dragged away—screaming, kicking, biting. The doctor, now speaking Yiddish, reassures Henya that, without treatment, her daughter will not be allowed to enter the country but that there is a remedy.

Petrified, Disha is taken to a large room on the opposite side of hall, where she witnesses other victims in various stages of "hair styling"—men, mostly stoic; women, some hysterical; others in a somnolent stupor. There are kids howling for their mamas.

A woman doctor begins the process of removing Disha's lush hair, at first smiling at the child. She then lifts several curls and cuts them with scissors, handing one curl to Disha as a keepsake. Disha smiles and takes the submission. One by one, curls fall to the floor. Disha is now calm, but when the doctor begins the final shearing process—shaving her entire head with a razor—Disha's ear-piercing screams echo throughout the chamber, encouraging all the children, and a few more of the women, to join the choir.

In the meantime, the doctor turns to Henya and asks her to remove her sheitel, the mandatory wig worn by Orthodox married women.

"No, I can't do that. You see, I'm not allowed to take it off. Only my husband can see me that way. No!"

"I must insist," he asserts.

The doctor recalls his own mother who, a mere fifteen years ago, had been similarly detained by a doctor making just such a demand, and so he understands what Henya is feeling. In part, his impatience has to do with the painful memory of his mother's humiliation and shame and with his need to distance himself from "these people."

As a German Jew, and one who worked hard to fit in, he considers himself far superior to these Jews from Eastern European stock, who are so uncultured, loud, and, for the most part, embarrassing. He feels they give all Jews a bad name—wearing wigs and yarmulkes, and with filthy lice! Anger and shame overtake whatever empathy he fleetingly felt for the small family before him.

He insists, once again, that Henya remove her sheitel. Just as his assistant reaches to remove her wig, Henya sheds the passivity that she, and all Jews, had to assume to survive the tyranny of the czar and his minions.

"Don't touch," she admonishes. Impetuously pushing his hand away, she removes her sheitel. Henya is stunned by her own reckless gesture and the commanding sound of her voice. She is reminded of Faigel.

The humiliation of being forced, or touched by a man, feels more degrading to her than revealing her natural hair. *What could be bad or wrong about what God has given me?* And yet, once removed, in spite of her justifications, generations of tradition are etched onto the tablets of her soul, and she feels queasy with guilt. She automatically covers her hair with both hands. *I look the way I looked before I married Mendel*, she thinks.

Could this be any worse than the cross-examinations she endured with the Russian regime? She thinks not. Henya vows never again to wear a sheitel. Never again to follow any authority's rules, unless they are also consonant with her own. She determines to toss it in the first trashcan she encounters after she leaves the station. *Or maybe into the ocean. The same ocean that took me to my new life and new customs will be the same ocean that drowns the old*, she thinks. "So much for Jewish doctors," she whispers to Bessie.

"In America, they do things differently," she reasons to Bessie, trying to convince herself of her newly forged perspective. "And now I'm an American. I can think for myself. I'm a slave to no one. Not to doctors, not to czars, and not even to my husband. Well, maybe a little with him. But an American wife, no?"

Chagrined, the doctor does a perfunctory examination of Henya's head and, eager to rid himself of this unusual woman turned a ferocious tiger before his eyes, he quickly dismisses her with a wave of his hand, without a word.

Shorn of the beautiful black curls that once adorned her head, Disha returns an hour later to her mother's side. The young attendant returns, wearing a surgical dressing on his hand and a surly expression, the result of Disha's protestations.

Before they walk away, trying her best to sound convincing, Henya tells Disha, "Your hair will grow back in a little while. My mama used to say that hair grows back stronger when you cut it. It's important we should look happy, so make a nice face for the doctors."

Then Bessie removes her babushka and ties it around Disha's head and holds her briefly in an embrace. "Now you look like a real American girl." But Disha is not to be pacified, for, in her mind, she looks more like a Russian peasant—those old ladies dressed in black, with wrinkled faces and dried-up hands, working the fields in their babushkas.

Once more, they have averted the dreaded chalk mark: *SC* for scalp, *G* for goiter, or an *X*—writ large—for suspected anything. Suspected of what? No matter. They are suspects and feel as guilty as if convicted of a horrendous crime. The only crimes they have committed, however, are arriving as impoverished immigrants, not speaking or understanding English, and being born in a country that spurns Jews.

Henya does worry what Mendel will say when he sees her in this unorthodox state. And Disha—what will he think about that? Her musings are interrupted when she realizes that they have successfully reached the next station. *Mazel tov*, she thinks.

First Disha, then Leib, then Marya, Henya, and Bessie move slowly and solemnly through the line, barely breathing for fear of displeasing the new doctor. He is a grim little man who continues the hunt with the vigilance of a dedicated agent of the czar, pursuing those suspected of harboring revolutionaries. This search demands the honed skills of a specialist in loathsome maladies, on the lookout for symptoms of venereal disease or leprosy or favus— at that time, misdiagnosed as leprosy rather than a fungal disease that modern medicine would cure with drugs. Immigrants receiving that diagnosis are immediately quarantined, hospitalized, and more often than not, deported. With a curt grunt, he waves them on and turns his focus to the next person in line.

One, two, three, four, and five proceed to the third and final medical destination, unaware they are facing the most frightening of all inspections: the so-called buttonhook test. Bessie, however, had been forewarned by her aunt and audaciously volunteers to be the first. She's determined to show the *kinde* how brave she is and to serve as a model for how they should behave.

"The eye man," as the immigrants call him, holds an instrument designed to ease shoelaces around the metal hooks of ladies' button-top shoes—the latest fashion. As Bessie steps up within an arms reach of the doctor, his assistant holds her head firmly from behind with rubber-gloved hands as the doctor hastily flips her eyelid inside out. She screams in shock and promptly faints, which induces the very reaction in the children she was valiantly endeavoring to avoid: ear-shattering shrieks and attempts to escape.

Henya follows, determined not to faint for fear of deportation. Then comes Avram. By the time Disha and Leib reach the doctor's gloved hands—the very gloves that have manipulated hundreds of eyelids—they are bawling, their contorted faces a mass of tears and snot. And then it's Marya's turn.

Henya now feels in her guts Abraham's plight when ordered by God to sacrifice his son, Isaac. Henya tries to contain Marya's struggling body so the Herr Doctor Specialist can administer torture by buttonhook. But there is no divine intervention, no angel from Heaven to spare Marya from this barbaric deed. She howls for her mama.

The doctor pronounces them free of trachoma but pauses at the end of the examination, puzzled by the sounds emanating from Marya's throat, more like whale songs originating from the depths of the ocean floor than a human voice.

"Come here, little girl. Tell me your name," he asks, first in English, then in Yiddish.

Marya shows no signs of comprehending his appeal. She is determined to reach her mother's side and jerks her arm out of the doctor's grasp. When he fails to capture her attention, he orders Henya to instruct the child to say her name.

"*Gottenyu,* please help me," Henya prays silently.

She explains to the doctor that her child, while on the boat, suffered from a fever and that her ears are plugged as a result.

"Please tell her to say her name," the doctor commands. Marya responds to her mother's instructions with the same guttural sounds. "No language," he deduces. "Definite signs of mental disease, most likely retardation with severe hearing loss."

He takes his chalk and begins to mark an *X* contained in a circle on her back.

Henya and Bessie do not know the significance of the stigmata, but they know it is bad. Very bad! They plead with him to stop writing and erase the mark. They hang on his coat sleeves; they cry and throw themselves at his feet; they wail and kiss his hands; they appeal to him as a father, as a Jew, as a good doctor. Everyone is staring.

More out of his own need to rid himself of this mortifying confrontation rather than pity for their predicament, he puts the chalk in his pocket, rubs his marking from her back, and waves them on their way to the legal interrogation line on the opposite side of the hall, the final impediment to freedom. "Let someone else deal with this," he whispers to the doctor on the adjacent line. "For this we went to medical school?" He looks up to find Henya still standing nearby.

"May God bless you, and may you live to be a hundred and twenty," Henya whispers through her tears as she takes the doctor's hand in hers. "I will remember you for the rest of my life. Thank you, doctor."

The doctor shifts uneasily, aware of the stares from his colleagues. He clears his throat and gently pulls his hand away. He hastily turns to the next supplicant, trying to keep his emotions in check and to hide his tear-brimmed eyes. He makes a mental note to call his mother.

At the final inspection, a Yiddish-speaking young man, barely older than her Shmuel, Henya guesses, wearing eye glasses with lenses so thick they make his dark brown eyes look like ripe black olives, asks, "And so, Mrs. Kolopsky, can you tell me how old you are and the ages of your children?"

"Well, mister," she answers, "I have forty-seven years and my little one here, she has five. Her name is Marya, and Avram, my son, has fourteen years. He's a good boy. And Disha, *mein tuchta,* has about ten. She's very unhappy because, you see, she had her hair shaved. And Leib, my youngest boy, has eight. I have two other sons already in America, working, and another daughter who's married. Doing very well. My husband, he's a rabbi and . . ."

"Yes, ma'am. Who is this other child?"

"Bessie? We met on the boat. She's not my child."

Bessie volunteers that she is twenty-three.

The inspection continues with questions—twenty-nine of them—about where they were born, whether anyone had ever been jailed or arrested, their financial and marital status, who is to meet them when they debark, how they are going to support themselves, where they would be living, whether they have the twenty-five dollars required to enter the country. He asks whether Henya has a job waiting for her. It's a trick question, for it is illegal to have made previous employment arrangements.

Luckily, Henya doesn't understand the question because of the inspector's inept Yiddish.

"Excuse me," Henya responds. "Sometimes I don't understand. Where did you come from? Poland? Are you a Litvak?"

Clearly, his language is lifted from the past, rusty from lack of use or recently learned for this occasion. The demands of the tens of thousands of immigrants waiting to pass through this entry portal strain the New York authorities' capabilities and tax the overworked examiners, some of whom take this job out of the need for work. By and large, they are decent people but stressed beyond their competence and forbearance.

After she has satisfied him with her answers, he says, "And now Mrs. . . . uh, uh . . . Kolopsky, I'd like you to read a passage. In what language would you like to read? Russian? You come from Russia, right?"

"Uh, mister, I'm a Jew, not Russian. So I can't read Russian. Where we live, Jews don't speak Russian. We speak Yiddish.

"You can read Yiddish, yes?"

"Doctor," she sighs, "when my mama died, I was only a little girl, but I was the oldest daughter, and I had to take care of my father and brothers and sisters. My brothers went to cheder, religious school, every day, and they learned to read and write, not girls. Then I got married, and I had to take care of my family. I had seven children; one died. And my Marya is just five, as I told you. So, you should forgive me, but I never learned to read. Maybe in my new country, I could learn to read. When I was alone after my husband left, I learned some Russian words. And he is practicing English writing now so he can teach me. He's a teacher, you know, and a rabbi."

As the inspector picks up a piece of yellow chalk to tag Henya's back, Bessie interrupts. "Listen, Mrs. Kolopsky is very smart. She learns fast, so give me the card with the Yiddish writing, and I'll teach her to read it. You'll see. She'll read it."

The exasperated inspector hands them the written passage and indifferently waves them off. "Okay, okay, but you'll have to go to the end of the line when you return. Next!"

An hour passes before they again reach the head of the queue, all the while with Bessie encouraging, cajoling, repeating, scolding, and drilling the words into Henya's angst-laden brain. When next they greet the inspector, Henya recites from memory the few sentences written on the two-by-four card. Bessie stands behind Henya, silently mouthing the words.

"Okay, now move on, all of you. Over there. Here is your landing pass." He pauses and adds, "And good luck! Next!"

With such determination and persistence, is it any wonder that so many immigrants made awesome contributions in their fields of endeavor? Later, Bessie would learn of the German physicist, Albert Einstein; the Armenian painter, Arshile Gorky; Levi Strauss, the German clothing manufacturer; Irving Berlin, the Jewish-Russian songwriter; and the Italian bodybuilder, Angelo Siciliano, who, as Charles Atlas, taught a generation of scrawny American boys how to keep the bullies of the world from kicking sand in their faces.

Henya leaves the Great Hall and enters the waiting room. She feels her breath coming in spasms and her throbbing heart about to burst through her chest.

What if I don't know my Mendel? she worries. "What if he doesn't know me?" she cries to Bessie. "No sheitel and I've grown old and skinny in the year he's been gone. It feels more like ten. And he's a real American now; after all, he's a regular businessman selling goods from his own pushcart and talking to American people every day."

"Okay, okay, I know you're nervous, but go already," Bessie answers.

Brushing her skirt down and smoothing her wind-tousled hair, she thinks, *He could be ashamed of me.* She collects her family around her, and together they march to the reception platform, where she spies a small bearded man standing inconspicuously at the railing, dressed in a black waistcoat, an overcoat, and a black hat. He is looking for someone.

"Oh, it's my Mendel," she nudges Bessie. "There, look."

Alongside him stand two clean-shaven young men and a stately, very well-dressed young woman wearing a black dress and a beautiful black felt hat with a long red feather. Next to her stands a real American, black-coated and wearing a fedora and black leather gloves. His expensive black shoes shine.

Henya's feet are glued to the ground. Her legs and arms hang like cement, defying motion. She can barely breathe the salted New York Bay air as she comprehends that the small gathering consists of her husband and older children, greenhorns no longer. Mendel, Levi, Shmuel, Faigel and her husband, Yosef, have magically transformed themselves into all-Americans. She will learn that Shmuel is Stewart; Levi, Leon; Faigel, Faye, and the dashing man standing beside her, a good six inches shorter than his wife and holding flowers, is Faigel's husband, the erstwhile Yosef, now Joe.

Bessie gives Henya a shove, and she walks shyly, nervously, slowly to her husband, leaving the children with Bessie. Two small people walk toward each other, then stand face to face for a moment before they spontaneously reach out to embrace.

"Henya," he whispers in her ear.

"My Mendel," she responds and rests her unadorned head on his shoulder.

II: THE NEW WORLD

Chapter 6

THE NEW WORLD: GREENHORNS, GREENBERGS, WHAT'S THE DIFFERENCE?

1934

"Henya, what are you doing, *vas machst du*? You sit for over an hour, staring at nothing. You make tea and don't drink it, and now it's cold. So what are you thinking?" Mendel asks, basking in his own distracted thoughts. "Always thinking, thinking. It's getting late; the sun will be going down, and then Shabbos is over," he says, stretching and stifling a yawn. "Time for my nap."

"You know, Mendel, I was thinking about the time when I first came to America. I was forty-six, maybe forty-seven. Marya was five—that I know. Maybe four. So young. I thought I was old then, but now I'm really an old lady. Look at these hands. Sixty-seven. Mama never got to be sixty-seven. She had it so hard all her life. Died before she saw her grandchildren. Isn't that what makes old age bearable? Mendel? Are you listening?"

Mendel nods as he sits on the cot, removing his shoes and yarmulke, readying himself for his Shabbos snooze.

"So many veins and lines and wrinkles," Henya continues. "I

laugh when I think of how I used to make fun of Papa when I was little. Sitting on his lap, I'd pull up the skin on his hand and watch it slowly sink, like a feather falling, like this. I thought it was so funny. He'd laugh, my papa. Look, it's the same with me but not so funny now. Mendel, are you asleep?"

"Yes, just squeezing my eyes a *bissel*," he answers.

"You looked so American then, hat and all, and a trimmed beard; I was afraid you would think I looked like a greenberg and be ashamed."

"Greenhorn," corrects Mendel with some irritation.

"Greenhorn, greenberg, what's the difference?" Henya retorts, shrugging her shoulders.

For a moment, Mendel sees the ghost of his younger wife as she tosses her head and makes that familiar gesture. He visualizes his wife as she stood at the landing gate, looking so small, weary, and foreign, holding tightly to Marya and their three other children. Then, he still nurtured fantasies of becoming the famous rabbi that his father had predicted. "I'm going to close my eyes for a bit."

"I'll wake you when it's time to light the Havdalah candle," Henya tells him. "Last night I put a chicken stew in the oven before *benching*. Disha, uh, Dora says she might come if Saul gets home from work early. And don't give me that face. You know he works on Shabbos. Anyway, we haven't seen the *kinderlach* for a while. They grow up so soon."

Mendel removes his gray flannel slippers, with cutouts to make room for his overgrown toenails and bulging corns, lies down on the cot, and is soon softly snoring.

New Jersey, she thinks. *So far away. Hindel Hyah—Hannah—I know. It was wonderful that they lived with us those four years—crowded it was. And then when they moved to Fort Lee when Saul got the job in the laundry, I hardly saw them. Fort Lee. Strange names. And now even farther away. But the little one, Beulkah—Roberta—I don't know her. She doesn't know me. I don't understand her, and she doesn't understand me. Saul doesn't like I should call them by their Jewish names, but I'm only talking to myself. So, I'll just clear the table and put the oilcloth down. I wonder if there's seltzer in the icebox. Saul likes it. And cream soda for Hannah. I guess Roberta will like soda too.*

Who knows love unless you've lived a lifetime together. Such a good man, not perfect, but . . . she thinks, glancing at her slumbering husband as she sets the table on the chance that Dora and her family will join them. The aroma of the baking chicken fills her nostrils.

Henya feels great solace in these established rituals with Mendel, exchanges that bind people who have lived, loved, argued, and known each other's every gesture and mood for so many years. They anticipate each other's thoughts; they can, and often do, finish each other's sentences. It is a predictable and reassuring routine that she relies on. She thinks she loves him more now than when they married.

I'm a little tired myself, she thinks and sits down on the flowered upholstered chair, a gift from Faye when she bought her new set. She closes her eyes, and her mind drifts to the time two years after she first planted her feet on American soil. In reality, there is no such soil in her cement environment. In fact, there are no trees on her street, not even a shard of grass or a weed sprouting between the cracks of sidewalk to soften the bricks and mortar of her landscape.

1916

Abe is now a manly sixteen years old. Neither he nor his brothers wear the traditional beard of orthodoxy, nor do they observe the ways of their parents. Dora, at twelve and bleeding almost a year, looks quite the beautiful young American woman with high cheekbones, porcelain skin, and a thick mane of curly black hair. Her breasts are budding. Leib, who had been dubbed Lenny by the principal when Henya had first registered him for school, is ten. Everyone adores him because of his good looks, sunny disposition, and pleasing nature.

"Look, Mrs. Kolopsky, first let me tell you something. Leib is no name for an American boy. Lenny! Now that's a fine American name," Mr. Steen had told her, "my brother's name, in fact—a doctor and making good money, I might add. Respected. So if it's good enough for him, isn't it good enough for your boy?"

Henya quietly acceded to the principal's authority, unaware of the psychological harm that such a change leaves. "After all, he knows what's best. He's gone to a college," she reasoned later with Mendel when he objected.

Without the language of the land, but for a few English words, and only the Yiddish spoken in the tenement and at home, Dora, who renamed herself on her first day of school, and the newly anointed Lenny and Abe had been placed in the first grade in order to absorb their new tongue. They hated being banished to the lowest grade with the "little kids" in the gloomy basement of the school building. Dora and Lenny, because they were quick and because the schools were overcrowded with new immigrants, advanced a grade with each passing month. Not so Abe. Impatient and restless, he struggled to learn his lessons. At fourteen, he quit school. He could read with difficulty and write but learned very little else.

"I don't need nobody telling me nothing or sticking me with those little brats just out of diapers," he justified to Joseph, his brother-in-law, when he asked for a job. Joe put him to work sweeping floors and doing handyman tasks at his flourishing bloomer factory.

But now, when Marya turns seven and Henya tries, once more, to enroll her in school, she is greeted by more of Mr. Steen's words of wisdom.

"Mrs. Kolopsky, haven't I always given you good advice? Dora and Lenny are doing well. Like I told you last year, take the girl home and teach her to do something useful. Show her how to make beds and clean house and maybe cook a little. She'll be a help to you, and maybe she can make some money working as a maid. Let me say it plainly: she's retarded, Mrs. Kolopsky, slow, mentally challenged. She'd be taking precious space from the other kids who can learn to read and write. And, by the way, have you thought about changing her name to Maryann or Muriel? It's very important for Jews to blend in to this great American melting pot. To do that, we've got to give up our old-fashioned ways. Give up beards, yarmulkes, sheitels, Yiddish, and, for God's sake, above all, old-country names."

Just one generation removed from immigrant status, Mr. Harold Steen, MA, formerly Herschel Bernstein, is desperate to distinguish himself from the most recent wave of immigrants, especially those from Eastern Europe. His favorite axiom is "Fit in, don't make waves, swim with the tide, or you'll sink with the swarming masses in the boat."

Working three jobs so his sons could get an education, Mr. Steen's father, Israel Bernstein, a tailor from Germany, toiled daily as a janitor at their tenement residence, helping to defray the rent for their apartment in the bowels of the building. He took in needlework to finish after supper when the family slept, and taught Hebrew to the children at a neighborhood cheder every Friday and Sunday afternoon. Mr. Israel Bernstein, father of Harold Steen, MA, dropped dead of a heart attack the day after his youngest son graduated from City College of New York. With his life's goal accomplished, he could now rest in peace at Baron Hirsch Jewish Cemetery on Staten Island. Like Henya, he spoke only Yiddish to his mortified sons.

With the bits and pieces of language she has acquired over the past two years, Henya is puzzled why Mr. Steen suddenly talks about melting pots. She does, in any case, understand that he wants her to change Marya's name and finds the words—a combination of Yiddish and a smattering of English—to make it known that she will never change this one's name.

"No. Marya good name. *A shaynem dank, zol zein gezunt*; thank you very much, she should live and be well."

She hurries out of the building, holding her child's hand in her own as she blinks away hot tears of disappointment, humiliation, and fury. Her dreams for Marya's education have evaporated, along with the vapor from Mr. Steen's melting pot.

"Smart, he may be," she grumbles to Marya, who, with her limited audible range, hears her mother's muffled voice. "But with all his brains, he is *farbissener*, an embittered fool. He should be ashamed. Just because he goes to school and gets fancy letters after his name doesn't make him smart. My husband, without his learning, is wise. And who knows a child better than her mother? I know my Marya. The nerve of him calling you retarded. If only I had words to tell him." Marya whimpers in pain and yanks her hand out of her mother's viselike grip.

The Kolopskys live in a three-and-a-half-room, street-level apartment in Brighton Beach, which boasts a direct view of the little beige stucco synagogue across the congested and noisy thoroughfare. Fifteen floors of similarly configured apartments rise above theirs, populated mostly by Jewish immigrants, with a scattering of Italians and Poles, their families, and boarders. Mendel and Henya are a couple of the more privileged tenants who share their flat with only their four children Lenny, Dora, Abe, and Marya.

The buildings that encircle their apartment—similarly crammed with émigrés—deprive them of daylight. From her small kitchen window, neatly framed with hand-embroidered curtains, Henya is inured to the sight and smell of newspaper-wrapped garbage falling from the sky. Like bombs dropped in wartime, they explode on the sidewalk beneath her window with a thump. The hundreds of stairs it takes to reach the basement where the garbage pails are stored deter the overworked housewives from negotiating them at day's end.

The neighbors know better than to pass the open windows, and cross to the other side of the street, thus avoiding the anticipated onslaught. Some even open their umbrellas on sunny days for protection. Not so the unsuspecting outsiders who are often pelted by the airborne projectiles that rain down on them. At dusk, when most of their household tasks are finished, the women congregate on the stoop to witness the naive visitors' ordeal. The kids gather on the rooftop to aid and abet these air-to-ground attacks. Often, Abe is the ringleader.

The kitchen, which houses a small stove and icebox, the latter a recent gift from Stuart and Leon, is sparkling clean, as is the remainder of the sparsely furnished apartment. Henya, with the help of Marya, scrubs, whitewashes with lime, and polishes the walls, windows, and floors, or whatever surface can tolerate their ministrations—in part, a futile attempt to keep the bedbugs at bay.

In the small parlor, Dora's narrow sleeping cot fits snugly against the far wall, next to the small dining-room table, used for that purpose only on Shabbos. The table is also a gift from Faye and Joseph, after their purchase of an extravagant ten-piece set made of Philippine mahogany. Always protected by a canopy of plastic, it serves as a place for Dora and Lenny to do homework. Sometimes, it accommodates a mattress when there is an overnight guest, perhaps the brother of a neighbor's friend or a very distant relative who arrives from Odessa unannounced. Abe, when he isn't working and when he isn't spending his nights carousing with his new friends from Joe's sweatshop—cutters, basters, pressers, and trimmers—sleeps on a makeshift mattress that he places under the table on the floor close to Dora's cot. Lenny sleeps on a thin mattress on the kitchen floor.

Dora frequently complains to her mother about the arrangement.

"I don't want him sleeping right next to me anymore, Mama. At times, he scares me, especially when he smells of schnapps. Sometimes, when he thinks I'm sleeping, he puts his hands where he shouldn't. Make him sleep somewhere else," she implores.

"I'll tell him to stop, but there's no place else for him to sleep," Henya responds. "What should I do, send him out to sleep on the street? Maybe in the kitchen, and Lenny can sleep next to you. Now don't tell your Papa; he'll kill him."

Henya and Mendel share their cramped bedroom with Marya, who sleeps on a folding bed.

"Just like the old country," Mendel chides. "Still sleeping with Marya in the same room. Nothing has changed since we came from Odessa."

"Except we don't do it anymore," Henya teases. "There we always did it, even with the children nearby." Mendel is taken aback by the brashness of his wife's words.

"Well, sometimes on Shabbos," she proceeds, ignoring his slack-jawed expression, and tickles him in the ribs.

"Where do you hear such talk?" he asks, feigning shocked perplexity.

"I hear it on the street, sometimes from your own sons. Some-times when I sit on the stoop to pluck my chickens, the boys play their games. Abe says the bad word, your own son. But why is it bad?" she asks coyly, knowing full well that it is not a fit topic for a lady, especially an Orthodox Jewish lady. Especially the wife of a rabbi—she still thinks of him that way. Often, she tries to get a rise from her husband as a way of connecting—a shared intimacy; it makes her feel like a real American.

"It's not nice and especially coming from your mouth." After an awkward silence, Mendel counters, "But I didn't know it still matters to you. You never said."

"Who has time to talk," Henya rejoins.

Feeling chastened and uncomfortable talking about such a delicate subject, he sulks for a while and then blurts out, "It's a duty for a husband to give his wife pleasure. So maybe I haven't been doing my duty. I have failed HaShem. It was better when I didn't think you cared."

After several moments of quiet introspection, Mendel looks shyly at his wife and declares, "But it doesn't work the same anymore, Henya, especially with Marya there."

"Don't worry," Henya says, trying to sooth his distress. "It's okay; I was just teasing. We've done it plenty. And sometimes," she says, with the emphasis on sometimes, "I like talking and joking better than doing."

Together, the couple relishes a furtive laugh that heals Mendel's wounded pride. Henya does enjoy their infrequent moments of closeness and would welcome a bit more "dallying," but she refuses to further humiliate her husband.

"Ah, Mendel, Mendel. I've got a big mouth. Now you feel bad. And I feel bad because you feel bad. A nice place to live, enough food, no Cossacks knocking down the door." She considers telling Mendel about what Dora told her but fears that, with his temper, he will kick Abe out, and then what would happen? *He's had a harder time than the rest of them*, she thinks, *not so smart or good-looking*.

"And Faye and Joe live in a fancy house in Brooklyn with their daughter," she continues. "And now another on the way. The last time we saw her, she was wearing a fur cape. Imagine, a cape made out of fox. In Russia she'd be like the czar's wife. Well, she is a bit, what with Joseph having over thirty people working for him. Thank God it wasn't his place that burned down and killed all those people. The Triangle fire, Faye called it. People trapped inside a building—even children—so many jumping out windows. Such heartbreak, I can't think about it. So, I was saying, Dora and Lenny go to school and learn English. They read and write. There's nothing to complain about. Soon they'll be ashamed of their greenhorn mama and papa."

Bored with homework and reading, writing, and arithmetic, on the one hand, and eager to meet boys, have fun, date, and join the idealized world of young adults, with money to spend on pretty clothes, Dora quits school at sixteen. No one objects. Not Mendel. Not even Henya.

"I can read and write, I can do my sums, and I'm pretty good at that. I can even do them in my head. So I don't need more school. I want to start living a little," she explains to her mother, who is in awe of her daughter's knowledge.

"I'm going on seventeen, and I'll be an old maid if I stay in school with all those little kids. My friends are working, and some are even keeping company with boys."

Her big brothers Leon and Stewart, both married, encourage their sister to go out in the world. They tell her to work, buy pretty clothes, save her money, help out Mama and Papa. "You should have a good time, meet a nice Jewish husband, and start a family. Like Faye. Look at her," they assert.

Dora is five foot two and barely ninety-five pounds. Now that Abe is driving a cab and no longer employed at Joe's place, she accepts her brother-in-law's offer to work at his factory on the Lower East Side. Her job is to stitch elastic to the waistband of ladies' bloomers. She falls in with the thirty-odd other sewing machine operators who toil in the noise-filled, sooty, windowless, freezing or sweltering, claustrophobic surroundings, working five and a half days a week for twelve to fourteen hours a day. Assembly-line human machines, all.

These women, aged from thirteen to sixty-six, are hard-pressed to produce both from within, in their need to support themselves and add to the family coffers, and from without, because of the boss's need for bigger and bigger profits. The women earn five to six dollars a week, while the men make seven to eleven, but without labor unions to protect them, and with no notion of sexual equality, they go along because that's just the way it is. They hear of other workers, even women, disgruntled and speaking out against the injustice of their conditions and wages, but this contingent, for the time being, seem content to collect their weekly salary.

Dora is swift and agile. Soon she outpaces her coworkers, those with many more years of experience. And although they envy her connection to the big boss, and her beauty, and begrudge the money she earns because of her larger yield, they succumb to her fun-loving ways. She makes them laugh.

Sadie, the older woman who sits next to Dora, takes her under her strong wings and treats her like the daughter she never had. As they share their day-by-day tribulations, gossip, and family stories, Sadie tells Dora about her favorite nephew, Saul, who works as a plumbing apprentice in the city.

"Such a nice boy, Dora. Serious. Honest. Hardworking. Good-looking too. He loves his mother, and that's a good sign. Maybe you'd like to meet him someday? I told him about you, and he said he'd like to meet you."

Dora deflects Sadie's frequent invitations to introduce them. *Who needs to get serious, especially with a serious boy?* she thinks. *I've had enough serious; for now, I want fun and laughter and excitement. I want to wear pretty dresses and hats and shoes. I want to go dancing—kick up my heels.*

"Listen, Sadie, maybe someday," she tells her. "I'm in no hurry. I'm only seventeen, but maybe later I'll meet your Saul, when I'm ready to settle down. He sounds like a good boy. But who knows, he shouldn't wait on me."

With her constant joking, singing, laughing, and dancing in the narrow aisles on their all-too-brief and infrequent breaks, Joe takes her aside and warns her to stop being a show-off. Each week, she proudly presents her mother with six dollars for room and board. With what's left over, she begins to accumulate a small wardrobe of the latest styles in clothing. And a small savings account.

As she snips and stitches throughout the day, rhythmically pumping the foot treadle that powers her heavy-duty sewing machine, one of Joe's new purchases, she loses herself in fantasies of becoming a fashion model or Adele Astaire, a tap dancer who danced on Broadway with her brother, Fred. Once, absorbed in her reverie, she catches her index fingernail in the needle but hides the bloody wound for fear that she will be punished, or fired, for spoiling the prized fabric.

Sadie wraps Dora's finger with a piece of her own fabric and then conceals the bloody evidence in the brassiere that holds her generous breasts. The nail, with its permanent ridges and fissures, will evoke Dora's anger until her dying day, like a shrine commemorating all the abused factory workers of the world. She never forgives Joe's callousness after hearing Henya's reproach.

"What do you want from me?" he responds. "If she's so careless, what do you want from my life? I tell them all to be careful, but they all do it every now and then. It's part of the job. Tell her to pay attention. Maybe you should know what it costs me when someone ruins a pair of bloomers? I have other things to worry about, like a payroll and unions trying to break me, trying to unionize my workers."

Dora is keenly aware of the attention she attracts and of the admiring glances she receives in the subway, in the trolley car, and wherever she ventures. As she walks down the street one day, dressed in her most recent acquisition—a navy blue gabardine dress that exposes her shapely knees, with a matching fake-fur-trimmed coat and white flannel cloche that shows only a few ringlets of her dark hair—she catches sight of a pair of shoes in a store window. It is Shabbos, but she determines that it can do no harm just to take a look. *Looking can't hurt; I won't buy*, she promises herself.

"Well, hello there, miss, can I help you with anything?" the shoe clerk inquires. Dora looks up to see a beautifully dressed, handsome young man in his mid-twenties, wearing a gray silk suit and smiling appreciatively as he welcomes her.

"I want to see those black patent-leather shoes you have in the window, the ones with a strap that buttons across the instep. I take a size four and a half, but I may have grown a little, so maybe you should measure." Like Cinderella, she sits down and offers him her foot, along with her most winning smile, and then looks down shyly.

"Gladly. It's the latest style."

As he puts the shoe on Dora's foot and takes the buttonhook from his pocket to fasten the strap, Dora suddenly yanks her foot away and covers her mouth to muffle a scream.

"No, no. Take the shoes away," she pleads.

"But miss, they're the shoes in the window, the ones you said you wanted to try on," he insists.

"Just take them away. I changed my mind, and please, please put that thing in your hand—the buttonhook—put it away," Dora insists as an involuntary shudder ripples throughout her body.

"Okay, okay, but say, haven't we met someplace before?"

Recovering, Dora giggles.

"Oh, come on, I've heard that line before. You can do better than that."

"No, really," he continues. "Do you ever go dancing at the dance halls? I think we've met there," he sweet-talks.

"What do you take me for? I'm not that kind of girl. Oh boy, my papa would kill me."

"Well," he asks, "do you like to dance?"

"I love to," she responds with great enthusiasm. "Do you know how to do the black bottom, or the Charleston? I just learned it from the gals at work."

The clerk prolongs their playful conversation by insisting she try on one shoe style and then another. And another.

"You know, with your tiny feet, I'll bet you could be a shoe model. I know a few people in the business that I could introduce you to," he cajoles as he slips a red silk sandal on her foot and gently slides his hand over her ankle.

She loves the touch of his hand on her foot and the way he looks at her. She is aware that other customers have entered the store but that his focus remains steadfastly on her.

"There, don't they look lovely? No one else could wear them the way you do."

She feels even more like Cinderella after the ball with the prince, trying on the glass slipper. She veils her growing excitement with an air of nonchalance and wonders if he can see her heart beating wildly underneath her blouse.

Well, you're some smooth talker, you know. I bet you say that to all the girls."

"No, only to the beautiful ones. Say, how would you like to go dancing with me sometime? Or have lunch? And by the way, my name is Freddy. Fred Cohen. What's yours?"

"Dora."

"A beautiful name for a beautiful girl."

Dora departs feeling as though she is walking on the cotton candy she recently tasted at a funfair she attended with her friend

Minnie. Her heart thumps loudly in her chest, like the rat-a-tat-tat of a drum in a marching parade on the Fourth of July. She is light-headed and stops to lean against the wall of a nearby building. She throws her head back and laughs. She can't wait to tell Bessie and Minnie about her adventure. For the first time ever, she gave a man, this handsome stranger, her address at work. She closes her eyes and prays that he will live up to his word and take her to lunch.

Whoever heard of being taken out to lunch? she silently squeals. She feels so sophisticated and grown up. She is thrilled and reassured to realize that he is Jewish. Freddy Cohen. A nice Jewish boy. *Mrs. Fred Cohen*, she repeats. *Maybe Papa will let me keep company. I will even if he says no*, she thinks defiantly.

Theirs is a torrid but chaste love affair. He introduces her to macaroni and cheese, creamed spinach, and chocolate milk at Horn & Hardart's Automat on Broadway and Thirteenth Street. He describes it as a "beautiful example of Art Deco architecture." She doesn't reveal her ignorance of whatever subject he introduces, but will often ask Bessie, still believing that Bessie knows everything. And, mostly, she does.

"He's so smart," she tells Minnie. "He knows so many things. And I love his deep voice. Imagine, for a handful of nickels, we eat banquets fit for kings and queens."

"Especially since they're his nickels," Minnie retorts.

She delights when the small glass doors open to reveal delicious pastries and pies and sandwiches to be had for a few coins and a twist of the dial. She giggles when Freddy puts the nickels into the waiting slot and commands, like Ali Baba, "Open Sesame." She is totally in love with him.

One Sunday afternoon, she calls in sick to Joe. Freddy takes her for a ride on the Staten Island Ferry where she sees, for the first time since her arrival in America, the Statue of Liberty.

Forty-five minutes and ten cents across the five-mile expanse from lower Manhattan to Staten Island and back provides ample time for whispered exchanges and the opportunity to hold hands, hug, even kiss when no one is looking.

Freddy surprises her with little gifts: a frosted cut crystal locket with a diamond the size of a grain of sand at its center, a pair of leather gloves, a stuffed animal. He promises her the world.

"And one of these days, I'll buy you a diamond ring that will cover your finger from here to here. And a diamond necklace. And a diamond . . ."

Dora interrupts, "Freddy, I don't need diamonds. You are all the diamonds I need. I love being with you. You make me so happy. I've never known anyone like you. You're smart and funny. I love you."

On Saturday nights after sundown—after Mama lights the Havdalah candles—he takes her to dance halls, where they gambol until just before midnight. He is her Prince Charming, she his Cinderella; she is his Ruby Keeler, he her Dick Powell. She is mesmerized when he holds her in his arms or when he whispers "little nothings" in her ear.

Five years later, when Dora reaches her twenty-second birthday, Freddy is still promising Dora a world of fun, fur, and diamonds.

"Someday, Dora, I want to give you the moon and the stars and the clouds. I'll buy you a mansion, and we'll have servants, and you won't have to sew bloomers at Joe's factory anymore. We'll go to Paris and Rome."

"Freddy," Dora says in a tone that surprises both of them, "you don't understand. I don't want the world or the stars. I don't need diamonds or fur coats or mansions or servants. Really. All I want is to be with you and to be your wife, Mrs. Freddy Cohen. So tell me if that's going to happen, because if it isn't, we'll have to stop keeping company. I mean it, Freddy."

"Ah, baby, listen. I have to make my mark in the world," he wheedles, taking her hand and putting it to his lips. "You just gotta be a little patient and believe in me. It's our future."

"I'm listening, Freddy. I've been listening for five years now. Now you listen to me. I'm almost twenty-two, and I want to know what your intentions are. All my friends are married and having babies already, and soon I'll be a dried-up old maid. And my brothers keep *hoching* me. So tell me. Are we going to get married? And I don't mean next year; I mean now. You don't have to answer today. Just let me know, Freddy. Tomorrow. Next week. Otherwise we're through, and I mean it this time. I know I've said it before, but this time it's for real."

Always optimistic, Dora expects to hear from Freddy the next day. Or the next. She waits three days. Then a week. And finally a month. She never hears from him again.

"So listen, Sadie," Dora proposes several months after her confrontation with Freddy. "What about your nephew? Is he still single? Is he keeping company with anyone? No? So fix me up with him. I'm ready. It's Saul, right?"

～

"Hello, Mama? Mama, yoo-hoo, we're here. Why are you sitting in the dark? Are you all right? Saul is parking the car. But look what I have: some peaches from our tree. And apples too. We picked them right before we left. You've never tasted anything as good. Sweet like honey. Sorry we're late. Roberta fell asleep right before we were supposed to leave, and I let her sleep for a while. She gets cranky when she's tired. And there was all the traffic on the bridge. But never mind, we're here.

Where's Papa? Let's turn some lights on. Here, can you hold Roberta so I can take Hannah's sweater off? Oh, Papa is still sleeping. Nothing wakes him up. Watch, he'll say he wasn't sleeping, only squeezing his eyes."

Henya reaches out to take the sleeping child from Dora's arms and watches with pride as she looks at her daughter's real American beautiful family. *Who would have thought?* she reflects.

"Mendel, wake up, Dora and the *kinde* are here. It's time for Havdalah."

"Who's sleeping? I was just squeezing my eyes."

Chapter 7

SAUL: AN HONEST MAN OF FEW WORDS

1926

"Saul is everything Freddy is not," Dora confesses to Bessie over tea at her best friend's place, a cozy but cluttered walk-up apartment she shares with her husband, Max, on the Lower East Side. Papers, books, and newspapers are strewn on the floor, sofa, and table that serves as a desk and a place to eat. Her apartment is an hour subway ride from Henya and Mendel's apartment.

"He's kind of short. Well, not short exactly. He's taller than me by five inches but shorter than you-know-who. With Freddy, I always had to look up. So funny, when we danced I always ended up with a crick in my neck. It felt like I was gawking at his *pupik*," she says, laughing.

Bessie snorts. "You said it. Definitely a pain in the neck. And elsewhere, if you know what I mean."

"I guess that's the story of our relationship, a great big pain in the neck. Yet, I hate to admit this," Dora imparts, "I still have dreams about him too."

"It's months already, and you're still having dreams? That's bad," says Bessie as she makes Velveeta cheese sandwiches on Wonder Bread for their lunch.

"I can't figure it out either. I mean, why? The last year we were together, I was miserable. We kept arguing about getting married. I was a nag. A real nudnik. But just the other night, I dreamed that we were on a big boat, in the middle of the ocean, and there was no one around, and there was this big hole in the bottom of the boat, and the waves were huge, like skyscrapers. There was a big leak, and we were being pulled down into the hole. You know, like what happens with water going down the drain in the bath tub, only the noise was like a big steamship sinking. We were never on a boat together, except when we took the ferry to Staten Island. What do you think of that?" Dora asks as she reaches for a sandwich.

"Well, I'm no psychologist, but I did take a psychology course, and they mentioned a Viennese doctor named Freud. A Jew! He says that dreams have meanings that we can't understand unless we interpret them. And you interpret them by what he calls *free association*. They're symbolic and have their own language. I mean they stand for something else that your mind doesn't want you to understand, because you really don't want to know. He calls it the *unconscious*. So maybe you felt like your relationship with Freddy was going down the drain and becoming dangerous, like you were drowning, or that the world was coming to an end. Freud says that tall buildings stand for male genitals. And holes stand for a woman's genitals. Get it? No? Well, as I said, I'm no psychologist, so what do I know?"

"I get it all right, but it's filthy! I'd never dream that. I'd say this Freud was a dirty old man. But do you really think dreams can say all of that without our even knowing? Amazing. Because it is true that I didn't want to know that it was kaput, all washed up, and I kept hoping that he would change," sighs Dora. You know, Saul is a man of few words, but from the start he showed he liked me. He didn't say it—like Freddy who gushed words all the time—but I could tell by the way he looked at me."

"I'll say he's quiet," nods Bessie. "Those few times we met, he barely said anything. But you know what they say about still water running deep. So with Freddy, going back to the dream, you were overtaken by big waves of emotion that were drowning you. You were losing yourself. And with Saul, he doesn't make big waves. Maybe a little boring but definitely steady. Not like Freddy. But what about male and female genitals, or what would you like to call them?"

Sitting at the kitchen table with their heads almost touching, these two women reflect the comfort that friendships of long standing provide. Their conversation radiates warmth and love, at times interrupted by laughter or a playful slap on the forearm, a shrug of annoyance or irritation, or a sulking silence. The thirteen-year disparity in their age evaporates. The differences of yesteryear, when Dora was a child of ten and Bessie a woman of twenty-three, disappear.

"I'm going to ignore that question and especially that you think Saul's boring. He's not one for talking for the sake of talking. He doesn't gossip and just listens when I talk, and he doesn't fool around the way my family does. You know, come to think of it, I've never heard him laugh out loud—you know, really laugh a belly laugh. He has one of those tight-lipped smiles, as if he's trying to cover up bad teeth. And, believe me, he has nice teeth—nicer than mine—straight and white. He brushes them with baking soda. And sometimes," continues Dora, taking a bite of her sandwich, "he doesn't understand what I'm even laughing at. He looks at me like I'm meshuga. And I think he thinks my family is batty because we're always nudging each other and laughing about things. Well, mostly Stewart and Lenny. And yet, I think he likes it. So different from his family. Maybe, like they say, opposites attract.

"Freddy could talk your ears off about nothing, but I liked it because the way he told a story made nothing sound exciting. But then there was the Freddy who told lots of fibs."

Bessie interrupts Dora with contempt. "Fibs? He told you out-and-out lies for over five years. Five years he was going to marry you! Five years he was going to give you a ring! Five years he was going to pay back the money you loaned him! Five years he was going to find a job that would make him rich—get out of selling shoes. Five years taking away your youth, and then he disappears without a word. That man was no good. I will never understand what held you. And you say you still think of him. Are you out of your mind? But maybe this is where Freud comes in."

Dora places her half-eaten sandwich on her plate and stares pensively out the window. Hester Street at this time of the day is teeming with hordes of humanity: children returning home from Yeshiva Day School; housewives shopping at Gertie's Bake Shop, at the last minute, for a sweet finale to their supper; Orthodox men departing the Bialystoker Synagogue, their prayers for the day at an end. As the sun begins to settle in the western sky, it casts a rich shadow upon one half of Dora's figure so that, in her silhouette, she resembles a Rembrandt portrait, with its muted tones of brownish-red amber.

Bessie takes another sandwich from the platter. "You want another, Dora? Or a little more tea? So tell me, did you ever, you know, do *it* with him?"

"I can't believe you're asking. How can you even ask? You, of all people, who's known me since I was ten years old. No! Never! I would never do that."

After a silence, Dora whispers, almost speaking to herself. "Well, maybe I wanted to, but I just couldn't let myself. Although, God knows, Freddy kept pushing. He even said once, 'you shouldn't buy a car without driving it first.' I said, 'I'm no car.' I'm glad I didn't. I'd feel worse now if I had."

"That bastard, you should excuse my French. But the reason I thought that is because it would explain why you stayed with him for so long," Bessie justifies. "You were so crazy about him. You know, like you felt guilty or felt like damaged goods. But let's change the subject. So what about Saul?"

"Hey, just a minute," Dora blurts out. "Don't think you're going to get away with that one, wise guy. So tell me, did you, before you were married? I mean with Max?"

Bessie's face turns a stippled crimson, sprinkled with red polka dots.

"Oh, you did, you did," Dora exclaims. "I knew it. And you're the one who feels guilty, and if I did it too, that would make you feel better."

With eyes cast down at her lap, Bessie explains, "Look who's the psychologist now. It happened late one night when we were studying. We used to get so tired working during the day and then going to school at night and studying all the time. We thought we'd just lie down and close our eyes for a bit before we began to study again. It was our big final exam the next morning. We had to pass. Money was running out."

"Yeah, yeah. So go on," encourages Dora.

"We were on the couch and fell asleep, and then, before I knew it, we were doing it. Mind you, Max never forced me. He would never, and he would never talk about test-driving a car. That's so crude—so Freddy. It just happened. And that was the beginning. And shortly after that we got married. We both felt guilty. But it really wasn't wrong. We were in love and had all intentions of getting married—just not then. That was five years ago. I was thirty, almost thirty-one. It was time."

Dora sucks in some air and asks, "So, did you like it that first time? Did it hurt?"

"Well, it hurt a bit, and I bled a little, but honestly, Dora, I actually had to ask Max if that was it. I said, 'Honey, did we just do it?' And he laughed. Then I laughed. It was his first time too. So, between you and me, I could live without it, but Max likes it and feels deprived if we don't do it once a week. And we do, mostly on Shabbos. It's the only time my atheist husband gets religious on me. He says it's a mitzvah."

A silence ensues, and then Bessie implores, "You must promise not to tell your mother."

"It's our secret. But you were the one to bring it up, you know. So, back to Saul. He's honest, as I said. Sometimes too honest, if you ask me. Like he told Faye that she was a yenta when she was gossiping about Stewart's wife, Yetta. Always minding someone else's business, he tells her."

"No, he didn't?" laughs Bessie, covering her mouth with her hand, feigning shock. "I like him better already."

"Yes, really, he did. I tell him that he doesn't have to lie, but he doesn't always have to tell the whole truth, especially when no one is asking. Like he told Papa the other day that religion is the opiate of the masses, whatever the hell that means. Papa didn't get it, but he knew it wasn't good, and they got into a fight. Once I took a piece of silk from Joe's place—just a small, teensy-weensy piece. I wanted to make a scarf out of it for Mama's birthday, but when Saul saw it and asked where it came from, he made me promise to take it back. And then I had to sneak it back in my lunch bag so no one would see that I had taken it in the first place. But it got all smeared with the oil from my sandwich, so I couldn't return it, and Mama didn't get her scarf. Saul said it was stealing!"

"Well, isn't it?" Bessie chastises.

"Stealing! What do you talk? Look what Joe has stolen from

me over the years! He stole my fingernail. Look. I hate to look at it. It looks like a smashed bug. Everyone always comments and then says, 'ugh.' He's always pushing us for more. Refuses to talk to the unions; God forbid we should get more money. He does well for Faye, and I should be glad for that. But he's no angel either. But could I ask you another question?"

Bessie looks suspiciously at Dora. "What now?"

"Well, you know when you have sex and then at the end you're supposed to have a—uh—climax? Well, did you? What's it like?"

"Listen, Dora, I'll give you the short answer, but after that, no more. It's too personal. Between Max and me. No, I've never had one, but then lots of women don't. But enough, enough."

"Okay. Thanks, Bessie. We were speaking of Saul and how blunt he is. Another thing about him that's good, he never spends a cent unless he has the money to pay for it. No borrowing. Me, I'm a little cheap myself, so that's not so bad. No arguments about money. And he can fix anything. He has golden hands, as they say. Toilets, faucets, windows, you name it, he can make it like new. He's fixed Mama's stove for her."

"Well, he certainly is different than Freddy. Money just slipped through his fingers, and it wasn't even his own money." Bessie wipes a crumb of bread from her mouth and places the empty plate into hot, soapy dishwater.

"Who knew that Freddy was always borrowing money from friends to buy his clothes or to place bets at the horse races? I should have known," Dora declares, "because he borrowed from me and never paid me back. But Bessie, I figured we were going to get married, so I made up excuses. To myself. I've never told anyone."

"When you love someone, it's like being blind. That's another thing I learned in my psychology class. Falling in love is like being a little crazy. Freud said that. I just hope you learned from it," Bessie chides.

"People tried to warn me, even his friends after a while, but I didn't listen. You remember how fussy Freddy was about what he wore. He had to wear only silk suits with a silk handkerchief hanging out of his pocket. He said, 'It's important for a man to look a certain way in order to get ahead.' He said, 'You never know when you'll meet someone with a connection.' I mean, I like clothes, but for him it was his life."

"I remember, and I also remember warning you about it." Bessie pours more tea into their now empty cups. "You want more lemon? Or sugar?" she inquires.

"So Freddy was a clothes horse, and Saul doesn't care what he puts on his back, only that it's clean," Dora reflects. "That's sometimes good and sometimes bad. Like when I want him to dress up, to put a suit and a tie on, he refuses. And he always has to have a shirt with a pocket on it. He says he has to have a place for his pens and his cigarettes."

"Oy, men!" they say, almost in unison. They look at each other and laugh until the tears course down their cheeks.

"It seems to me," Bessie says with a sigh, "that you are well rid of that jerk. You would have had nothing but trouble. Think! Why was he jealous? You want my opinion? I'll tell you anyway. Because inside he was thinking about what he would do and how he would act. He got jealous because he didn't trust himself. Why else would those thoughts come into his head? I wouldn't trust him as far as I could throw a feather from my duster, which reminds me, I should use that duster here—look at all the schmutz."

Dora regards Bessie with wonderment. "How did you get so smart, Bessie? You seem to know everything. Always did. Even on the boat coming here, Mama told me."

"When I took that course in psychology at college, I read something about people who are suspicious—it's called paranoia—and how they don't trust others because they assume everyone thinks and acts the way they would themselves. That's called projection. Which brings me back to the subject of education."

"We weren't talking about education, Bessie. And don't start."

"Never mind! I just wish you weren't in such a hurry to get married. You're smart too, although you don't know it. You could go back to school and at least get your high school diploma. You just never know when you will need it. Look at what Lenny did. Got his diploma, and now he's almost finished college and he's going to go to medical school, or at least, he's applying. It's still hard for Jews to go medical school, so who knows with those quotas? Strange, we came here from Russia to get away from all that, and now it's the same thing. That's not altogether true; I could never have gone to college there and certainly never have become a teacher."

Dora brushes her friend's too-familiar tirade aside.

"Please. Don't start. I know it by heart. But you forgot the part about an education being like an insurance policy because you never know what happens in life, and you can always earn a living. Blah blah blah. You were always so determined, from the time I first met you. You always pushed yourself. Not me, so please don't waste your breath.

"But I have something more important to tell you. Take a deep breath. Saul and I are going to get married. In December. December eighteenth, in fact. No one knows but you and Minnie. Not even Mama. She's taking me to look at the hall she got married in. Saul doesn't want to move in with Mama, but we may not be able to afford to live on our own. Maybe when he gets a real job. And how would you like to be my bridesmaid? You and Minnie? Surprised?"

"You bet I'm surprised," exclaims Bessie. "In fact, *shocked* is a better word for it. You just gave me chapter and verse about the ways you are different from Saul, and now you're telling me you're getting married. After knowing Saul for less than six months, you're going to tie the knot? For Pete's sake, what's your hurry, Dora? You're only twenty-two."

"Whenever you don't agree with me, you get mad. I'm not a kid anymore. I've been working and making my own money since I was sixteen. No one is perfect. Maybe his down-to-earth ways are good for me. It is time for me to settle down. But listen to this," Dora says, taking Bessie's hand. "Isn't it just like him? He didn't even propose to me. He says, 'So when are we going to get married. It's time.' He's right. What am I waiting for? Sure, sometimes I think I could get bored, but then, as I say, no one is perfect. You never had doubts about Max? How many couples do you know that have fun after they get married? Do you and Max have fun? I don't see a lot of laughing going on here. Only get up, go to work, come home, eat supper, go to sleep, get up, go to work, come home, and eat supper. Freddy was as perfect as anyone could be for me, and look how that turned out."

Dora sits silently for several moments, dejectedly gazing out the window. "You know, I was heartbroken. Really, my heart would actually hurt. I couldn't eat or sleep for weeks. I thought he loved me. After I said what I said to him, I kept on waiting for him show up. And sometimes I'd walk past the store and—I swear, Bessie—I thought he saw me, but then he'd look away. I did that for months, even after I was keeping company with Saul, until one day I saw him with another girl. That did it. He was finished with me," Dora continues. "Threw me away, just like a piece of garbage."

Bessie reaches over and pats Dora's cheek. "Okay, it's okay. Here's my hankie. Blow your nose and wipe your eyes. I'm sorry I yelled at you. You know how I can be sometimes. It's because you're like a kid sister to me. I want nothing but the best for you. Okay, we all have to learn our own lessons. So about the wedding?"

"You know what? Saul doesn't believe in God. Between you and me, I'm not so sure myself, but I keep my mouth shut. He says if there were a God, he'd find a cure for diabetes so his mother wouldn't suffer. He worships her."

"You should be glad," Bessie says. "People say that if a man loves his mother, he'll love his wife and make a good husband and father."

"Yeah, that's what his aunt told me. He says everyone loves her because she was always doing things for other people, until she got sick. Like if someone was sick, she was there with the soup, or she would take their kids back to her house. And it made no difference to her whether they were Jew or Gentile. And she had her own six kids. The older boys, Sam and Matt, are gone, but the younger girls are still there—and Seymour, Saul's kid brother. Saul doesn't much care for his father though. Says he was very strict with him and his brothers. He would whistle between his teeth to call the boys home so the whole neighborhood could hear, and if they didn't get home in a few minutes, he'd take the belt to them. Saul says he'd never touch his own kids."

"Good thing," Bessie exclaims. "I don't believe in hitting kids, although sometimes in my class I get frustrated enough so I want to."

"His father was born in Hungary. So was his mother, but she came when she was much younger. He came here in his forties. Speaks with a heavy German accent. He was looking for a pot of gold, like all of us, and found bubkes. He went from being a Hebrew teacher in Budapest to making cigars in Connecticut and then to working in a saloon. And to drinking too much, Saul says."

"Don't be ridiculous," Bessie asserts. "Jews aren't drunks."

"I've heard that too. He says it doesn't take much to get him drunk, just one or two shots of schnapps. Saul says it's not a happy marriage. He thinks it was arranged. Anyway, just when she can have a little peace, what with the older boys married and only Saul, his younger brother, and the two girls at home, she gets really sick. And the doctors say there is nothing more they can do about it. No medicine."

"I know a teacher at school who has diabetes. Once, she went into a blackout, right there on the classroom floor, and then she never returned," adds Bessie.

"So when he was fighting with Papa, he told him that he thinks keeping kosher is ridiculous and doesn't believe it has anything to do with being a good person. He says he doesn't need a book to tell him what is good and bad or right and wrong. He says there are plenty of Jews who keep kosher and then steal from their friends or relatives. He says it's okay for me to keep kosher, but I shouldn't expect him to. Then Papa mumbled something about Saul sounding like Shimshon. Why would he bring up that guy in the Bible—didn't he bring the temple down?"

"Yeah, Samson, a physically powerful man—not too smart—who brought the temple down," answers Bessie. "But he's right about some religious Jews cheating. Mostly they do because they had such a hard time in Russia. They're terrified, so they do what they think is necessary for survival. But, you know, there are plenty of religious Jews who don't cheat. And goyim who cheat and goyim who don't. You can't make those generalizations. It's what causes all kinds of prejudice. Like Jews who are money grubbers or Negroes who are lazy or Chinese who are cunning."

"Well, Papa wouldn't cheat. And I think my brothers wouldn't cheat, and if Saul's life depended on it, he wouldn't cheat. But right or wrong, I couldn't put a piece of pig or other *traif* in my mouth. He promised to stop fighting Papa. I believe him; he's a man of his word. So Bessie, what are you thinking?"

"You ask what I think, but you have already made up your mind. But if you really want to know what I think, I'll tell you. I think you are marrying Saul on the rebound. I think it's too soon after Freddy. You're still crazy about him. Every other word out of your mouth is Freddy this and Freddy that. You dream about him. Do you think you may even be marrying Saul to get back at Freddy?"

Dora shrugs. "Don't be silly. I really like Saul; he's a good man. He'll be good to me. He'll make a good father. I trust him."

"Or do you think," Bessie continues, on a roll, "you may be hoping that when Freddy hears about your plans, he'll come charging on his white horse and beg you to marry him? I hope not, because I don't think that's fair to Saul. But, Dora, I just worry that you're settling. I was thirty when I got married. Everyone warned me I'd end up an old maid. Your mama said I was giving up my life to be a teacher. But I made up my mind to go to school to get my teaching certificate and to make something of my life. And that's when I met my Max. And good man that he was, he agreed that it was the right thing to finish college. That's love. Even so, no man was going to keep me from making something of myself."

"But I'm not you, Bessie. And being a wife and mother isn't making something of myself? You ought to be ashamed. So *hock mir nicht kein chinik*."

Bessie ignored her and went on. "I worked hard, but look at me now: a teacher, an immigrant. Look at the respect I get. What's your hurry is what I want to know. You know what they say? Men and trolley cars come along every sixty minutes."

Chapter 8

SHATTERED DREAMS

1926

Saul is, as his Aunt Sadie claimed over the years, a very good man—honorable, intense, and stubborn. What Sadie hadn't told Dora was that he was shy. On their first date, just a week following Dora's exchange with Sadie, he arrived at Mendel and Henya's apartment holding a flower but then stood at the door, smiling, flower in hand. Frozen. Dora impetuously reached out to retrieve his stifled offering—a carnation—and pulled him into the apartment. Weeks after this date, he revealed to Dora that he was following Sadie's instructions to bring flowers.

Dora is drawn to his reliability, his strength, and the sense that he will protect her, no matter what. There is something about his quiet but stalwart demeanor that calms the ever-present anxiety she daily lives with, anxiety that she masks with jokes and singing and playful banter. At that time, no one spoke of trauma and the way traumatized victims concealed their wounded soul. No one wrote of survivor's guilt, with its resultant dissociation, until Lifton's masterful research on the survivors of the Hiroshima bombing. And the Holocaust.

Saul wastes no words; he is deliberate to act—but when he

does, it's full speed ahead, damn the torpedoes. One evening, while taking a stroll on the boardwalk, he relates an anecdote about how, a few years ago when looking for a job, he was waiting on one of the lines, along with scores of other men, to submit his application. He approached an interviewer, who looked at his application and remarked that he was just the kind of man they needed. But after looking more closely at the application, the man asked Saul if Sussman was a German name. When Saul's response was a terse no, the man took Saul's application, which had been on one pile, and moved it to the bottom of another pile. "I'll call you if I need you," he barked and hastily called out another name.

In telling this story to her brother Leon, Dora inquired, "So what do you think he does? He gets on another line with a different guy, but this time, he writes down Patrick O'Brien, the movie star's name, rather than Sussman. The guy says that Saul looks good to him and tells him where to report the next morning. Then Saul throws the whole table over and shouts, 'Kiss my ass, you anti-Semitic sonova bitch.'"

She likes his loyalty to the few friends he has and the quiet devotion he shows to his mother and younger siblings. She likes that he was born in Bridgeport, Connecticut, an authentic citizen of the United States of America. No greenhorn.

She is attracted to his boyish good looks, from his black hair that falls over one eye to his big, brown eyes—"as big as saucers," she often says—and cute pug nose, like his father's. She likes that people are always mistaking him for an Irishman. They think he looks a bit like Thomas Mitchell, she recounts to friends. When they are together, she begins to enjoy the peace his silence allows—a peace that she had never known. She admits to herself that what she feels for Saul is not what she experienced with Freddy, but she also knows that their relationship will not have the excessive ups and downs she had with him.

The wedding is to take place on December 18. Minnie and Bessie have their bridesmaid outfits, which Bessie actually makes for them. It's her wedding gift to Dora: beautiful dresses with shoes to match. Minnie's is a pale blue chiffon over peach silk, and Bessie's, peach chiffon over blue silk. They plan to wear fresh violets in their hair. Dora has saved over five hundred dollars, which will cover some of the food and the rental of the hall. She puts a one hundred dollar deposit down to reserve the room. She learned from one of her coworkers that in America, the woman's parents pay for the wedding. Saul insists he will pay for the liquor and, of course, their honeymoon. Her future sisters-in-law, Blanche and Rosalind, volunteer to make their mother's recipe of chicken *paprikash*.

"It's good and really very simple to make," Rosalind says. "You take two tablespoons of *schmalz* and put a cut-up onion in together with three or four cloves of garlic, crushed, and mix it with red pepper flakes and lots of paprika. Then you cook it until the onion gets real soft and golden. Then you add the cut-up chicken with a cup of water—or if you have leftover chicken soup, that's even better —and cook it for over an hour. Then you add tomatoes, cut in small pieces, and stir the whole thing and cook it a bit longer. That's how Mama makes it. It's an authentic Hungarian dish and, believe me, no caterer could make anything any better. The secret is in the paprika. It has to be genuine Hungarian paprika— smoked—very fresh. And then, at the end, you have to add a touch of Hungarian sherry. It's Saul's favorite dish, so you need to know how to make it."

"Whoever heard of cooking with sherry?" Dora relates to her mother. "But what do I know of cooking?"

Henya says she's never heard of the dish. She tells Dora that her own mother made stuffed cabbage, and that might also be good to serve. She volunteers to make it.

"Rosalind—they call her Roz—says they'll have to make it in batches to feed thirty people, but she and Blanche, that's her older sister, can do it. 'It's nothing,' she says. Everything is easy for her. Like her brother, everything is easy. She's a real balabosta."

The youngest child in Saul's family, Rosalind is the one most like her mother: good-natured, competent, independent, and down-to-earth. She has Saul's face but with long, black hair, which she wears pulled back in a bun. She is, in spite of her youth, the little mother of the brood of six siblings—four boys and one girl beside herself.

Bessie proposes to make *kasha varnishkes*, and Faye will buy a wonderful wedding cake from a very fancy-dancy bakery shop, that's what she calls it, near her new home in Brooklyn. Once Faye invited Dora and Bessie for lunch and gave them a tour of the house. They claimed they got lost. They viewed, in awe, the kitchen with its two sinks, two iceboxes, and three sets of dishes: one for milk, one for meat, and one for Passover. Bessie and Dora laughed in the retelling about all the furniture, even the lamps, that were covered with plastic so that when they sat, it sounded like they were passing gas.

Stewart and Leon plan to bring a case of schnapps. To that, Saul comments, "I can just hear their wives squawking, 'Too much money.'" And Abe is to bring some of his friends at the cab company to play music for dancing. Although he is not Dora's favorite brother, he turns out to be "not such a bad guy, just as long as he's not sleeping next to me," she tells Minnie. "One plays an accordion and a harmonica, and the other plays a mandolin, or maybe it's a fiddle—who knows the difference? It's going to be fun. I'm even teaching Saul to do a few steps of the foxtrot. Two left feet, he has."

Dora's planned wedding day celebration comes close to the Cinderella fairy tale she had once read. Saul, her not-quite princely prince, has halfheartedly agreed to buy a new dark blue suit from Robert Hall. He refuses, even though it comes with the suit, to wear the vest. She tries on her white satin dress with lace trim and dances around her parents' small apartment but refuses to put on Bessie's beaded tiara, one that she borrowed from one of her teacher associates, when her friends ask her to model it.

"Are you kidding?" she says, kissing her fingers and expelling three gusts of air through her pursed lips. "*Kenahora*, you want me to jinx my wedding?"

But the event is not to take place, despite Dora's refusal to tempt the evil eye. Cinderella's fairy godmother will not appear to transform a pumpkin into a stately wedding coach, nor will she slip her size four foot into the proverbial glass slipper. Her wedding dress is to remain covered with a sheet filled with mothballs, taking up room in her cedar hope chest until her older daughter marries some twenty-one years later. Bessie and Minnie sell their dresses to a friend who will use them for her bridesmaids. Shattered are Dora's dreams; broken is her heart.

In October 1926, two months before Saul and Dora were to marry, Saul's mother falls into a diabetic coma. Though insulin has been discovered, it is not soon enough to reach the rural town in Connecticut where Hannah lives. And dies. She slips from coma to death with only a sigh. Just like Saul's mother not to disturb anyone.

Saul never forgives himself for not "going to the ends of the world" to find the magic elixir that would have saved his mother's life. He is inconsolable, as are Hannah's other children, especially Roz, and the small community, which held her in high esteem.

At her funeral, deeply depressed, full of rage, and wracked with groundless guilt, as the final shovel of dirt falls on his mother's pine casket, Saul explodes, "So much for God!" His older brothers must restrain him from jumping into the grave. At twenty-two, he crumbles to his knees and weeps, caring not a whit who is there to observe or who might call him a sissy. It is the first of only three times in his life he surrenders to such strong emotions.

Dora wants to go on with both the wedding plans and the celebration, but the Sussman family, with Rosalind as ringleader, threatens not to attend unless the plans are drastically revised.

"My mother is dead, and you want to have music and dancing? Not on my life! Get married, okay, but out of respect for her, no party, please. No flowers, no dancing, no music," Rosalind threatens, "or we won't be there."

Mendel and Henya are in total agreement with Rosalind's directive, and so Dora grudgingly forfeits her down payment on the reception hall. She forgoes the multilayered wedding cake, settling for a miniature version, and puts her wedding gown and silk shoes into her cedar hope chest, along with the sheets, pillowcases, and embroidered tablecloth her mother-in-law finished two weeks before dying.

On the day of the wedding, at her father's insistence, Dora, accompanied by Bessie and Minnie, visits the mikvah——the traditional ritual bath used to purify women. *At least*, Dora thinks, *I'm not going to wear a sheitel after my wedding.* Although she has seen remnants of that custom in the neighborhood.

Before the small group leaves Henya and Mendel's apartment for the synagogue, Bessie and Seymour, Saul's younger brother, witness Saul and Dora's signing of the ketubah, the two-thousand-year-old traditional marriage contract. Saul signs with a steady hand, while Dora can barely manage her signature, her hand is trembling so. She recognizes the life-long commitment she is making to a man she barely knows.

Mendel performs the simple ceremony at the synagogue which he attends and had hoped to lead so many years ago. Instead of her gown, Dora wears a navy blue street-length dress, and Saul, his navy blue suit, as they stand beneath the chuppah. Rosalind, Dora's maid of honor, stands next to Seymour, Saul's best man. Dora, at Saul's request, holds a picture of his mother throughout the ceremony. She wonders if this means he will be married to both of them.

The ceremony begins with Dora circling Saul seven times—symbolizing the seven days of creation and the sacred space of the home they are about to build—and ends with Saul slipping a thin, unadorned gold wedding band on Dora's right forefinger while awkwardly reading from a piece of paper his father-in-law-to-be hands him.

"Behold, you are consecrated to me with this ring, according to the Law of Moses and Israel."

Mendel chants the wedding benedictions, ending with the seventh:

"*Soon may there be heard in the cities of Judah, in the streets of Jeru-salem, the voice of gladness and joy, the voice of bridegroom and bride, the grooms jubilant from their canopies and the youths from their feasts of song. Baruch ata Adonai, who makes the bridegroom to rejoice with the bride.*"

Shyly, Saul kisses his new bride on her cheek as Seymour places the napkin-wrapped wine glass under Saul's foot for him to break—a reminder of the sadness at the destruction of the Temple in Jerusalem. As Dora hears the shattering of glass, she thinks of what else will be shattered tonight. Unable to contain their typical Kolopsky gusto, Dora's brothers break out with a raucous mazel tov, but Mendel's frown and Rosalind's shushing quickly restrain their ardor.

Following the ceremony, the wedding party and guests—the small gathering of brothers, sisters, aunts and uncles—having been warned to contain their merriment, solemnly cross the street to the Kolopsky apartment.

Saul and Dora retreat to her parents' claustrophobic bedroom, where a platter of food has been placed for them to break the fast, and by unspoken consent, they put off the rite of deflowering. They sit on the bed and taste the chicken, the cabbage rolls, the kasha, the slice of wedding cake. They take a sip of sweet wine left for them. Saul takes her hand and toasts to "My wife, Mrs. Sussman." Dora knows she married the right man.

There are no photographs to memorialize their wedding or party, and at Saul's insistence, Dora halfheartedly agrees to postpone their two-day honeymoon to Niagara Falls. It is a trip postponed until, in 1965—when she is sixty-one—they will cruise to Hawaii on the Princess Lines. And eight years later, when Saul retires, he will move her to Honolulu, kicking and screaming.

Chapter 9

GENERAL WASHINGTON AND THE SUSSMANS OF NEW JERSEY

1939

Little does Saul know when he moves his family of four to Bergeneck in 1939 that exactly one hundred and sixty-three years before, General George Washington, riding his favorite horse, Nelson, departed from his headquarters in Hackensack, passed through Bergeneck, and witnessed the more than six thousand British troops snaking their way up the Hudson River, buoyed by their soon-to-be-fleeting success.

Neither does he know that a stone's throw from their recently purchased black-shuttered, yellow-painted wood and red-brick home, the demoralized Continental Army crossed a nearby metal bridge in retreat from their catastrophic loss at Fort Lee—that very town from which the Sussmans were departing—wearily trudging in the mire of a freezing rain, bootless, and dressed in muddy and threadbare uniforms as they marched on to an unexpected military triumph in Trenton, New Jersey.

And neither does he know that the Lenni Lenape Indians once

inhabited the area of a nearby village called Achkinckeshacky, or Hackensack, several miles from their newly acquired property. It is a region saturated with history and the lore of the birth of the American nation, one that his children will learn from their history books.

What he does know is that he has to escape the stultifying environment of his in-law's claustrophobic apartment in Brighton Beach, with its stench of sidewalk garbage and the strident street noise of trolleys, hucksters, and hoodlums. Also, the constant babble of foreign tongues invading his monolingual brain. More importantly, he has to flee from the confinement of Orthodox Judaism's uncompromising laws that shape every aspect of life, from birth to death: what food to eat or not and on what plate; how to dress; what shoe to put on first (the right, but do not tie the laces); when to work and when not; how to have sex—when and when not to; how to prepare and dress the body for burial; where to be buried; how long to mourn. He feels physically and psychologically straight-jacketed. Rather than a comfort, it feels more like the iron discipline meted out by his father, from which he escaped years ago. *No more whistles to obey*, he determines. *Now I come and go when and as I please.*

The advent of the Northern Railroad in 1859 and the completion of the George Washington Bridge in 1931—the engineering achievement of Othmar Ammann, an immigrant from Schaffhausen, Switzerland—provided a passageway over the Hudson River from Manhattan to northern New Jersey and to the once sparsely populated community of Bergeneck. The township of Bergeneck, six and a half square miles of meadowland—transformed itself from rural farmland and swamp into a thriving New York City rural community with a paid police force and fire department, new hospital—Catholic—library, post office, and even junior college. Saul jumps at the chance to resolve his prison-like predicament and moves his family to New Jersey. As far as Dora is concerned, it might as well be the moon.

He had previously experienced his wife's tortured dread of change when, in 1931, he found a top-floor, four-room garden apartment in Fort Lee, New Jersey, thinking that his wife would appreciate having a bedroom just for the two of them and one for two-year-old Hannah. She cried and pleaded not to leave the now familiar environment she had known since her arrival from the old country and not to separate from her parents and siblings. Saul disregarded her tearful protests—a practice he would repeat many times over as the years passed—and with the help of Seymour, moved his family out of the Kolopsky apartment.

"What do you want from my life, Saul? How can you do this to me—take me away from Mama? Who do I know here? You go to work but I remain here. Alone."

And once again in 1933, after securing a substantial increase in salary in his new job as production manager for Hudson Valley Laundry in Jersey City, he moved his growing family to a ground-floor, five-room apartment in the same complex. This move brought fewer protests from Dora. At that time, she was pregnant with their second child and welcomed the convenience of more room and no stairs to climb.

The move to Bergeneck is not a happy event for Dora; rather, she experiences it as a tragedy. Although a mere six miles from Fort Lee, her response is tears of remorse. She doesn't speak to Saul for days and continues her grievances for months.

"I have to take one bus and two different subways to go to Mama's. Our neighbors hate us. They hate Jews. I hear them talking about the kikes who have moved onto the block. No kosher butchers, and I have to get on a bus with my hands full, schlepping groceries and, all the while, keeping my eyes on the kids. I have only two hands, you know, and I don't drive. You just drive away, but me, I'm stuck here with no one but stuck-up neighbors who look at me like I'm a freak—I mean it—like I have horns. And don't tell me to learn to drive. Roz tried to teach me, and look what happened. I could have killed the guy on the sidewalk and myself."

"Jesus H. Christ, Dora, how long ago was that? You didn't step on the brake, that's all." Saul interrupts. "You gotta step on the damned brakes. And as far as the neighbors go, let them all go to hell! Who do they think they are anyway? A lead-footed cop that pounds the beat! An assembly line worker at Ford! An elevator operator who puts on a suit, like he's working at a bank, and then changes into a monkey uniform when he gets to work—cap and all! He looks like the midget calling for Phillip Morris. They'd be on the bottom of the dung heap if they didn't have Jews and colored to kick around. They even hate Roosevelt—call him a Jew. A bunch of ignoramuses. Well, they can just kiss my sweet ass."

Shortly after they move in, Dora tells Saul that a little kid on the block approached Roberta, thinking she was a shiksa because of her blond hair and blue eyes, and whispered in her ear that there were Jews on the block. "Imagine, Saul, he called her a dirty Jew when she told him she was Jewish. He could only have heard that from his parents. She ran home and asked if we are dirty."

Saul had not informed Dora that before moving in, there had been a little Jewish matter to be reckoned with when he put down the asking price for the home, the remaining sixteen thousand of his hard-earned dollars—all of their savings, except for Dora's hidden stash secreted out of her weekly food allowance. He knew then that Jews were as unwelcome as the colored folk in this community of working-class Christians, at least in this area near the swamp.

The developer, Antonio Inganamort, made it very plain, when he not so subtly persisted in pressing Saul to reveal the origin of his name.

"So, what kind of a name is Sussman, eh? Sounds German? No, can't be German; that's with two *n*'s. Yours is with one, right? So where are you from?"

For once, Saul ignored the advice he gave to his children to "hit first and ask what they mean after" and made the disingenuous retort to Inganamort, "My people came from Connecticut and before that, Hungary. And before that, who knows? Do you have a problem with that?" Inganamort said he had no problems with Hungarians and that Saul needn't be so thin-skinned.

Inganamort did have a problem, though, not only with "kikes," but also with "niggers," "Chinks," and "Pollocks." Fortunately for the Sussmans, Inganamort also needed to sell the last remaining home in the small development he had built on an abandoned baseball diamond near the swampy marshlands, populated with mosquitoes and cattails—so named for their foot-long brown spikes, which kids break off to puff like make-believe cigars. He wanted to get on with his next and more lucrative upscale project on the other side of town, the prosperous area where the council members lived, as well as the mayor and the wealthy businessmen and professional men—those who commuted to their skyscraper jobs in Manhattan. They were bankers, lawyers, stockbrokers. Inganamort was drawing up plans for his own Tudor-style brick home on that side of town as well, so he accepted Saul's check, despite the *n* missing at the end of his name.

Later, Saul's youngest daughter encounters Inganamort's son, Bruce, at Longfellow Elementary School, when he explains he did not invite her to his second grade birthday party because she's a "filthy Jew and a Christ killer." Roberta asks Dora if the Jews killed anyone, and, she perseveres, she's not filthy because she takes a bath every night. And years later, when Roberta approaches Bruce at her thirty-fifth high school reunion, trying to be friendly, she tells him that her family lived in one of his father's housing developments. He says, "Nice," and quickly walks to the group who had been in the "rah-rah" crowd to describe, in great detail, the skyscraper he built in New York City.

Although there are no signs displayed on the borders of Berge-neck proclaiming, as there are in Miami Beach and environs, that "Jews and colored" are not welcome, one has only to tote up the number of churches that serve a population of 25,275 to get the covert message.

Presbyterian Church, St. Anastasia, Christ Episcopal, Bergen Methodist, Baha'i, Community Church of Christ, St. Mark's Episcopal, and St. Paul's Luti. A Jewish house of worship is nowhere to be found. The statistics say it all. Jews! You are not welcome. Go back to where you came from: to the old country.

The Sussmans move into their six-room suburban tract home in September 1939, a date coinciding with Germany's ground invasion of Poland and the start of World War II. Dora and Saul are thirty-five; their girls, Hannah and Roberta, eleven and six.

In April 1940, Adolf Hitler invades Denmark and Norway with his now familiar military tactic of "lightning war," or blitz-krieg—a word that promptly infiltrates the American vocabulary. The Germans bomb Paris in June, and Benito Mussolini, *Il Duce*, enters the war on the side of the Nazis and coins the term *axis* to represent the strength of their Fascist alliance. The Battle of Britain begins in July and culminates with another strike of German lightning—and with the first German Luftwaffe air raids on Central London. The onslaught of German bombs wreaking mayhem on the English citizenry corresponds with passage in the United States of the military conscription bill.

Saul listens to the nightly news on the radio and, without telling Dora, makes the decision to join the fight. Churchill informing his citizens "we will fight them on the beaches, we will fight them on the landing grounds, we shall fight them in the fields and in the streets" moves him almost to tears. He is similarly moved when he hears his president, Roosevelt, warning his countrymen that they have "nothing to fear but fear itself." And Saul admits to no fear.

The drumbeat of Hitler's marching army reverberates in America. Americans' awareness of the growing menace is heightened when they view the Pathe's weekly film clips of Hitler's SS troopers and Mussolini's Fascist Blackshirts strutting their staged ferocity for all the world to tremble. And tremble they did, including Saul and Dora.

In American homes across the country, radios are tuned into Gabriel Heatter and Walter Winchell. Families eat their evening meals in stony silence as they listen to Winchell's mesmerizing words of greeting: "Good evening, Mr. and Mrs. America and all the ships at sea."

They find little solace in Heatter's words of reassurance that "there's good news tonight, folks." They learn that German Jews over the age of ten are now required to wear a yellow Star of David with the word *Jude* on their clothing, identifying them as Jews, although that edict had previously been put into practice in Poland following *Kristallnacht* in 1938. There are reports of Jews being deported from Vienna, Germany, Alsace-Lorraine, and Poland to newly constructed concentration camps in Hitler's determination to detoxify German blood of its non-Aryan contaminants. And between 1939 and 1940, Hitler invades Poland, then Romania, the Netherlands, Luxembourg, and France, quickly followed by Belgium, Norway, Denmark, and Greece. In 1941, the Axis troops invade the Soviet Union in the largest military operation in human history, with over four and a half million troops, labeled Operation Barbarossa. The loss of life, some three million Russians, is staggering.

Der Stürmer, a Nazi newspaper, editorializes that ". . . judgment has begun and it will reach its conclusion only when knowledge of the Jews has been erased from the earth." In October 1941, Saul keeps the news from Dora that thirty-five thousand Jews from Odessa have been summarily shot. Most likely, her grandparents are part of that horrifying sum.

Indeed, there is no good news tonight or any night. Rather, anti-Semitism is on the rise both at home and abroad, with a striking lack of compassion for the plight of the thousands of European Jews being forced, yet again, to leave their possessions and their homes and being loaded into cattle cars for unknown destinations. But some know.

Ships carrying hundreds of Jewish émigrés are turned away from foreign ports. Jews are reduced to ashes in German crematoriums along with gypsies, socialists, homosexuals, Poles, mental and emotionally disabled people, and the few brave German citizens who dare to defy Hitler's 1935 Nuremberg Laws—laws defining Jews as anyone having three or four Jewish grandparents, regardless of whether the individual identifies himself as a Jew. A courageous Protestant minister named Bonheoffer will be hanged weeks before the German surrender for refusing to submit to the Nazi ideology.

Only four years past, Jesse Owens's Olympic victory in Berlin was a refutation of Hitler's notion of "Aryan racial superiority." And in the same year, Margaret Bergmann Lambert, the Jewish world-class high jumper who matched the world record of five feet three inches, was disqualified from jumping because of her religion. Two years later, in 1938, Joseph Louis Barrow, aka Joe Louis, the Brown Bomber, struck an additional blow to the chancellor's theory of supremacy when, on June 22, before a crowd of over seventy thousand, Louis pummeled Max Schmeling, the German heavyweight champion of the world, with a series of body blows that ended the rematch in two minutes and four seconds.

Years later, Jews will be blamed for going to their deaths like sheep to slaughter, without so much as a fight. The world will eventually learn of the 1943 Warsaw Ghetto uprising, in which 1,200 Jews, armed only with smuggled pistols, rifles, grenades, and Molotov cocktails, held off the bombardment of two thousand Waffen-SS soldiers, with their heavy tanks, artillery, and flamethrowers, for twenty-eight days, until they could no longer resist. The ghetto, along with the hopes and lives of the valiant fighters, went up in smoke and flames. No one could accuse them of cowardice.

The strange guttural-sounding names of these destinations will all too soon become unwelcome additions to the English vocabulary:

> Dachau!
> Buchenwald!
> Sobibór!
> Mauthausen!
> Ravensbrück!
> Auschwitz!

Nineteen-forty ends with another massive German air raid on London and with Saul's clandestine visit to the Hackensack Draft Board to enlist. Because his job as a production manager at the Hudson Valley Laundry keeps the fighting troops supplied with clean linen and is, therefore, deemed essential to the war effort, Saul is rejected.

Several weeks following his humiliating rebuff, with the children tucked into their beds, he confesses to Dora while sitting at the yellow Formica kitchen table the reason for his lousy mood and why he has withdrawn from her and the children into a dark cocoon.

"You don't care about us," Dora erupts in tears of confusion and anger, unable to support, no less understand, Saul's action and feelings.

"You enlist without giving us a thought? Did you even think of me? You'd walk out on me with two small kids? First you move me to this God-forsaken swamp—away from my family—and then, like a big *gantze macher*, off to war you go. Without telling or asking me!"

"Your family? Your family? I'm your family," Saul counters. "You're not a Kolopsky, you're a Sussman. Do you ever think beyond the nose on your face? For once, can you think about what it means for me not to be able to go to war—especially after my kid brother was drafted? You were saved by this country and cry whenever you hear that schmaltzy song 'God Bless America,'" he snaps, "but you want me to sit home on my duff and not fight?"

"Do you see Jack Coddington volunteering? Or Arthur Ziegler? He's a cop, and yet he didn't go marching off to fight for his country," Dora responds with mounting fury.

"That's because he's flat-footed. And 4-F," Saul's voice increases in intensity to match Dora's. "I don't have a so-called physical disability. It's the goddamned job and because I'm married with children that they rejected me. I volunteered, so don't compare me to that dumb cop or to that fascist coward bigot of a Republican across the street."

"Why do you always have to do the 'right' thing, Saul?" she pleads, her tone softening, her voice cracking. "Why is it you who has to make a stink because some colored man you don't even know doesn't get a raise at the laundry? Why do you have to risk our lives when you punch the guy because he calls you a dirty Jew? He could have killed us all. No, not you. Always fighting for the underdog. Telling Jack to go to hell because he doesn't vote for Roosevelt?" She starts trembling, "What if the army took you and then you died? The kids would be without a father. Did you think of that?"

"It's the navy! And you'd get a pension for life if it's money you're worried about. And I'd be dead and I wouldn't have to listen to your bellyaching."

Saul says that she never understands him and never will, and he walks out, slamming the front door behind him, shouting, "You should have married Freddy." One of Dora's blue-and-white porcelain figurines with ruffles on its skirt falls off the curio shelf in the living room and breaks. She picks up the pieces and places them on the kitchen counter for Saul to repair. When Saul doesn't return by ten, she gets into bed but lies awake in the dark, awaiting the sound of the car and the projected headlights dancing upon the bedroom ceiling. Hours later, he returns from the neighborhood bar with Jack Coddington—drunk, remorseful, and singing the only song he knows as he fumbles, unlocking the front door.

"Show me the way to go home. I'm tired and I wanna go to bed. I had a little drink about an hour ago . . ."

He has tied a handkerchief over one eye to keep from seeing double. Dora rushes downstairs when she hears him stumble over the umbrella stand in the hallway. She places her hand over his mouth to keep him from waking the children and uses all her strength to help him climb the stairs to their bedroom. Lying on the bed, he grins as Dora labors to remove his shoes and socks, his pants and shirt. Still singing, he pulls her down to him—"I'm tired and I wanna go to bed," she protests—and holds her tightly for several moments before turning her over to make love. Dora succumbs to her husband's boyish charms and tells him that it's a good thing he's so adorable. Lovemaking, not words or apologies, dissolves some of the bitterness of their many arguments.

~

Sixty million deaths occur as a result of World War II, including Saul's favorite brother, Seymour. At thirty-eight, in March of 1945, he is killed off the remote and formerly unheard of island of Okinawa by a Japanese kamikaze attack. Young Japanese soldiers leave their wives and children to obey Emperor Hirohito's declaration of war to fight their American counterparts in a forced marriage of suicide and death. Younger than Saul by three years, Seymour leaves his wife, Betty, and their six-month-old infant, Susan. He also leaves a hole in Saul's already aching heart.

The brothers had plans to go into business together after the war. Saul was to quit his job as production manager so they could open a small laundry in the working-class neighborhood of Guttenberg, New Jersey. They were to employ and train the unemployable—mostly colored men returning from the war—and bring economic vitality to the foursquare block community. No one would have to force them to pay a decent wage and bring dignity to the lives of their employees.

For the second time in his life, Saul weeps unabashedly. With his brother's death, unlike his mother's, there is no grave site, no black void in which to heave himself. Nor will there be a marker to signify that a brave young man died on this very spot. Only the cold, dark, hostile waters of the Pacific Ocean will receive the severed body parts that fall freely from the conning station lodged above the pilot house of the LST—a Landing Ship Tank—which are known to his navy brethren as "large slow targets."

Unlike Icarus's fall into the Icarian Sea after he disregards his father's warning not to fly too close to the sun, there is no Bruegel to memorialize Seymour's plunge into the watery sepulcher along with his fellow patriots. There are no survivors.

Typically, when Saul returned home every evening punctually at seven sharp, he rushed in to listen to his nightly news program on the radio. Tonight, he turns the car into the driveway at five and sits motionless for well over an hour, seemingly a statue with his arms over his head, resting on the steering wheel of his gray-and-black Buick that he recently purchased secondhand.

Dora views Saul walking trancelike across the green lawn, looking as though he might have been drinking, perhaps to celebrate the war's end—something he would never do and never allowed the children to do. He thumps on the front door.

Oh, he must have forgotten his keys, she thinks, not grasping that he had to possess them to drive the car. He looks at her, says nothing, and walks into the kitchen and sits at the kitchen table where his daughters are doing their homework. "What is it, Saul?" Dora asks, "What's the matter? Isn't it wonderful that the war is over?"

His daughters sit stricken, helplessly watching their daddy—their all-powerful and silent protector—as he sits at the kitchen table with a crumpled Western Union telegram, taken from his pocket, and makes strange noises. They can't tell if he's laughing or crying. Hannah and Roberta exchange wary glances as curiosity transforms itself into fear and then into a paroxysm of giggles. Dora finds their behavior bewildering, not comprehending that their laughter helps to mitigate the panic they feel seeing their father's collapse. Frightened herself, she scoots them to the living room, leaving Saul to fend for himself.

"I'm sorry to tell you this, but the telegram Daddy received informed him that Uncle Sy is dead." Dora struggles valiantly to continue, holding back her own tears. "You know Uncle Sy was in the navy and was fighting our enemies in Japan. He was very, very brave, but while he was on his ship, a Jap flew his airplane into his ship, and he and all the men on the ship were killed. He has gone to be with God."

"Is he really dead?" asks an unbelieving sixteen-year-old Hannah. "It can't be; I just got a V-mail from him. He said he was coming home soon."

"Is he in Heaven?" Roberta wonders.

"Well, maybe," Dora says. "I don't know if there is such a place. Maybe."

"Mrs. Strong, my teacher, told me that when we die we go to Heaven," Roberta persists. "She said that we either go to Heaven if we've been good or Hell if we've sinned, and there's a place called Purgatory where God decides which place we'll go."

"Jews don't believe in Heaven. And certainly not Hell," sighs Dora, feeling that she has reached the end of her ability, or patience, to explain. "And I've never heard of that other place."

"I don't want to die," cries Roberta, "I'm scared, Mommy."

"You won't die for a very, very long time," Dora responds, feeling short of breath, the result of her own death anxiety. She hates to think about dying and, at times, suffers painful attacks when breathing becomes difficult, when her palms sweat, when she suffers from diarrhea or nausea.

"I don't believe you; I know he's not dead," insists Roberta. "Hannah got the V-mail, and I just got the Peter Cottontail bunny he sent." With a growing weakening of her conviction, her lip begins to quiver.

Hannah has been sitting quietly during this exchange between Roberta and Dora. She looks at Dora and then at Roberta and blurts out, "But what about Daddy? He's all by himself in the kitchen crying. And poor Uncle Sy. He was only thirty-eight, and Aunt Betty . . . and their baby. Oh, jeez, this is terrible."

"You're right." As Dora returns to the kitchen, she hears the muted sobs from the living room grow louder. "Oh, God," she thinks, "what do I do now?"

Dora has always dreaded the fact that someday she too would die and does whatever she can to avoid thinking about it. Her oft-stated belief is that once you're dead, you're dead. To face the reality of death without the comfort of a belief in a hereafter means to confront the deepest, darkest void of despair and nonexistence.

She cannot bear to think of a world without her or her children or Saul, and when she does, her mental state becomes intolerable.

Her Judaism is of no solace. It consists of blindly following the rituals she once observed in her parents' home without any comprehension of their philosophical, historical, or even moral underpinnings. Girls and women were exempt from the obligations to learn Torah and Talmud, and from the performance of mitzvoth. Rather, they were relegated to sacred tasks in the realm of home and hearth. Dora recalls her mother's routinely avowed beliefs: "What could be more blessed than caring for your child or lighting the Shabbos candles or preparing food for those you love?"

Without fail, with her hands circling and then covering her eyes, Dora lights the Friday night Shabbos candles and, by rote, repeats the prayers that accompany it. She refuses to write or turn on the oven's flame and demands similar compliance from her children. She maintains a strictly kosher kitchen and never mixes meat, fleishig, with milk, milchig. She keeps the children home from school on the High Holy Days and even observes tashlik, the ritual casting away of one's sins into a body of water on Rosh Hashanah. On Hanukkah, she grates the onions and potatoes to make latkes and gifts the children with their annual supply of flannel pajamas for winter and cotton for summer. All this she does without reflection or curiosity as to its significance. The comfort it provides, however, does not extend to death.

When Dora can no longer ignore the muffled cries emanating from the children's bedroom, she mounts the stairs to find Roberta and Hannah lying on the floor, crying into their pillows to stifle their weeping.

At these moments, Dora wonders if she is cut out for motherhood. She feels overwhelmed with its relentless stress and longs for the days of her carefree youth. She thinks of the way she used to dance and sing and even idealizes the time she worked for her brother-in-law Joe in the bloomer factory. She wonders what she'd be doing now if she had married Freddy rather than Saul. She thinks of Bessie, who always knows the answers to everything, and tries to imagine what she would say or do.

"Okay, that's enough with the crying already. Now get dressed. We're going to get on a bus and visit Bubbe and Zaide. If you hurry, we can catch the next bus. Quick, quick. The first one dressed gets a piece of halvah. And maybe we can even see Aunt Bessie. I'll call her and tell her we're going to Bubbe's." She finds her anxiety abating as soon as she thinks of seeing her mother and of the slim possibility of talking to Bessie, the Cassandra of the Bronx, and her best friend.

"Yeah, we're going to Bubbe and Zaide's," shrieks Roberta. Hannah shushes her and reminds her about Uncle Seymour.

Roberta and Hannah jump up and run to their closet, discarding their pajamas as they go. Dora collects them from the floor and hangs them on the hooks Saul installed inside their closet door.

When she feels unstable and emotionally needy, Dora longs for the comfort and warmth of her mama's arms. She tears a piece from a brown paper bag—her mode of correspondence—and writes a note for Saul, who has left the house to make a condolence visit to Seymour's wife, instructing him to pick them up the following day. She guides her children out the front door and makes her way to the bus stop three blocks away, just in time to board the 167 bus that will convey them over the George Washington Bridge and to the subway that will take them to her beloved Brighton Beach. And home. Home to Mama.

Chapter 10

MARYUSA FREIDE: WHY HAVE YOU FORSAKEN ME?

1946

They think I'm stupid, but I'm not. They think I'm re-tard-ed, but I'm not. That's what that man told Mama—re-tard-ed—when she wanted me to go to school. Why didn't she explain to them—tell them all that just because I can't talk the way they do doesn't mean I'm stupid? They're stupid. Oh-oh, that's not a nice word. Dora says that's not a nice word, but if it's not, why do they call *me* stupid? Sometimes words go over and over in my head; I can't stop them. The words talk. They tell me how they should sound. And I try to say my words their way, but they don't listen to me.

People laugh at me too. I don't laugh at them when they act silly. Like when Shmuel did a round-and-round on his head and bumped into Levi's glass cabinet and broke it, I wanted to laugh because it looked funny. Everyone else did except Lena, Levi's wife. Owwwee, she was so mad. Her face turned red like my sweater. But it was a bad thing for him to do. So, back to words, I try to say what I see their mouths saying, but then it comes out all *fermisht*. Their faces tell me they don't understand me. Why is my way wrong and their way right?

I can't read, but Mama never sent me to school because of that stupid man who called me re-tard-ed. But she couldn't read either, and she wasn't re-tard-ed. All the others went to school. Avram went for a little, and he wanted to make money, so he quit. He drives a cab and makes lots of money now. But I can read some words. And I can hear some too, if they talk loud. They didn't know that at first. Sometimes I like not hearing so good. I like when it's quiet all around me. I look at words on the trolley when I go to work, like O-F-F or P-U-L-L or S-T-O-P, and then when I'm brave, I ask someone to say it. And sometimes—not always— the nice people on the trolley tell me, and then I know. Some just look at me and then look away. But sometimes I can even figure for myself, so I think that's smart. I think Avram isn't smart—that's why he stopped going to school—but he got to go anyway. He always talks loud, so then I can hear him better than the rest; I don't like what he says.

People talk about me and say things about me like I'm a child. No! Worse. Like I'm not there. "I'm here," I want to scream at them. "Don't talk about me when I'm here." I may not hear everything when they mumble, and, boy, do they mumble a lot. And I may not understand everything they talk about. But I know plenty. I know how to go to the bank and cash my check on payday. I know how to put money in my savings book. I know how Papa used to come into Mamma's bed in the night when it was dark and everyone was asleep and thump her. That's the noise it makes: thump, thump, thump. And he made noise too—sounded like he was crying, but when I asked Mama if Papa was crying, she got all upset. But it shook my bed like when trolleys go by. Mama said "shhhhh" to him. I made believe I was sleeping; I didn't want them to know I was hearing. I didn't want to make Mama upset.

And I know how Faigel—Faye—talked angry words to Mama when they fought. And then Mama cried. Why did everyone change their name? At work, they call me Mary. Maybe they can't say Marya. And I know how Levi and Avram used to grab the money that Papa got selling rags from his pushcart, and how they would throw his little purse from one to the other until all the pennies would fall all over the floor and roll under the chairs and tables. How bad that made Papa feel. He would chase after the pennies on his hands and knees and try to pick them up. He got so mad and would try to hit them, but they'd run around the table and laugh at him. "Look, Papa, look at all the money you made. Twenty cents. Ha, Ha, Ha!" That was not nice. Papa said the Bible says you should respect your parents. Sometimes he did cry.

And I know what Avram—uh, Abraham—does to me in the middle of the night is bad too. He holds my mouth so I don't make noise, and when he's done, he warns me if I say anything, he will hit me. He tells me "shhhhhh" the way Mama told Papa "shhh-hhh." No one is there, so why does he shush me? Sometimes he hits me for nothing. Says that's just to show me what he'd do. He scares me, so I don't tell. But someday I'm going to tell Shmuel so he'll say to stop. That's spelled S-T-O-P. Like the time Mama caught Abraham sneaking over to Dora's bed, when she used to live here before she married Saul, and touching her. Down there. Mama told him if she ever caught him doing that again, she'd cut him up with the big knife the way she cuts chickens up. She didn't tell Papa. Dora screamed and he stopped. Maybe next time I'll scream. Mama used to tell me that no one should ever touch me down there. I scream better than I talk. Now that's funny.

Sometimes when I'm talking to a boy at work, Shmuel yanks me away and then hits me after I get home. Why does everyone hit me? Mama tried to stop him, but he didn't listen to her. He yells at me, "If I ever catch you talking to that guy again, you'll see what I'll do to you." Like Avram. He's not my papa, so he shouldn't hit me. Papa never hit me. Well, what about Avram? Does Shmuel know what he does to me and what he did to Dora? Sometimes he smells like schnapps when he stops by. And sometimes he puts his thing in my mouth, and once he put it—I don't want to think of that, but it hurt. Sometimes he comes here in the morning when he's supposed to be driving his taxi. He knows the day I don't work, and he chases me around the room. Sometimes I run out the door and get away. Sometimes I don't.

Shmuel tells me that if anything ever happens when I'm at the laundry—if anyone tries to hurt me—I should tell him, and that if he's busy doing important things because he's a big boss and can't come, I should scream or call a policeman. So maybe I should call a policeman when Avram chases me or hits me again. Once, a nice man talked to me at the laundry. His name was Marco; we ate lunch together. Mama used to make me lunch, but now that she's dead I make it for myself. I make hard boiled eggs. Sometimes I take chicken and sometimes I drink coffee with milk in it, but I don't tell anyone because you're not supposed to have milk with meat. Papa always told me you don't mix meat with dairy. I don't know why, but most of the time I listened to what he said. But Marco was nice to me. Sometimes he helped me fold sheets. He asked questions all about me, like if I was a good girl and if I had enough money. And where I kept it because it should be in a safe place. He was worried about me. No one usually asks me questions about anything. So I told him I kept my money in a bank, thank you. "It's safe there," I told him. Once, he asked me if I could borrow him some money because he had some important business to do. I took him to my bank, and I gave him some. Not all. I gave him a lot though, and I let him touch me too in the closet at work, because I liked him. And because it felt good. Not like with Avram. Because he was a nice man and talked nice to me and asked me questions and didn't hit me.

But then Shmuel found out—I don't know who told on

me—and that's when he came to Papa's place—well it's mine now since Papa and Mama died—and hit me a lot. He cried. I wonder why he cried. He hit me and he cried. I cried too. I cried because he hit me and it hurt and because he was crying. He said he was hitting me for my own good, but it didn't feel good. Papa told me that we came here from far away on a big boat from a place called Russia. I don't remember that because I was little. Papa said I was five years old. Papa said that he came on a different big boat before we came. He came with Levi and Shmuel. Faigel came before that; she ran away to America with Yosef—they call him Joseph now. Joseph and Faye got married when they came to America. I came with Mama and Dora and Leib. And Avram. He wasn't Abe yet. And Dora wasn't Dora yet. I wish he stayed in Russia because then he couldn't do bad things. He doesn't hit me for my own good like Shmuel; he hits me to scare me so I don't tell on him. If I was five, then Avram was fourteen. And Dora was ten, and Leib was seven. See, I'm smart. But I used my fingers, so maybe that doesn't count. Mama said the name of the boat was the *Lusitania*, and it took lots and lots of days to get here, and so many people got sick, and it smelled bad because they got sick all over, and there wasn't any air because we were so close together in the bottom of the boat. Mama said the boat rocked up and down because the waves were big, like giants. Shmuel and Levi and Faigel sent Mama money to come. Papa too. That was kind.

Sometimes I go to visit Dora and Saul. Saul is nice. They live in a faraway place called New Jersey, but it isn't as far away as Russia. I have to take three buses to get there. It's a big house, not little, like my place. First Mama died and then Papa died. And Dora has a big dog. He has a big black tongue, and they call him Rover. He's a chow dog. Sometimes he scares me because he barks loud. I hear his barking, so it must be loud. He never bites me, but I still get scared. So I get on the bus and give the bus driver what

Saul wrote on a paper that tells the man who drives the bus where I need to get off. And then I have another piece of paper that I give to a different man who drives a different bus, the number 167, and it leaves from a place called the Port Authority. That's not in New Jersey; it's in New York. Lots of buses are there and lots of people rushing this way and that way, and I get on the right bus. And it takes an hour to get there. Sometimes I fall asleep. We go across the George Washington Bridge. I don't get off at Fort Lee though, where they used to live. When I fall asleep, the driver stops the bus and even comes to wake me up. I guess I don't hear him when he calls "Queen Anne Road." Then I get off. I walk three blocks with houses on both sides of the street, and trees, until I come to Dora's house. It's brick on the bottom and white on the top, with black shutters. It has a porch too. And a place where Saul puts his car. He can drive but not Dora. Sometimes we sit on the porch. Rover is in the back behind a white fence that Saul built, but he always barks and jumps up like he's going to jump over the fence. He can't because he was always running away so Saul made a wire that he clips onto a chain on Rover's collar. Dora has two kids, girls. Roberta loves Rover. She dresses him up in baby clothes. They are cute, but I think they look at me funny. I hope they don't think I'm stupid. I am their aunt, after all, and they should respect me. Sometimes Hannah—she's the big one—comes over and sits by me and smiles. She's nice. The little one, Roberta—Papa used to say she looks like a shiksa—looks at me funny. Sometimes she lays on the floor making paper dolls.

I go to work almost every day. Sometimes when I'm very tired, I don't get out of bed, but most of the time I make myself get up and go because I'm afraid Abe will come. I take wet sheets and put them on a big, hot machine—it's called a *mangle*—and it rolls the sheets around and around and they come out nice, dry and hot, without any wrinkles. I like their smell. Josie is at the other end to catch them, and she folds them. She's my friend at work. Sometimes I burn myself but not bad. Then after Josie folds them, someone else takes them away in a big cart, and I don't know where they go after that. Shmuel is the big boss there. Saul used to work there too, but he has his own laundry now. Everyone listens to Shmuel. They call him Mr. Kolopsky, not Shmuel. He tells everyone what to do, and he has a big office all by himself with glass around it and a door that sometimes he closes. And he has a phone too. Sometimes he lets me come in and eat my lunch with him. There's a lady who sits outside of his office; she gives me paper and a pencil to write on. She has taught me how to write my name. I practice writing my name, Mary Kolopsky, like Papa did. Sometimes she learns me a letter of the alphabet. Sometimes Shmuel takes me to a diner across the street—all white and black tiles— and he gets me mashed potatoes and spinach. I don't like the spinach, but if I eat it all up, he gets me ice cream. It's square and wrapped in wax paper. Strawberry, chocolate, and vanilla stripes. I like the vanilla best, so I eat it last. He watches me and sometimes tells me stories the way Papa used to. I don't remember anything about Odessa—that's the place in Russia we lived in. Mama said I was too young to remember. Now I'm thirty-seven. Mama said it was bad there and that there were bad men who came and hurt people. They hurt people because they were Jewish. I don't understand why they did that. But she said that we are very lucky to be here in America. I miss her so much. I think she loved me more than anybody. She would rub my back and kiss me. Papa would sometimes tell me stories about "the old country." He said he was important there and that a lot of people listened to him. And he didn't sell rags either. He taught boys and studied Torah—that's a holy book. I like the story he used to tell me about a man named Samson who was so strong that he pulled down a big building. After he told me that story, he looked sad. I guess Papa was a boss like Shmuel.

He used to take a pushcart around the streets here and try to sell the rags that he collected the day before. He doesn't do that anymore because no one bought them. Well, he really doesn't do it anymore because he's dead, but even before he died, he stopped and didn't do very much except sit and pray and go to shul. I like the boardwalk. It's very near our place. Near the ocean. I like the smell of the ocean. They have a man under the boardwalk that sells knishes. He has a cart too, but he must make money because he's been there a long time. When Papa wasn't at shul, he prayed and read his little book, and sometimes he practiced writing his name over and over again on the inside of his siddur. Papa must have liked to write his name because he smiled when he finished. I can write my name too. I said that already. Sometimes Dora tries to teach me to read. It's hard. Mama never learned to write. I speak English, but she couldn't. We spoke Yiddish, but it didn't matter because she usually knew what I meant even when I didn't talk. She was always working—pulling feathers from the chickens, making dinner, giving Papa lunch, making tea, and cleaning. It was Shabbos when she died. She fixed the house all nice and clean and set the table with the Shabbos tablecloth—it's lace, and I still have it, and sometimes I put it on the table just like Mama used to—and she put the chicken in the oven to cook and lit the Shabbos candles, and then she fell on the floor. She made a big bang. She never got up. I cried, "Mama, Mama, get up. Please get up. Please, Mama, get up." And then Papa came home from shul and found her on the floor—I was sitting by her and crying—and he started yelling, "Henya, Henya. Help, please help me." And then a big white truck came, and two men in white came and took them away, and then Shmuel and Levi and Avram and Faigel came, and they cried and tore their hair and their clothes. So I tore my clothes too. And then people came over with food—people I didn't know, from Papa's shul. They brought food and covered the mirror, and we all sat on wooden crates, and I didn't go to work for a week. And we all cried. They put Mama in a box, and they put her in the ground, and Papa started crying and said something about "my little Yonkel." I don't know little Yonkel or why Papa was calling little Yonkel. Maybe that's a special name he called Mama. Dora came to stay with us for the week. Not Saul. Dora was very sad. She cried a lot. She said she lost her best friend. Then she cut Papa's toenails and went home.

I miss Mama more than Dora because she lives with Saul and Hannah and Roberta. I'm all alone. Papa died a little while after Mama died. He said he wanted to be with Mama and said something about Yonkel again. And Shimshon. Who is he? I should have asked him then about Yonkel, but he was sad, and I didn't want to make him more sad. When I get very sad and lonely, I put on a record that Papa used to play on our Victrola—it has a white dog on it with his head to one side and black ears. I wind it up and put it on. It says, "*Eli, Eli, lama sabachthani.*" I still have it, and I am very careful because I don't want to break it. Papa told me it's written by a man called David. He said he was a king a long time ago who was a poet, and when he was a little boy, he played a harp and killed a giant. Josie, my friend at work, calls him a Messiah, but she called him by a different name, Jesus. She told me he was asking his father why he had forsaken him because he was dying and his father didn't help him. She said he was God and lived here on earth for a little while, but when I told Papa what she'd said, he said Jews don't believe that, and I shouldn't listen to her. He said there is only one God and that he lives in a place in the sky. Papa said the poem this King David wrote was a very sad song and that was why he was crying. It must have been very sad because every time he played it he cried. Even when Mama was alive, he cried. I can close my eyes and see my Papa sitting on his chair by the Victrola and crying while he plays the record. I wish I asked him about Yonkel. And Shimshon. It's too late now. I feel sad now thinking about my Papa, so maybe I'll feel better if I put the record on. I will think about my Papa— and my Mama—and I'll ask them to tell me why they left me here all by myself. I wonder if that's why that man—that Jesus—was calling out to his father, because he didn't want to be left all alone. Maybe Papa was crying about his papa? Papa had a father; maybe his name was Yonkel. He was very sad and missed his papa too. And Mama. I miss them so much.

> My God, my God, why hast thou forsaken me?
> Why are thou so far from helping me,
> And from the words of my roaring?

Chapter 11

DORA: SCORCHED EGGS, MEMORIES, AND SHATTERED GLASS

1990

Huddled behind a threadbare chair, Disha, a dark curly-haired child, shivers with fear as the sound of soldiers' booted strides comes closer. She hears the truncheons striking doors or whatever unfortunate object finds itself in their path. The pained yelp of a dog trumpets one of their victims. And then: "Yid, yid, Christ-killers! Kill the dirty Jews!"

"Mama," she screams as the door explodes with thunderous force, toppling the mound of furniture stacked against it to keep the assailants out; they snap like delicate, miniature tables and chairs that populate a child's dollhouse.

Eighty-two years later, Dora awakens to her own smothered scream and to the shouts of garbage men clearing the detritus of her neighbors' lives as they make their weekly rounds.

"Vey iz mir! I must have fallen asleep."

The acrid odor of burning food invades her nostrils. She wonders where she is but slowly, slowly recovers her whereabouts as she looks around the familiar living room overflowing with cherished possessions that joggle her memory.

"The eggs!" she whispers, placing her hand to her cheek, and staggers to the kitchen and sees the remains of the scorched pan and charred eggs sitting on the still-glowing stove burner, with its shattered shards of eggshells precariously hanging from the surrounding walls and ceiling. "I could have burned the house down with me in it . . . So, it would be so bad if I went? How long can a person live? Saul gone; my brothers and sisters dead. Eighty-six years, almost blind. And dangerous. And here I am talking to myself. What a mess! What a mess!"

She sets the small, rutted aluminum pot in the sink filled with hot, soapy water, wipes the egg fragments from the stove and wall, looks at the ceiling, shrugs, and returns to the living room and collapses in her rocker, struggling to eradicate the memory of the nightmare image of carnage and the ever-present reminder of death.

"So many years ago and still that same dream. A nightmare. Odessa. Only in my dreams do I remember that place. But why should I remember? It was nothing but misery. Roberta asks why I don't speak Russian. Why would I want to? She shows me pictures a friend took when she was there and asks if I know where it is. 'It's Odessa, Mother,' she says, like I should know. How would I know? Sometimes she can be a nudnik with her questions about the past. She thinks she's in court. Always questions and more questions."

With great effort, she shuffles her slippered feet back to the kitchen table and sits down to an improvised lunch of canned vegetable soup and a hunk of challah, the bread she bought for the evening's Shabbos meal. Taking but a few swallows of the soup, she pushes aside the bowl and opens the oven door to make certain that the vegetable tzimmes hasn't burnt as well. *At least*, she thinks, *my dinner shouldn't taste like ashes.*

"I can't eat. That dream takes appetite away," she says, talking to herself, "but I'll be hungry later." She returns to the comfort of her wooden rocking chair, well worn, like an old sock, from years of sitting, depressed in just the right places.

A Whistler-like portrait in gray and black, Dora rhythmically rocks back and forth in the chair she has known intimately for what seems like an eternity. This small, still strikingly handsome white-haired woman stares into the space of time past as she absentmindedly strokes the worn armrest of the rocker. She smiles as she recalls the home she lived in for more than forty years with Saul and their daughters. Such a long time ago.

"So different, like night and day they were, those kids. One afraid of her shadow; the other afraid of nothing. Hannah serious, with her face in a book, and Roberta, getting into mischief. Always doing splits and headstands and cutting school. Who would have thought she'd become a lawyer? The troublemaker, a lawyer; the serious one, an artist. Well, maybe that's not so strange after all. The troublemaker understands how it feels for another troublemaker, and the serious one expresses her deep thoughts in works of art. Huh! I sound like Bessie. I've got to call her."

Dora thinks of the ways Saul encouraged Roberta to be a tomboy. She pictures the trapeze he hung in the doorjamb when she was barely two and how he let her swing by her arms until she cried out "uncle" and how, eventually, she learned to pull her body into an upside-down arrow, feet up, head down, smiling and looking to him for approval. Like a sloth, she would hang in that position for five minutes or more, until Saul took her down as Hannah stood wistfully, looking at her baby sister's achievement with admiration and awe. And just a little envy. Roberta, even at that young age, knew what she had to do to enchant Saul. And to make up for having been born a girl.

Dora reflects on the time when Roberta was three and Saul

threw her into the swimming pool at Paramus on one of their Sunday excursions and how she came up sputtering but determined to laugh through her fear. She refused to cry "uncle," the signal she knew would stop him, when Saul squeezed her knuckles. She knew he liked her spunk, and she so needed his approval and love.

It wasn't right, she thinks, *how he ignored me after Roberta's birth and how he told me that I never gave him anything he wanted.* And then she smiles, recollecting how the nurse told him off as they were leaving.

"Listen, Dad, take a look at this beautiful little girl. You should be ashamed of yourself, acting like a spoiled child. If I were your wife, I'd throw you outta here. So she's not a boy, but she's got all her fingers and toes and can see and hear."

It didn't help, she thinks. He was so stubborn. He was always to feel the deprivation.

She glances at the silver-framed image of two young girls, residing on the table beside her rocker—the older of the two with thick jet-black curls framing her sweetheart-shaped face, with saucer-like brown eyes; the little one's hair the color of butter and eyes like the sky at twilight and skin as pale as moonshine.

"Eh, those were the days," she says to the photograph. The image, one that Saul captured of the girls with his new Brownie camera, is now somewhat faded with age and brown spots, like her hands. Hannah stares solemnly into the camera; Roberta smiles and looks adoringly at her big sister. They had stopped for a break at a drive-in restaurant on their way to Miami, where they were meeting Lenny and his family, in their newly purchased but used 1941 black-and-gray two-toned Buick coupe. *He wasn't a bad father,* she thinks. *It's just that he wanted a son. He liked it that we named Hannah after his mother, but he wanted a son to carry on the Sussman name. He even told Roberta that she was the biggest disappointment of his life. Imagine. We had moved to Hawaii, and they were visiting.* She looks again at the photo from their first family vacation.

Hannah read the road signs aloud as they entered the city.

"NO COLORED OR JEWS."

She remembers her shock and fear and Saul's fury after first being welcomed at the motel, the one with the flashing red vacancy sign, then given the clerk's disclaimer that there was, in fact, no vacancy after Saul wrote his name on the reservation form. She wanted to go home, but Saul wouldn't hear of it. That was the first time Dora experienced an inexplicable feeling of imminent death, what the doctors later labeled a *nervous breakdown.* Her heart beat as though it would explode out of her chest; her lungs felt near collapse; her palms sweated profusely. "I must lie down," she said to Saul, who was in the middle of a very rowdy quarrel with the clerk. Dora climbed into the back seat of the car to restore her equilibrium.

The Golden Land, she thinks. *Hannah must have been, let's see—it was 1940, so I must have been thirty-six, so Hannah was eleven or twelve and Roberta, five or six Ah, who can remember? My mind is a muddle. The best times of my life,* she reflects, *when they were little. They were so sweet. I would look at them as they slept in their beds and think they looked like cherubs. But could I enjoy it? Always worried about fitting in. Always feeling like an outsider. I still do, even though there aren't many left to fit into. I guess that never goes away. Always looking to see how everyone else was doing something or not doing something. Not Saul. Born here, so why would he worry? He was always standing up to someone. I was always shrinking.* She remembers the car accident. The girls were in the back seat, and some man cut Saul off on Degraw Avenue and clipped the left fender. Saul got out of the car and before you know it, the man was calling Saul a dirty kike. *Well, no one did that to Saul,* she thinks and smiles with pride, recalling the image of the man sprawled on the ground and her pleading for Saul to calm down. Saul calmed down when he got the man's apology.

"He never knew what hit him," she says, laughing as she addresses the photograph.

"You had some father. He always taught you girls to hit first and ask later what they meant. That's my husband—your father—may he rest in peace . . . The girls insisted we should cremate him because that's what he wanted. I stood my ground, for a change. But, ah, what's the difference; when you're dead, you're dead."

Dora begins to stroke the arm of the rocking chair and thinks of the day she made the decisive purchase. It was Adeline, her next-door neighbor—Addie, she called herself—who instructed her in the ways of her new, new world in the suburbs.

"*We all* buy our furniture there," she said. Dora understood what Addie meant by "we all." It refered to folks born in America, not foreigners—especially Jews—like her. She recalls how Addie's mother spoke with an accent. But it was Scotch. Being a Scotch immigrant, not Russian and certainly not a Jew, made all the difference to Addie.

Oh, Saul! You had to move us to New Jersey with its pigs and smells and swamps—Secaucus, Weehawken, Hoboken, what names!—away from Mama and Papa. So what we had near Mama wouldn't be a two-story brick house with shutters—what good are shutters anyway?—and a backyard with peach and apple trees and a fenced-in pen for a dog. Who needed a dog, with his hair all over the place? Just more work for me. In Brighton Beach, at least I could walk to Mama's every day. And there were kosher butchers and a shul across the street and people like me. I heard Yiddish in the streets. And no one called me a dirty kike or a greenhorn. We were all greenhorns then.

Still, she yearned to be like "them," like Addie or Addie's sister, Elsie, who lived across the street—to speak the way they spoke, without an accent; to wear their kind of clothes; to drink Manhattans with cherries or rye and ginger ale after their husbands returned from work; to make the food they made—pineapple upside-down cake—not *traif* though; and to buy furniture like they had in their parlors.

One day, while waiting for the clerk to bag her groceries at the A&P supermarket on Queen Anne Road, she turned the pages of a magazine near the checkout counter with dreams of transforming her home. Making it like *theirs*. Once, she even bought a *Woman's Day* when she happened upon a picture of a forest green-walled living room. So beautiful, like a velvet jungle.

Maybe Saul can paint it, she thought. *That man can do anything with his golden hands. Turns the basement into a playroom, with its orange and blue square cardboard ceiling and walls that look like real wood. Builds a white fence in the backyard. Plants a Victory garden. What can't that man do?*

Willing herself to act like the other women in line who would casually make such a purchase, Dora, with a small flourish, dropped the magazine in her shopping cart along with her groceries, fervently wishing the other women were looking.

Several weeks later, Dora approached Ye Olde Furniture Shoppe on a typical humid summer day in Jersey. She paused to ponder the lettering of the wrought-iron sign hanging over the entrance as she wiped her brow.

"S-H-O-P-P-E? Huh? I could have sworn it was S-H-O-P," she whispered, looking around for reassurance that no one had heard her talking to herself. She did this frequently, mostly to rehearse what she was about to say. She searched her green felt pocketbook and took out a piece from the corner of a brown paper bag, which she carried with her for just such occasions, and a knife-sharpened pencil to scribble in her artless penmanship: S H O P P E.

"I'll ask Addie. No, Saul. He would know." She felt smugly satisfied when she thought that she was married to a real American, and smart.

The brass bell on the glass-framed door tinkled as she tentatively entered the claustrophobic store. She patted down her beige linen dress with its stand-up collar to erase the wrinkles from the bus ride from Bergenwood to Hackensack. A dank odor sent a shudder throughout her body. It reminded her of something. But what? The agitation was familiar. She knew it belonged to another time, another place. She hoped she wasn't about to get another one of those attacks. Her new doctor, Dr. Fechner, called them *anxiety attacks*. He was a nice man—a German refugee. Called what she had in Florida a nervous breakdown and gave her iodine to put in her milk each morning. She breathed deeply.

Tables, chairs, lamps, hassocks, and loveseats strewn about like pick-up sticks, a game her children love to play by the hour, left a narrow pathway for Dora to maneuver. Stricken with queasiness and the fear that she might have another collapse, she turned to leave.

"Good afternoon. May I help you?"

Too late. She regretted coming alone, but she couldn't turn and run now. Once again she thought of Addie and tried to emulate her stately bearing. She would hold her head high and breeze through the door with a condescending gesture, waving the man aside, as if she owned the place. *Just like a queen*, Dora imagined.

Addie represented everything Dora was not. A tall, handsome woman who appeared to Dora to be strong and invincible. She did everything Dora feared to do or even to think of doing: She drove a car—a baby-blue convertible Chevrolet—steering with her right hand while smoking a Lucky Strike in her left. She painted the shutters that bracketed the windows of her cottage while perched on a stepladder, her auburn hair piled high on her head, the ever-present cigarette suspended loosely from her plum-painted lips—with fingernails to match. She baked pineapple upside-down cakes and blueberry pies and told shady jokes about a man's body "down there," followed by hearty peals of laughter. When the war came, she got a job spot welding in an assembly plant. Dora never learned exactly what that meant, just that it was what Addie did and that it must be grand. The factory even used her as the model for a "Rosie the Riveter" poster that Addie hung prominently in her living room, framed. Saul had made the frame. *That man, what can't he do?* thought Dora, somewhat jealous, and imagined herself as the woman in the frame.

Addie even divorced her husband, Arthur, an Errol Flynn lookalike who, despite working as an elevator operator in one of New York's high rises, wore a neatly pressed charcoal-striped suit each morning as he set off for work, attaché case in tow. He also cheated on his wife.

She was the talk of the neighborhood when a strange man was seen frequenting her bungalow and then leaving in the early morning hours, before the neighborhood awakened. For two years they carried on this charade, and then she married him. And then Larry disappeared from the premises as mysteriously as he appeared. He vanished shortly after Addie was seen with one of her eyes blackened and her arm in a sling. He was no longer "lovey." She now called him "a sonova bitch."

Years later, Dora's conflicted adulation of Addie would end abruptly when Addie refused to accompany her as a witness when she applied for citizenship. "We have enough foreigners here. And Jews. Find one of your own, honey. I'm kinda busy now that I have a job."

The insistent voice of the shopkeeper interrupted Dora's tentative maneuvers between the aisles filled with dusty furnishings.

"Excuse me, how may I help you?" he repeated.

"Oh, my! Uhh, my friend Mrs. Taylor—perhaps you know her—tells me that you have really nice used furniture. She says I can trust you, so I thought I'd look around. I don't know if I'm going to buy right now. I'm just looking."

"Madam, we sell *antiques* here. If you're looking for 'used furniture,' I could give you the name of a store down the street for that," he remarked, trying to hide his disdain. "I do believe I remember your friend. A very attractive woman."

"Thank you, so I'll look around. A little crowded in here, isn't it? My husband just bought us a house in Bergenwood. Have you heard of it? Used to be a baseball field. We moved from Fort Lee."

Dora turned away and placed her hankie over her nose to quell the growing squeamishness. She passed tables laden with dishes—some chipped, others rimmed with gold—and chairs perched precariously on top of other chairs and tables. Her eyes spied silverware, pewter mugs, vases, and crocheted antimacassars.

Who would buy such dreck when you can go to Sears and pick up something no one's used? she wondered. There were lamps of varying shapes and sizes, some wearing their shades askew, reminding her of a Frenchman's beret that her brother Abe wore. She uttered a faint exclamation when she spotted a wooden rocking chair hidden behind a black-lacquered screen featuring two painted Chinese ladies standing demurely, their eyes lowered, the lower half of their faces covered with open fans; mustachioed warriors wielding swords held high, astride hefty horses; and flame-shooting dragons.

Now I see what he's talking about. This is not a piece of junk, she mused. *The wood just needs a little polishing. And that chip I don't mind at all. It needs a cushion. Yes, definitely a new cushion. Saul will hate it. First he'll say it isn't comfortable! Then he'll say he doesn't care if it's a wooden crate as long as he can put his head back without me nagging him about making a mark. Okay, he's got other places to sit.*

In one of her uncommon gestures of defiance, Dora determined to buy the rocker. She loved it and had to have it. When she saw the salesman standing beside her, looking bemused, she sensed she may have been talking out loud again and resolved to stop that bad habit.

"This is a genuine copy of a Bentwood Rocker. As you know," he said, knowing she knew nothing at all about Bentwood Rockers, genuine or otherwise, "the Bentwood Rocker was invented by a Viennese carpenter named Thonet in the late nineteenth century. This is indeed a gem. No one would know the difference. You have very good taste, madam. Your friend would admire it."

Dora's mind drifted to concerns about how she was going to pay for it. The salesman brought her back to the present with his historical treatise.

"He developed a method of bending solid wood with steam. Truly remarkable. No one had ever accomplished anything like it. A creative genius in his own right, don't you agree?"

"Uh-huh," Dora replied without thinking or caring about how this furniture maker bent wood with steam. But she reminded herself to tell Saul, who would be interested. *He would like that*, she thought. She realized she hadn't asked the price.

". . . Art Nouveau era . . . Tiffany . . . Thonet . . . a factory in Moravia . . . very valuable, but for you," he added, "I can let you have it for twenty-five dollars. It's quite a bargain, believe you me. I see that you admire it"—he also saw her wince when he mentioned the price—"but I like to think that my pieces will live in a good home, so for you, twenty dollars. Did you say you live in Bergenwood? I drive by there—nice little town—on my way home to Leonia and could easily drop it off."

Dora siphoned one dollar and fifty cents from the twenty-dollar weekly food allowance that Saul gave her so that, in a little more than thirteen months, her authentic copy of a Bentwood rocker rested proudly in the corner of her newly painted, forest green-walled living room. Addie liked it so much that she painted her living room that precise shade of green.

A razor-sharp pain in her chest and neck jolts Dora back to the present day. Numbness travels down her arm as she feels the blood thundering to her head; her breath comes haltingly. She mouths, "Just like Mama, on Shabbos," and she slumps to the floor, dropping the picture of Roberta and Hannah. Its protective glass shatters, like her dreams—and nightmares—of yesteryear.

~

Roberta sits staring at her computer screen, blank now for well over two hours; she picks at a piece of ragged cuticle as if it's the most pertinent task of the moment.

In between attempts to finish a legal brief, she has already cleaned the refrigerator, re-alphabetized her file cabinets, and weeded out clothing from her closet. She has piles of old newspapers and empty bottles at the door for recycling the next day. She is just about to attack the children's bookshelves when, to her relief, the phone rings, interrupting her writing impasse and demanding her immediate attention.

"Hello," Roberta says.

"Roberta, sit down. I have some news. It's bad."

"What? Oh, my God. What's happened? Is it Mommy? I had an uncanny feeling."

"Now, don't get upset, I mean, I know you will, but Mommy is dead. I had been trying to call her all day; she'd said she wasn't feeling well. When I couldn't reach her, I asked the manager to look in on her. She said she wasn't authorized to go in without a family member, so I went over. Roberta? Are you there?"

Unable to speak above a whisper, Roberta tells her sister that she is listening.

"So I drove right over and was about to go in with her, but Mrs. Beasley said she thought it might be better for me to wait outside. Mrs. B. found Mommy on the floor next to her rocker with that picture of us that Daddy took on the way to Miami lying next to her. The apartment smelled something awful. It turned out that Mommy had a dish in the oven and it was burned to a crisp."

"Oh, Jesus, Hannah, I didn't call her this week. Oh, God! I said I was going to call her and take her out for dinner, but I didn't. I feel like shit! I kept putting it off. All because of this stupid brief. Shit! I feel just awful. I'll come right over now."

"Actually, Roberta, I don't think you should. I wish I hadn't seen her like this. She hit her head when she fell, and there's blood and glass all over the carpet. I just hope I don't always remember her this way. It's okay not to come. Really. Bert's on his way now, so he'll be here with me when they come to pick the body up. At least she didn't suffer. Just like with Bubbe. Are you there? Say something, Robbie. I'm just so sorry I had to tell you this way."

"I just can't believe she's dead."

Chapter 12

ENDINGS AND BEGINNINGS: A NEW GENERATION

1990

Menacing clouds hover darkly overhead, threatening to release their liquid matter upon the heads of the small group of people circling the yawning hole in the ground as they listen to the black-suited rabbi reflect upon the unknown life of the occupant of the casket: Dora Kolopsky Sussman. Hannah had enlisted her own rabbi to perform the funeral service and even writes the sermon for him.

The funeral director hands out giant-sized black silk umbrellas to protect the congregated assemblage from the light mist falling. There are only enough guests to form a minyan—if one counts the women—as the rabbi begins to intone the mourners' Kaddish, the ancient prayer dating back to ninth-century Persia.

> *Yisgaddal v'yiskadash sh'mei rabbo B'ol'mo di v'ro khirusai v'yamlikh malchusai b'chayaichon ooyomai chon . . . Oseh sho-lom bimromov, hooyaaseh sholom o'lainoo v'al kol Yisrael; v'imroo omain.*

Much has changed since the death of Dora's parents, when

only her brothers and other male members of the minyan had been granted the privilege of saying this prayer. Now, her daughters chant the Aramaic words, along with their husbands, friends, and Aunt Bessie, Dora's sister of the heart, who can barely mouth the familiar words between her uncontrollable sobs. At nearly one hundred years of age, she arrived in a wheelchair, with the help of her caretaker, Clara, declaring that nothing could keep her from coming. The sisters stand protectively on either side of her.

Such a pathetically puny gathering to bear witness, mourn, and commemorate the life—and death—of a woman who walked the earth for some eighty-six years. Or was it eighty-eight? With no birth certificate and conflicting dates on other documents, including her departure from Mr. Steen's middle school, the sisters will never know.

As Hannah and Roberta pack up the apartment in Los Angeles that Dora occupied since Saul's death fourteen years ago, they uncover a deteriorating document in European-style script, handwritten in German, Russian, and French, listing her date of birth as 1902, which would make her eighty-eight. There are other papers, records, and mementos stored in a small wooden box, the remains of a long-ago gift from Saul for a birthday or Mother's Day or perhaps to celebrate an anniversary. Hannah claims to remember the occasion as Mother's Day.

"Daddy bought it for her and it was filled with candy, or maybe it was cookies."

Through her child's eyes, Roberta recalls a beautiful, cobalt blue, star-shaped container sprinkled with silver dust—another gift from their father—that held an assortment of sweet-smelling fragrances and body powder nestled in the same blue-colored satin fabric, but she cannot bring to mind the container her sister now holds.

They find it tucked away in the corner of Dora's closet. Its lid features a picture of multicolored-flowers, resembling an old English print, wood-framed in rubbed sienna and covered in glass. It contains sepia-toned studio portraits of Minnie, Bessie, and one of Dora's favorite nephews, Stewart's only son, Harold, handsomely attired in his World War II officer's uniform. As a kid, Roberta had a crush on him and remembered his sweet offer to loan her his saxophone when she decided she wanted to play in the school band. That was the only chair available.

There is a picture of a very young man neither woman can identify. It looks like a relative, someone from the old country, with an uncanny resemblance to Zaide Mendel. On the back of the picture, faded with time, the name *Shimshon* is scribbled. Alongside, the word *Samson* is written clearly in a different hand, confidently. There is a mottled social security card, Saul's death certificate, dated January 13, 1976, Roberta's report card from Mrs. Howell's second-grade class at Longfellow Elementary School, and a fragile letter of discharge certifying Dora's exit from Public School 63 in Manhattan.

"Hey. Hannah, look at this. It looks like a passport, but it has everyone's name listed. And look, Mom's name is Disha here, not Dora. But the really bizarre thing is that her birth date is listed as 1902, and here, on her school's discharge letter, it's 1904. It's in French and German—I knew my French would come in handy someday: '*Le porteur du présent bourgeoise de Witelisk, de la commune de Tonrage, Mme. Henya Kolopsky, avec des enfants Avram, 13, Disha, 10, Leib, 7, et Marya, 5 ans en foi de quoi ce passeport, confirme' par l'apposition du scelle, est donne' pour voyager librement on pays étrangers.*'"

"Nice, Roberta, but would you mind translating?" Hannah exclaims with impatient sarcasm.

Roberta takes a breath and clears her throat, as though preparing to address a live audience. "Okay, it says, 'The bearer of the present citizen of Witelisk, in the district of Tonrage,'—I don't get it; didn't they come from Odessa? Well, anyway—'Mrs. Henya Kolopsky, with her children Avram, 13, Disha, 10, Leib, 7, and Marya, 5 years at the time of this passport, attested to and confirmed by the affixed stamp, has permission to travel to a foreign country.' Something like that. So you think she was trying to make herself younger than Daddy? It's only a few years, but maybe it meant a lot back then, you know, to be younger than your husband."

"Maybe, but it wasn't like her to lie." Hannah ponders. "If anything, she told the truth, her truth, when she shouldn't have. And she wasn't that vain either. I mean, she always liked to look nice, wear the latest style, at least when she was younger, but she didn't have the kind of vanity to lie about her age. I think. On the other hand, she kept the incest with Uncle Abe a secret until last year, when she told you about it. Boy, I still can't get over that one. You just never know about these things. I don't think a kid can ever know who his parents really are. Or, for that matter, even one's mate. Or mates—plural—if we're talking about you."

"Oh, that's a good one, Hannah," Roberta rejoins, her laughter merging with that of her sister's but quickly turning into sobs. "I still can't believe she's dead. And that this is what's left of her life. A few pieces of flimsy paper. That will be us someday, you know."

They are left to wonder if their mother did indeed misrepresent her age to Saul's Aunt Sadie so many years ago, when she stitched bloomers in Uncle Joe's factory. At that time, at twenty-two, Dora had already entered the realm of spinsterhood. They thought it was more likely a lapse on the part of their grandparents, having birthed seven children, not counting the little boy who died. Or it might have been a manifestation of the way the Russian government regarded the birth of Jewish children? Ciphers. Just Yids. Why keep records of people considered on par with animals? Or below. The Russian aristocracy did love their dogs and horses, as the paintings in the great museums established, with their rat-sized dogs sitting on their mistresses' laps.

Henya and Mendel kept track of important dates, referring to them as "the time of the big fire," or "the terrible flood," or "the year that the drought destroyed the crops because of the water shortage," or "the year that Yonkel died." Or it could have been the confusion caused by the czar's insistence on preserving the Julian calendar.

Gregorian or Julian, what does it matter now? We know that this woman was born and then she died; we also know that she lived and was buried in a hole in the earth. Two years, or two hundred, in relation to infinite time—forever and ever in the cold, damp ground—obliterates any reason to fret over such trifles.

Dora was the last living member of the Kolopsky family in America, although there had been talk of another branch—a wealthy professional cluster consisting of lawyers and doctors living in Boston. But they were only words emanating from Dora's lips: "My uncle Schmedia, a very wealthy man, and his sons, the doctors, David and Meyer." No one had ever met or had any evidence of their existence. The sisters would discover, some years later, through a previously unknown relative living in Pittsburg, the chapel built by the brothers at Brandeis University to honor their parents. In the entryway to the chapel, Schmedia's portrait hangs and bears a remarkable likeness to Dora's brother Leon, even to the full head of white hair and light blue eyes.

Mendel, as so typically happens, followed Henya to the grave within a year of her death. After she died, he no longer instructed the recalcitrant nonobservant passersby in the ways of Jewish law. Nor did he talk very much when his children visited. His day consisted in reading his siddur and occasionally crossing the street to go to shul. With his eyes dimmed by cataracts, he didn't see the car that hit him.

Faye died of a brain aneurysm as surgeons attempted to eradicate the clot that caused her paralyzing stroke. Joe remarried six
months later, much to the consternation of his two children. Abe
died of a sudden heart attack as he sat watching television, and
Stewart of lung cancer, the price for a lifetime of smoking. Lenny,
the doctor, died of a stroke in his sleep.

Dora outlived her adored younger brother, Lenny Kolopsky,
MD—adored except for a brief rupture in their relationship when
he remarried several months after his wife, Bella's, death.

"She wasn't even cold in her grave," she spat out with bitterness. "What? You couldn't wait to *schtup*? She's so beautiful,
this new one, with her *mieskeit punnum*? Or maybe because she's
rich and lives on Park Avenue?"

Dora didn't understand why her brother reacted with such
ire, reverting to a language he had put aside so many years ago,
"*Ikh hob dir in drerd*," as he slammed the receiver into its cradle
when she tried to call him at Hannah's insistence. Dora thought he
should call her and apologize for telling her to go to hell, although
apologies for the Kolopsky family did not come trippingly off the
tongue.

"I was telling the truth," she insisted when her daughters
reproached her for bad manners. "Everyone else makes nice to
him because he's a doctor. What, he couldn't wait for a year? How
must his children feel? It's their mother, after all. He fawned all
over Bella when she was alive and then forgets her, poof, like that,"
she said, snapping her fingers, "like she never lived. Who knew he
was such a delicate flower that he couldn't hear the truth."

Dora felt vindicated when, two years later, Lenny's bride
booted him out of her lavish Manhattan condominium on Fif-
ty-Seventh and Park Avenue—along with his new life of dinners at
the Russian Tea Room nearby—following a series of minor strokes
he suffered. She was afraid that he would exhaust her considerable

financial resources. Dora didn't hesitate to remind Lenny of his haste to marry as he recuperated at his son's home. He died within two months of his wife's abandonment.

Marya—well, no one knows why, how, or exactly when Marya died. Stewart found her in her bed, worried when, after several days, she didn't show up for work at the laundry. Lenny found a tattered bankbook stashed away with her underwear, reflecting a balance of twenty thousand dollars, which would more than cover the cost of her funeral. There was a broken record on the floor, lying alongside her bed, her father's recording of "Eli, Eli." She left the remains of a lifetime of frugality, fortitude, devotion and audacity.

The adopted member of the family, Aunt Bessie, as Roberta and Hannah call her, remains very much alive and vital. Max, her husband, left her a widow after being hit by a taxicab just prior to the lavish sixtieth birthday celebration she had planned for him. Stunned and grief-stricken, she continued to teach. When, at six-ty-five, she did eventually retire on an assistant principal's pension from one of the better Manhattan public schools, she immediately volunteered to tutor English and American history to the flood of new Russian immigrants, those fleeing yet another round of anti-Semitism overseen by Premier Khrushchev in 1956. Her rep-utation was of a demanding but caring and generous teacher with high standards and expectations, especially for the young women in her class, to whom she preached and, at times, loaned money and provided home-cooked meals of stuffed cabbage or meatloaf or beet borscht swirled with sour cream curlicues.

"I got a call from Aunt Bessie yesterday with the strangest request," Roberta recounts to Hannah in her daily phone call. "She wants Mommy's rocking chair. First of all, though, do you or your kids want it? I certainly don't."

"Why in the world would she want that?" Hannah inquires. "It doesn't go with the modern furniture in her apartment. And the pillow is falling apart."

"I asked the very same question, and she said she wanted something to remember Mommy by, and, with some emotion I might add, she said that the rocker was the only thing Mommy ever stood up to Daddy about. She said she remembered when Mommy bought it and how excited she was and how she saved her food money to pay for it. But when she finally got it home, Daddy spoiled it all because he didn't like it. She said that, for her, it signified what Mommy might have become if she hadn't settled in life."

"Hmmm. That's so interesting. I get the feeling—and always have—that Aunt Bessie didn't like Daddy. Maybe she was right, that had Mommy waited and finished school, she wouldn't have been so afraid of her own shadow. But it's unfair to judge by today's standards. That's what most of the women did then. I mean, who in that generation went to school? Bessie was the exception, and yet she was older than Mommy."

"Yeah, I guess we forget," Hannah adds, "Mommy came to this country without language, without education, humiliated when she's put in a classroom with little kids half her age, and not understanding a word of English. She had to absorb a different culture, and then with only a few years of education, she quits school to work in a factory to support herself and her parents. Now that I say that, I don't think I gave her enough credit. Makes me sad, you know? And Daddy didn't help. Aunt Bessie's right. He was so critical of her."

Hannah, from the beginning, felt closer to her mother. Unlike her father, she had a sense of humor; she was always interested in hearing about what they did. And she thought she was beautiful, a Dorothy Lamour lookalike, without sarong; while Roberta, in her anti-Semitic phase in her teens, thought, erroneously, her mother's nose was too big for her face. She seemed to focus on what wasn't there, what she couldn't do well, rather than the way she survived in this hostile and strange environment in which her father dumped her.

As a child, Hannah hung on to her mother's side. Whenever possible, she clutched her hemline, as if to reassure herself of the permanence of their connection, and patiently waited for Dora to finish a conversation with a neighbor, or an activity, or whatever she was doing. No separation for her.

Roberta, on the other hand, unconsciously determined who and what she would be or do in repudiation of her mother. Only later in life would she concede that some of the very qualities she possessed and enjoyed—her love of dancing, of music, of knowing and singing the words to all the musicals and songs of her mother's era, reflected her mother's fancies. She so wanted not to be like her, she so wanted not to be Jewish, she so wanted not be confined to Judaism's "nonsensical" restrictions that she turned a blind eye to her father's flaws while idealizing his strengths and identifying with his atheism. She looked to him for protection but ignored his lack of warmth and silence and criticism, and she even turned to him for help with her various "girl" projects, including sewing and knitting.

When she needed to be fitted for a dress she was making, she solicited his help. Only his extended arms were big enough to hold the skein of yarn she would wind into a ball for the sweater she was knitting. Or for the argyle socks she was making for her current boyfriend. And when a tennis match was scheduled for her high school tennis team, he was the one to check the strings of her racket and, when needed, restring it. She based her conduct on what she believed would garner his approving nod and always sided with him when a squabble erupted between her parents. The sides were clearly delineated: Roberta, her father's not-quite-good-enough surrogate son, aligned with him, and Hannah with Dora. She never won in her attempt to be the son he never had, the biggest disappointment of his life.

Later, in her several unsuccessful attempts at psychotherapy and finally a full-blown Freudian psychoanalysis—couch and all—her analyst suggested that her inability to understand her mother's struggle, coupled with her life-long battle to win the affection and approval of her father, most likely played a major role in her choice of husbands and her failed marriages.

"Well, I guess," Roberta reflects, "she had reasons, but in her passivity, she warded off lots of anger and aggression. And when it came out, it came out passively. She never made it easy for Daddy to do anything, to take the risks he wanted to take. Remember how she carried on when he wanted to quit that laundry chain so he could start his own laundry? My God, you'd have thought we were about to live on the street. Scheesh!"

"You know, Roberta, sometimes it gets tedious hearing nothing but gripes about Mommy," Hannah sighs, "never understanding how she may have felt. It's always about Daddy and you. Get a life! Weren't you supposed to get over all that after your five years of analysis? When do you stop blaming your parents and start taking responsibility for the life you are living? Not everything that happened is Mommy's fault. She grew up in poverty; she had no education, for God's sake, and did the best she could. We didn't turn out so badly, you know. How do you account for that?"

"And she never let him forget that he moved her to New Jersey, away from Bubbe," Roberta continues, her face blanching. "Imagine wanting to stay in that rotten ghetto? I think he'd have been a very different man if he had married a different woman. Someone more adventurous, someone who would have encouraged, or even challenged him to do more, rather than fight his every move to advance."

Moaning, Hannah argues that her mother stood up when it counted to her, though "maybe not when it was important to you. Can you possibly empathize with her? In reality, the rocker wasn't the only thing she stood up to him for. She was determined to keep a kosher home in spite of his outright hostility to it. There, you must admit, she put her foot down. He not only rejected but also denigrated anything smacking of religion, yet she continued to light Shabbos candles every Friday night of her life, with him always scoffing in the background."

"Okay, okay. She had her tough side," admits Roberta. "I guess you're right. I need to get over this, as my shrink said. But as a kid, I just hated that we weren't allowed to write or draw or sew on Shabbos. All the things I loved to do. That turned me so against being Jewish. And living in that anti-Semitic atmosphere. Do you ever wonder what it was that drew them together in the first place?" After a long silence, she continues, "But what about the rocker. Should we give it to Aunt Bessie?"

"But still, don't you think," Hannah persists, "that some of what you call her passivity had to do with her background? You always say how environment determines character. Well, look at her childhood. So getting on a plane or doing anything new or going on a vacation and spending money—all that has links to that frightened little kid. From that kid's perspective, Grandpa abandoned her when he went to America and took her older siblings with him. She comes to this country and can't speak or understand the language. And after two or three years of school, she quits and works in a factory. It's like she used up every bit of strength and courage to assimilate, with nothing left over for anything else. I call that resiliency."

"But remember," Roberta interrupts, "when she'd return from a vacation—and this really got to me—carrying on like she was going to her death beforehand, she'd return and rave about it, insisting that she always felt that way. I think we both suffered as a result, me in my way, my stubbornness, you in yours. Who we have become has been shaped by both of them, for good and bad."

In high school, Hannah was an academic star: honor roll, straight A's, Merit scholar, and conforming. "Goody two-shoes," Roberta called her, in part to diminish her own lack of academic accomplishment. At twenty-one, four years after high school graduation, having worked in Manhattan as a secretary, Hannah married her high school sweetheart, Bert, and moved to a neat suburban tract home with a backyard and swings, seesaw, sliding pond, and barbecue—a mere ten miles from Dora and Saul. Hannah and Bert raised two children, and in 1977, following her father's death, she published her first poem in a little-known poetry journal:

Tall

Towering

Redwood

Ever mighty, a giant to the small child,

Climbing skyward,

No more

Battling winds, tornadoes, hurricanes,

A Force of Nature. Cancer.

He was only a fragile limb. A defenseless man

The giant redwood topples

Leaving a Memory, a Myth, a child's shattered Fantasy

Forever

Silent

Roberta excelled in two endeavors: athletics and troublemaking, though the trouble she made was mostly for herself. Once, caught smoking a cigarette in the girls' bathroom at school, she sheepishly departed the toilet stall, with telltale smoke streaming from her nostrils, to find the principal, Miss Hill, glaring at her. Busted! She loves recounting these adventures to her friends and kids.

On another occasion, she and her steady boyfriend declared a personal holiday to hear Sarah Vaughn sing at the Paramount in New York City, and naively, Roberta returned to the campus to rehearse a play in which she had a minor role. Once again, Miss Hill was there to greet Roberta as she opened the door to the auditorium. Her parents were advised and she was suspended for a day. Busted once more!

She was a cheerleader, not an honor student. A champion tennis player, no straight A's for her. Rebellious rather than submissive, she forged her identity in opposition to Hannah's, and her mother's, and in the process made decisions she would regret in the future. In actuality, she didn't think she could compete with her sister's intelligence and beauty and sterling reputation.

"Oh, you're Hannah's baby sister" was the enthusiastic refrain from teachers at the beginning of each school year, typically followed by their cutting comments as the girls' differences were discovered. "Well, Roberta, it's hard to believe you and Hannah are woven from the same cloth. You should try more to emulate her."

"You're right. I'm not like her. I'm me, and I'm glad of it," Roberta responded with a clenched jaw that held back tears of fury from the rebuff she unknowingly produced.

At twenty, on her own, she moved from the East Coast to Los Angeles, in part a reaction to a painful breakup with her boyfriend and first lover. Several years later, after working at a series of low-paying administrative jobs, she enrolled in college and graduated summa cum laude, surprising everyone, most of all herself. She entered law school, then married and divorced her constitutional law professor, some sixteen years her senior—with whom she had had an affair—but not before giving birth to two children: a boy and then a girl—a girl child who was wanted, not the disappointment she was to her father. She specialized in immigration law.

Several years passed before Hannah and Bert and their two children tired of the eastern winters and joined Roberta in the sun-drenched, palm-treed, rose-colored tropical setting of Southern California, with its miles and miles of beaches, bistros, and freeways.

Saul and Dora followed two years later, but Saul hated the congestion and smog, the noise, the freeways, and the materialism. He fell in love with Hawaii following a cruise that he and Dora took and insisted on moving to Honolulu, where he swam, snorkeled, gathered seaweed for the marinated salad he learned to make from the Japanese fishermen he befriended on the beach, and, as he said to anyone who would listen, "was a beach bum." He started a little business doing small repairs for the neighbors in their condo. The money, he said, paid for his two-pack-a-day cigarette habit.

Saul found his element in the laidback existence in Hawaii; he was happy and carefree for the first time in his life. He worked a little, fished a little, swam a little, listened to radio talk shows, and even called in to vent his rage at "the dirty old men who make the wars," while Dora, lonely for her daughters and grandchildren and going blind from her neglected glaucoma, grumbled until the day that Saul died from throat cancer seven years later. She purchased a Los Angeles condo within a week of his death, leaving the arrangements for shipping his body to her sons-in-law.

"Oh, Hawaii was such a beautiful place. Paradise. You've never seen anything like it. Friendly people. Palm trees. Beaches. Sand. I loved living there, but after Saul died, he should rest in peace, what could I do but move back here to be near my daughters?"

"I can't believe my ears," Roberta whispered to Hannah as they overheard their mother talking to one of her new neighbors after returning from Saul's memorial service, held, at Dora's insistence, at the local synagogue.

"Did you hear her? All the while she was there, she made Daddy's life miserable with her complaining. She is such a phony."

"Was," Hannah counters, "she *was* a phony. Whatever. He dragged her there against her will. She didn't want to go. She didn't know a soul there. He didn't either, but the difference was that he never needed anyone, the loner that he was. And she was going blind too. He never took her needs into consideration; it was always what he wanted to do. Period. End of report. His way or the highway."

"I guess. But she got her revenge," retorts Roberta, "when it came to following his explicit wish to be cremated and to have his ashes thrown in the Pacific in Hawaii! That time she did it her way. Buried him in the ground."

"You know that Jews don't cremate their dead. He was dead, and she was the one that had to live with it. One shouldn't rule from the grave."

"She always seemed to divide people. Look at us, even now it's happening. Talk about ruling from the grave. Have you noticed that every time we talk about our parents, we end up repeating their dynamics? I take Daddy's side, you take hers. We both get so damned defensive and stubborn. It's contagious. That's the pattern. So what do you say we both try not to do that anymore? Let's bury it along with Mommy. How about a hug, and let's give the rocker to Aunt Bessie. After all these years of loyal devotion to all of us, especially to Mommy, and even to Bubbe when she was alive, she deserves it. Right?"

III. BACK TO THE BEGINNING

Chapter 13

THE MISSING PIECE

1995

The gaps of knowledge Roberta perceives concerning her ancestry at times leave her with a baffling sense of solitude. She feels alone, despite the home she shares with her boyfriend of two years, Dick, and despite the regular visits of her adored grandchildren and children. When there's a break in her busy routine, she searches online for clues in the assorted Internet sites: The Mormon Genealogy Library, The Church of Jesus Christ of Latter-Day Saints, The American Jewish Historical Society, Yiddish Scientific Institute. These endeavors reveal nothing of consequence. No Kolopskys, or any ending in *i*, are to be found anywhere.

When her attempts fail to materialize a promising clan member, she has the sense that she is plummeting into a black hole that, upon entry, closes tightly, leaving her feeling trapped—endlessly tumbling, head over heels into the timeless pitch-blackness of depression. Not exactly depression but adriftness. She insists there has to be a sign somewhere, a name, a reference. Something. *There has to have been a seed that began it all. Some Adam and Eve. Or Erda and Wotan. Something cannot come from nothing. Now who said that?* she wonders. *Democritus*, she recalls. *Didn't he write that nothing can come from nothing? I think so. Or am I thinking of* King Lear, *when he tells Cordelia that nothing can come from nothing? Gotta look that one up*, she tells herself. *Anyway, the point is that I had to have come from someone or somebody.*

Her obsession with her family's history began when, in 1976, she read Alex Haley's novel *Roots: The Saga of an American Family*. The following year she sat transfixed in front of her newly purchased Magnavox console with its enormous twenty-five-inch screen, watching, along with her two teenage children and 130 million other viewers, ABC's television miniseries. For eight consecutive evenings, she and the world were mesmerized by the images on their television screens.

She wondered, who was her Kunta Kinte? Who was that first forebear that launched her family tree? She longed to know and to be known, to discover and be discovered through the lives of those bearing her DNA, as if that knowledge would somehow lend significance and structure to her own life—would fill the mysterious void that popped in and out of her consciousness.

Roberta's obsession was further motivated when she read an article in the *New Yorker* that went on at length, as only *New Yorker* profiles can, about the recent spate of twin births. Yes, it held, it had to do with the new "assisted reproductive technologies" and treatments that zealously implanted an excess of fertilized eggs in the uterus as a way of ensuring the survival of at least one viable embryo, which often resulted in the birth of two—or three or four—newborns. That made sense to her, but she was taken aback when they offered an alternative hypothesis.

The article described, in passing, the latest research on the phenomenon of the "vanishing twin syndrome." The authors claimed that there had been many more multiple pregnancies than previously recognized that ended in early miscarriages—at times, so early that no one realized the existence of multiple fetuses. Now, with the advent of sonographic techniques, it was easy to document such events. She was fascinated by the description of the not-so-rare occurrence—one in eight births—of what was labeled "vestigial twinning" or "parasitic twinning" or "the vanishing twin" phenomenon. Intrigued by this notion, she felt the need to dig further into the subject.

As she continued her search, she stumbled upon a piece written by a woman professing to be a "womb twin," who held that all her life she had experienced an absence of something that she could neither explain nor verify, but with the recent research on "missing twins," she was now persuaded that her fantasy of having shared a womb with a sibling was not as delusional as she had been led to believe by the several psychiatrists she had consulted over the years.

Riveted, Roberta went on to read about medical anomalies that came under the rubric of *doppelganger*. There were Siamese twins, where the splitting of an ovum produced two whole people joined, tragically, by a piece of skin. There were individuals carrying within them embedded body parts—an arm, a foot, or a leg. She chanced upon an exposé describing a *fetus in fetu:* a fetus encapsulated in a cyst containing bone fragments of teeth and, at times, hair. Was she, she wondered with fascinated horror, perverse in this pursuit, or was she trying to understand something important that she had somehow intuited about herself?

She rushed to the telephone to call her sister to share her findings and to allay the anxiety she suffered. She thought maybe she was crazy to have such thoughts.

"Remember when I had that stricture of my urethra, and Dr. Spitalny told me that I had four kidneys? And remember how I argued that that was impossible because people have only two kidneys? I was taking a biology course at the time, and there I was instructing my urologist. But he showed me my x-ray to prove it. Well, if I were a womb twin, wouldn't it explain that doubling up? I mean, how would I have gotten four kidneys otherwise? Fully functioning, he said. And why would I have a 'redundant colon'? Yes, that's what the doctor told me after my colonoscopy. I have enough colon for two, she told me. And she said it made the procedure much more difficult. I told her my theory, and she laughed. Four kidneys! A redundant colon! God, who knows what else? It just makes so much sense, and more importantly, it feels so right that I was a twin and, as the article alleges, I absorbed him."

There was silence at the other end of the receiver. Hannah was speechless.

"Did you hear that I called it a him?" Roberta continued, "I think that's right though. Sometimes you gotta listen to your gut. Wouldn't that explain this need I have to find our ancestors? It's not just that I'm looking for our family's roots; it's a displacement from trying to find the other part of me, my twin. Plato talked about being split apart at birth and then having the need to search for our other half for the rest of our lives. Of course, he was talking about a *soulmate*, but jeez, Hannah, do you think I ate my twin? Stop laughing. Everyone laughs, but I'm not joking."

When she informed Ted, her ex-husband, of her theory, he too laughed but good-naturedly and teasingly told her that it was quite plausible, since she was definitely trouble enough for two. "And maybe even enough for triplets," he chuckled, quite pleased with his joke. "Do you think you were once triplets? How about quadruplets?"

She was convinced of the truth of her hunch and stopped trying to sway others. She put aside the scientific journals with a sense of closure and returned to trying to unearth her family's roots. *If that's what it takes to fill me up, so be it*, she determined.

She fantasizes about her lone forebears—the Eve or Lilith,

the one who came before Eve but was too dominating a mate for Adam—who supplied the recessive genes required to produce her blond hair and blue eyes and her five feet seven inches, those traits that she both loves and hates—loves because with them she feels special, hates because she feels a creature from outer space.

No, it was not the iceman—the sperm about which everyone tormented her poor mother, including her loving aunts and uncles who called her a shiksa. The neighbors taunted Dora with questions about the milkman. They laughed as her mother cringed and secretly cried in the cold fury of helplessness. Nor is it the other explanation: the myth that one of her ancestors was a Tatar, those thirteenth-century Mongol invaders whose claim to fame was the bloodthirsty warrior, Genghis Khan. It was in this rumor, as a child, that Roberta first heard the word rape.

The evidence for her Tatar legacy? Her prominent cheekbones, the very cheekbones she inherited from her mother, and her blue eyes, eyes that popped up once in each generation: in her Aunt Mary and one of her own children. At times, she complains to her friends or to her children or, more recently, to her lover (at her age, and after two husbands, she refuses to call him her boyfriend and hates the term significant other) that for all the world she might as well, like Athena, have sprung from her father's forehead. Lost to her are the generations that came before her grandparents, who represent the scaffolding of her selfhood. Everyone tells her it's no big deal, but for her, it is a big deal. A very big deal indeed.

While in law school, Roberta envied a friend who completed an assignment in their Immigration Law class to chart their family genealogy by calling her seventy-year-old mother to investigate her history. Two weeks later, a large parcel arrived filled with tissue-thin rubbings representing over thirty gravestones garnered from the Old Burying Point Cemetery, established in 1637 in Salem, Massachusetts. The rubbings were embossed with the

names of the men, women, and children bearing the same sur-
name and DNA as Joni. Mrs. Wheeler, once again, reminded
her that her Puritan ancestors comprised one of the first waves
of immigrants to leave England in 1630 to make their home in
southeastern Massachusetts and that over half were dead within
the first year of their arrival. *Hmm*, Roberta thought, *the most fit
of the fittest.*

Roberta's first response was awe, then anger, and finally envy
and sadness. She felt cheated. Not only did she envy the retrieval
of Joni's family history, but more importantly, she longed for a
mother who could take on such a challenging commission with
enthusiasm, confidence, competence, and triumph. She felt as
though she had been punched in the stomach. Twice.

At seventy, Mrs. Wheeler, with a ham-and-cheese sandwich
crammed into her faded green canvas backpack along with a
sketchbook, charcoal crayons, and other accoutrements required
to fulfill her daughter's charge, had boarded a bus near her home in
northern New Jersey and spent the next two days nestled among
her relatives' gravestones on hands and knees, protected by her
gardening kneepads, carefully and lovingly creating the rubbings
to send to her daughter.

Even if she'd had illustrious ancestors, even if there were tomb-
stones to rub, it would never have occurred to Roberta to consider,
no less to ask, her mother to embark on such an enterprise. It
brought back painful memories of seeking her mother's assistance
in fitting a dress she'd been making for the junior prom, only to
be stuck with a pin that ruined the fabric—a beautifully patterned
fuchsia silk moiré that she'd bought with her hard-earned money
from babysitting for the O'Neils, who paid one dollar for an entire
Saturday night's work, now stained with blood. She recalled, as a
thirteen-year-old, falling asleep on their couch while listening to
Aaron Copland's *Rodeo*, the theme song for "Music Until Dawn,"

turned up loud enough to cover the creaks and squeaks emanating from the cellar in the weathered house. It was then that she began to appreciate classical music. With her earnings from the O'Neils, she bought her first record, Chopin's *Polonaises*. She especially loved his "Polonaise #6 in A Flat" and played it constantly.

Viewing the rubbings reignited Roberta's longtime interest in her own family's history. As she pursued her quest, she infuriated her mother with a new barrage of questions about Dora's life as a child. Were you born in a hospital? What were your grandparents' names? Why did your parents come to this country? How come you don't know a word of Russian? Tell me what you remember about coming over on the boat? Do you remember what your street or your house looked like in Odessa? And what about the Cossacks, were you attacked like Uncle Stewart says? "Come on Disha," she chided when she lovingly teased her mother.

"Stop *hoken a chinik* with all your questions," Dora countered. "I've told you a hundred times if I've told you once, I don't know. And I don't care to know. Ask Uncle Stewart if he's so smart."

Roberta told her to close her eyes and to try to picture the place she lived. "Roberta, please. How do you expect me to remember things that happened so long ago? And stop with this closing your eyes stuff. You were a nudnik as a kid, and sometimes you still are. Just leave me alone with all your questions, will you?"

The more Roberta hit a dead end, the more she was determined to uncover her past, a quality she attributed to her father. She was on a crusade.

She called a younger cousin in Boston, Aunt Faye's grandson, who she heard was also interested in the family's genealogy and had, in fact, begun to collect the names and birth and death dates of family members. Marty's visit to Ellis Island revealed nothing much more than Roberta already knew. He too ran into a stone wall. Roberta finally made use of her joke about springing fully formed from the head of Zeus. He burst out laughing. "Well, at least someone in my family thinks it funny."

"Well, it couldn't have been Zeus. He was Greek, so it had to have been from Moses's head," Marty retorted.

They promised to be in touch when one or the other came up with another name or fact to complete the family enigma, like a piece on a giant jigsaw puzzle that one begins knowing it will remain incomplete.

Years passed. Saul died. Dora died. Marty's mother died. And Roberta's favorite cousin, Harold, died. It frightens Roberta because, although sixteen years her senior, he was a member of the generation of first cousins. Not once removed, as is Marty.

When she learns of Harold's death, she recalls the seriousness with which he accepted her request to borrow his saxophone. She was eight and he was going off to dental school. She recalls that he told her that although it was a very unusual request for a girl—especially a little one—to want play a saxophone, if that's what she wanted, he wanted her to use it for however long she needed it. She played for half a year and then stopped.

Roberta receives a phone call from an unknown cousin living in Philadelphia that had been in contact with Harold just before his death. Samantha is doing research on the Kolopsky family genealogy and is most interested in knowing everything about Roberta's family: their children, parents, grandparents, cousins, marriages, divorces, deaths. All. She shares the results of her more sophisticated search of the Ellis Island archives and the happy discovery of a completely different branch of the Kolopsky family living in Boston—and one, she mentions in passing, in Israel by the name of Keter, and another Bar-Levy, although she doesn't know when and who first moved there. They stay on the phone for hours exchanging bits and pieces of information. Samantha, who has a doctorate in chemistry, tells Roberta that they are descended from a famous rabbi, or a cantor, who lived in the same region of the Pale as Mendel and Henya. She is uncertain of the year but thinks he may have been Mendel's uncle or great uncle. She reads an elegy she discovered that someone, she's not sure who, wrote upon the death of a son.

Months later, as she sits at her grungy wooden desk stacked high with mounds of paper, folders, forms, depositions, and unopened envelopes, an Israeli-stamped envelope catches Roberta's eye. Written in bold European script and addressed to Miss Roberta Sussman, Esquire—her name two marriages ago—she picks it up and informs her assistant that she is going to her favorite coffee shop across the street from her downtown Los Angeles office, where they make café au lait with authentic chicory beans, whole milk, and heavy cream, the way they make it in New Orleans.

"And don't warn me about my cholesterol. Do you want me to bring you back anything? How about a beignet?"

She loves the look and the feel in her mouth of the rich foam that tops the strong espresso blend. She sees that the sender, someone by the name of Keter, lives in Jerusalem. She thinks the name sounds familiar but can't recall why. As she turns the envelope over in her hand, she thinks about an old client who moved to Israel several years ago. She wonders if he changed his name to something more Israeli. *He was a nice, likeable old codger*, she thinks, *but also a pest*, and she wonders what he could want now. She knows nothing of Israeli law. The tissue-thin envelope opens easily and reveals a handwritten letter whose self-confident characters suggest strength and determination.

Dear Miss Roberta Sussman:

You don't know me, but if you are related to Rabbi Mendel Kolopsky, then I am your cousin. I have been searching for lost relatives all over the world for the past twenty years, but only with the latest computer technology has it been possible to turn up several threads. And you are one. I'm hoping this leads to finally finding my relatives.

When an elderly cousin died a few years ago, I was given a trunk that belonged to his grandfather, also my grandfather. He had asked me to disperse its contents as I saw fit. At the time, I was very busy with business and family and put it aside, but recently, when I moved from one house to another and needed to rid myself of things I had collected over the years—I'm somewhat of a hoarder, you might say—I was reminded of its presence. When I opened it, among other things, I uncovered a journal written by, I believe, your grandfather Mendel's brother. I think it was his brother—it may have been a cousin—by the name of Samson Keter, but originally his name was Shimshon Kolopski. Yes, a different spelling, but you know how those things are. He would be my grandfather, so if Mendel is your grandfather, he would be Shimshon's brother and your great uncle, and that's how we may be cousins.

The journal—actually it looks like a memoir—is written in Yiddish, and since I don't understand Yiddish, I had to find someone to translate it. Not many people speak Yiddish nowadays in Israel since our language, as you may know, is Hebrew. It is my fervent wish that you are, in fact, my cousin and that this will be as interesting to you as it is to me. Would you please be so kind as to respond soon to this inquiry as I've waited for a long time to resolve the mystery of my family's past history?

Sincerely,

Reuben Keter

No longer engrossed in drinking her now cold mug of coffee, Roberta quickly places the mass of legal material she brought to read into her thick leather portfolio—a gift from her children—and reaches for her cell phone to call Hannah.

"Hi, it's me. Are you sitting? You're not going to believe this. We've got long lost family in Israel."

Chapter 14

THE LONG FLIGHT TO ISRAEL

1996

As the lumbering blue-and-white El Al plane settles down for its final approach to Tel Aviv's Ben Gurion Airport, Roberta and Hannah strain to see beyond the clouds to the ground below. Like little kids, they can barely contain their anticipation as they peer out of the window for signs of life, in spite of the pitch darkness that reveals only the distant illumination of the runway lights. The time is two thirty in the morning, and they've been flying well over fourteen hours. Fourteen hours and twenty minutes to be exact. Nonstop. Mostly without sleep. They've talked the night away, recounting tales of childhood, catching up on things their kids are doing, envisioning who and what to expect of their newly discovered relatives, reviewing their awkward-sounding names, and laughing as their tongues twist in unfamiliar ways when they attempt to pronounce the Hebrew syllables.

Ever mindful of the cost of things, Hannah had entreated Roberta to fly economy class, which means that Roberta's long legs feel, as she says, like the compressed bellows of a Hohner accordion—the one her kids played years ago. And just their luck, a six-week-old infant, held by a distraught mother sitting in the seat behind them, cried incessantly from the moment of departure—no doubt the result of a plugged Eustachian tube—until they neared their destination, when she fell into a peaceful and sound slumber.

Hannah and Roberta agree that, although distressing, it was neither the cramped quarters nor the mewling child that kept them awake but rather their exhilaration and apprehension. This is their first visit to Israel and the first time since childhood they've had the leisure of fourteen uninterrupted hours to while away in conversation—except for the weekend sojourn to Santa Catalina Island following Roberta's decision to divorce Jerome, her first husband. There, they hiked, rode bikes, happily observed the herd of American bison that roamed the island, and griped about "men." But that was fourteen years ago.

Not that they, as children, took advantage of the long, never-ending summers to explore each other's psyches. The five-year age disparity mattered then. What matters now and what dissolves the space of time and age is their shared past, and they contentedly talked about their childhood history, including complaints about their parents, declarations of guilt for crimes both imagined and real, and, for Roberta, the knowledge that Hannah knew her from the very beginning. "Even when I was a fetus," she exclaimed, "and you saw me as a swelling in Mommy's tummy." They still call their parents "Mommy" and "Daddy" but only when addressing each other. They agree it sounds too immature in the presence of others.

According to "Mommy," Roberta recalled, Hannah placed a giant pillow over her head shortly after they brought her home from the hospital because, as Hannah explained to Dora, "the baby is very cold, so I covered her with a pillow so she'll be warm." This announcement, delivered with casual pride by five-year-old

Hannah, interrupted Dora's short-lived respite on the toilet and, as the anecdote is told, like a sprinter racing a five-minute mile, she dashed to the crib, panties at her ankles, and removed the offending threat—a stream of urine marking her path.

"Like Hansel and Gretel," Roberta mused, "but with urine, not bread crumbs. You know, Hannah, I don't remember that, obviously. What I do remember is your reading to me. Sometimes the books you read scared me, like *Pinocchio* when he gets lost or when he runs away from school, seduced by a wolf. Or was it a fox? For months, probably more, I used to look under my bed to see if a wolf was hiding there. My very favorite book was *Mr. Popper's Penguins*. Remember? You read it practically every night. My imagination ran wild with the fantasy that we would freeze over our living and dining room, and then I'd buy a pair of penguins who would give birth to babies—hundreds of them. They'd scamper down ice slides on their rumps. And we'd join in. Come to think of it, I still have a fondness for penguins; they're the first place I go when I visit the zoo. And it was the first book I bought for my kids and the first I bought my grandchildren. And whenever someone has a new baby, that's what I send. Birds and humans romping on ice in complete abandon. In my mind's eye, I can still see the gray-blue background and the black lettering on the cover. Maybe it's a wish to recover the freedom of childhood. I think we limit our imagination when we grow up. What a shame."

Hannah reminded Roberta how she cut the hair off her Shirley Temple doll and how Roberta tried, without success, to reassure Hannah, who erupted in tears of grief and rage. "Don't worry. It will grow back." They hooted, sounding a bit like owls, barely able to catch their breath due to their hiccupping laughter when the conversation turned to how Roberta cut the hair off Hannah's first boyfriend's leg while seated at the couple's feet, ostensibly cutting out paper dolls. He and Hannah were too deeply engaged in conversation and necking to notice the "surgical procedure" until he reached down to scratch the tingle it created.

"His name was Charlie, wasn't it?" Roberta inquired between giggles.

"I can't believe you remember his name," countered Hannah. "I dated him for a month or so before I met Bert. I haven't thought of him for decades. I wonder whatever became of him. As I remember, he was a good guy. I seem to recall that he may have served in the Korean War."

"Yeah, he was cute and so was the other guy you dated after him. Arnie? Arnie something-or-other, right?"

Hannah said that Arnie came before Charlie and that she never dated anyone else after Bert.

As a teenager, Roberta confessed, she used to sneak into their shared bedroom closet after Hannah left for work to "borrow" a blouse or a sweater or a skirt to wear to school, and then she'd restore it to its proper place—by counting hanger placement—before Hannah's return in the evening.

"Did you really think I didn't know that? Don't you remember that I confronted you after I found a stain on my favorite dress?" Hannah challenged. "It was a gray crepe dress with a lace bodice. But since we're making confessions, Robbie—" Hannah admitted that she could have been a better big sister. She disclosed that because she had to work so hard to get anything, she just couldn't be charitable.

Hannah described how she babysat every Saturday night. And how she worked all summer throughout high school—picking tomatoes on a farm.

"I'd be picked up at five in the morning and then dropped off with my face caked with dirt and sweat. I did it so I could buy a pair of ice skates, and then Daddy made me buy black ones two sizes too big so that I would 'grow into them.' And to make matters worse, because they were so big, I skated on my ankles, and they called me a klutz—even Mommy. I couldn't bear giving anything to you for nothing," Hannah sighed. "I felt bad, but I just couldn't do it. It felt to me that you got off so easy."

Roberta reminded Hannah that she was just a kid herself. She thought that it might have been hard for her because their mother always insisted that Hannah let Roberta tag along. Roberta said all the right things to Hannah, trying to assuage her guilt, and yet, at times, she had felt that her sister could, indeed, have been more generous. She recalled the venom she'd felt when she announced to Hannah that she was going to be rich when she grew up and wouldn't give Hannah a dime.

"I cringe now when I think of how I tattled on you when you did something wrong," Roberta continued. "Not that you really did anything wrong. You always did the 'right' thing. Got the good grades. Made honor roll. No one ever called you a nudnik. You were one hard act to follow, Hannah."

"You won't believe this," Hannah continued where she'd left off, "but you know what I still feel guilty about? About not giving you my Girl Scout uniform and that my friend Ruthie gave you hers, even though she was four inches taller than even me. It came down to your ankles. I felt ashamed when I heard her tell you that you could have her uniform. She said she wished she had you for a little sister. God, I was so humiliated. And then Mommy went ahead and gave you mine anyway, without asking me."

"Yeah, not a good way to build a sibling relationship," reflected Roberta. "But do you remember? When I was cutting off all of your badges—and, God, you earned every badge in the book—I made holes in the sleeve. But hey, Hannah, I can't believe you still feel bad about it. I mean, should I feel guilty about pushing your Shirley Temple doll's teeth down her throat? Because I don't, you know."

The conversation shifted to the *raison d'être* of their journey. Roberta reread the letter from Reuben. Several months had passed since it arrived. She silently wondered what she would find when she met this stranger—her mysterious cousin—face to face. She worried that he might be one of those right wingers.

"I mean, what if he's for building more settlements? Or the wall? Or what if he's Orthodox and wears all that religious paraphernalia? And worse yet, what if he likes Bush? Now that, I really couldn't tolerate."

"Well, you could be just as concerned, my dear sister, should he turn out to be one of those lefty extremists, you know, the ones who espouse Palestinians *über alles*. The ones who always blame Israel no matter what. The ones who claim Hamas as innocent victims? Those who can't see Hamas's provocative acts even when they themselves claim responsibility for the devastation, like last year when they suicide-bombed the bus full of innocent victims and then the bus station the next week? I say a pox on both their houses. If only there were good guys wearing white hats and bad guys wearing black hats, whom we could easily assign blame to."

"But don't you mean guys wearing white yarmulkes and black yarmulkes?" Roberta smirked, obviously pleased with her gag.

The sisters' politics diverged somewhat, with Roberta leaning center left and Hannah center right. Roberta felt strongly that because so many of the Israeli immigrants were survivors of the Holocaust, they above all should bear in mind what had been done to them and should not repeat the persecution.

"To me, it comes down to what it means to be a human being, a *mensch*," Roberta continued. "Yes, it's true that both sides claim Israel as their legitimate homeland from biblical times, and it's also true that Jews have a justifiable grievance because of the historical injustices they've suffered, going back to medieval times, but it's because of those injustices that they should go to all lengths not to perpetrate injustices against others. I have to say, sometimes I'm ashamed of my own people."

"Even if some of those very same people threaten Israel's very right to exist—like Hamas? It's in their charter. And others claim that the Holocaust never happened—that it's a figment of the Jews' imagination?" Hannah argued. She detailed what Roberta knew only too well, how in the 1930s and '40s, the Jews were kicked out of Germany, Poland, Hungary, Romania, the Ukraine. "And where were they to go?" she asked.

"Look, Hannah, I am well aware that we are a people who have been evicted, convicted, cremated, enslaved, and perjured, but I also know that there are now over four million Palestinians and their descendants who were extruded from Palestine and are now living in intolerable conditions. Those kids have never known anything but this awful existence. What do they have to look forward to? So they strap a bomb on their bodies and become martyrs."

They had both read early Zionist history and knew that, in 1882, the first wave of European Jews immigrated to Palestine, then a part of the Ottoman Empire. Many of those very early immigrants wanted nothing more than to be left alone to study their religious texts and practice their faith and be supported by Jewish charities throughout the world. Then, with a surge of nationalism and the purchase by the Jewish National Fund of large tracts of land from absentee Arab landowners, followed by the eviction of Arabs from the homes they and their families had lived in for centuries, the seeds of the current violence grew.

"But tell me, Robbie, what did the Arabs do for their own kind? None of the Arab states granted citizenship to the exodus of Palestinian Arabs who did resettle in Arab nations. The Arab community used them as political pawns. And one last thing, look what the Israelis made of the land. Once barren and parched soil with nothing growing on it is now fertile and productive."

Roberta contended that when the early Zionists arrived in Palestine in 1897, there were hundreds of humble Palestinian villages, like Jaffa and Ramleh and Der el-Hawa and Haditha. And there were farmlands and olive trees and orange groves—and more than half a million Arabs and Bedouins and Druze living there. "There were people living in Palestine for centuries, unlike what Golda Meir claimed! Nothing there, indeed!"

~

The noise of the landing gear's release brings the sisters' discussion to a close. Soon, the giant wheels of the plane thump to the ground and then hop and abruptly grind to a halt on the tarmac moments later. A breathless silence ensues, cut short by relieved applause, and then, as though the worrisome incident never happened, the passengers quickly turn to the task at hand, that of assembling their personal belongings in the overhead bin and scurrying to the baggage claim area to be the first to collect their remaining suitcases.

With each turn of the carousel, a dozen or so perturbed passengers scrutinize the mass of brown, black, red, green, and blue bags that rotate before them like a mirage that tantalizes the parched throats of wanderers crossing the desert. Some bite their fingernails in nervous frustration, several grouse to themselves, others complain to their companions or to any stranger who happens to be standing close by. Quite a few stand sulking silently at a distance. Roberta thinks that this pattern of behavior reveals as much about the individuals' personalities as does a Rorschach inkblot.

Roberta and Hannah ogle the same large black travel case making its unremitting rounds, as if their scrutiny will somehow transform it into Roberta's missing piece. But with each loop around the carousel, the ribbon-bedecked bag—the plaid one Roberta attached to its handle for easy identification—is not to be found. She is close to tears as the carousel grunts to a halt, and it becomes obvious that her case will not materialize. She and her sister join the growing line of peeved passengers queuing up at the El Al customer service counter, where flustered agents strive to appease the disgruntled crowd. An elderly gentleman standing next to Roberta complains loudly to his wife. He talks over her attempt to placate him. The more she tries to pacify him, the more strident and disruptive he becomes until, unable to restrain herself, Roberta blurts out, "You know, sir, we are all in the same predicament, and you're not making it any easier for yourself or for the rest of us. So why don't you just cool it."

Stricken, he turns on his heels, mumbling to himself something about "pushy broads," and sits down on a bench by the far wall.

"Sorry about that," his wife whispers to Roberta. "He gets very nervous when traveling. He's really a sweet man, but when the unexpected happens, he can't handle it. I try to intervene, but being a Holocaust survivor—if you know anything about that, you'll understand—he has a need for predictability. When something out of the blue happens, he goes a bit meshuga."

The luggage, they are told, has inadvertently been placed on a plane destined for Greece and won't arrive until the following day. The unhappy El Al agent reassures the crowd that the airline will deliver their precious goods to their hotels the following day and further mollifies them by handing out small blue faux-leather pouches designed for first-class travelers, containing diminutive tubes of toothpaste, compact toothbrushes encased in plastic, razors, eye shades and earplugs, mouthwash, and shaving cream. They are equipped, it seems, solely for male passengers. Roberta is about to point out their gender bias but, thinking better of it, shrugs her shoulders and joins Hannah, who is in the taxi queue. All she wants is to be taken to the Dan Hotel in Tel Aviv. And to sleep for twenty-four hours. Or more.

The compromise Roberta and Hannah reached was that if Roberta agreed to fly economy, Hannah would consent to stay at a good hotel in a deluxe room with a view of the city. Not, however, Hannah asserted, in the deluxe deluxe room with a view of the blue Mediterranean. "I mean," she justified, "how much time will we spend looking out the window? We'll just be sleeping and sightseeing and visiting with our relatives."

"Ha, I still can't believe we have Israeli relatives. And here we are not knowing a word of Hebrew."

Chapter 15

MEETING
THE MISHPUCHA

Promptly at noon the following morning, the sisters are jolted awake by the insistent ring of the telephone. Groaning and knocking her glasses off the bedside table in her attempt to locate the phone, Roberta removes the receiver from its cradle.

"Hello?" She looks at the desk at the opposite side of their spacious, white-walled room, squinting as she strives to read the illuminated hands of the clock.

A deep baritone voice, speaking in heavily accented English, responds, "I hope I'm not disturbing you. I hope it's not too early, but I've been up since six this morning cooling my heels, as you would say, and couldn't wait another minute. This is Reuben, your cousin. I'm downstairs in the lobby. Rivka told me to wait until you called, but I couldn't."

Roberta can hardly get the words out between her own disorientation and exhilaration and Hannah's impatient attempt to pull the phone out of Roberta's hand. "Oh, no, no, no, not at all," Roberta responds. "We've been here eagerly awaiting your call," she lies, "but didn't want to bother you. We're both so eager to meet you and your family. I can't believe we're here. Just a minute, Hannah is so anxious to talk to you, she's tugging at the receiver. Here."

"Hello Reuben, it's Hannah. Oh my! I can't tell you how, how . . . pleased . . ." Hannah hands the phone back to Roberta, unable to contain the whimper coming from her throat.

Roberta and Hannah leap out of bed and hastily discuss what to wear as they apply their makeup, in tandem, at the bathroom vanity. They decide on dark linen pants and short-sleeved blouses rather than the more revealing sundresses they packed, reasoning that should they visit the Wailing Wall, they wouldn't want to offend the Orthodox men at prayer. Or perhaps even their cousin. At least that was Hannah's thinking. Before leaving their room, she elicits a promise from Roberta that she will not get into a political discussion about the Palestinian-Israeli conflict with their relatives, adding, "Roberta, promise that if we do go to the Wall, you won't insist on standing with the men. You're a guest in this country, so it's not the time for activism. Show respect. Sometimes you remind me of Daddy, always with his confrontations. So, you'll promise, right?"

The elevator doors open onto the large, well-lit lobby with a brown-and-yellow checkered pattern on its highly waxed marble floor. Standing near a massive, luminous wooden console in the center of the lobby, Roberta and Hannah observe a rather husky, ruggedly handsome man in his late sixties, nervously pacing back and forth and intermittently peering at the elevator doors. He bears a striking resemblance to what they remember of Uncle Stewart but for the shocking head of curly auburn-and-white stippled hair and his Goliath physique. His full white beard is neatly trimmed. He wears no yarmulke. No *tzitzit*. Nothing that would identify him as a Jew, no less an Orthodox Jew. When he smiles, the fissures on his well-worn face are liberated. The sisters walk silently toward this strangely intimate stranger, and he toward them, as if drawn by an invisible magnet. They soon find themselves enveloped in their cousin's brawny arms. A chorus of subdued sobs breaks the stillness. The dance of embrace and tears, interspersed with laughter and arms-length inspection, persists for well over five minutes, to and fro, until Reuben takes both women by the hand and guides them to the parking lot and to his black Peugeot.

"*Todah rabah,* thanks very much for coming. You'll never know how much this means to me and Rivka."

Standing around an oversized ebony coffee table, Roberta and Hannah are surrounded by concentric circles of large, small, young, old, blond, brunette, redheaded male and female folk. Relatives all. Laughing. Crying. Talking. Questioning. Interrupting. Opining. Interrupting. Arguing. Interrupting. Eating. Drinking. And interrupting.

The table is laden with bowls of yogurt, hummus, black olives, pickles, chopped liver, tabbouleh and tomato salads, baba ghanoush, platters of sliced cucumbers and hard-boiled eggs, oranges, knishes, pita bread, kofta kebabs, feta cheese, and dolma. Bottles of scotch, rye, bourbon, seltzer water, diet Coca-Cola and ginger ale line the sideboard, guarding their posts like silent sentinels, along with paper plates, napkins, plastic forks, knives, and cups. A hint of burnt coffee permeates the celebrants' nostrils. This is breakfast in Israel on a mid-Sunday morning.

Reuben and Rivka smile with pleasure at the assortment of family members gathered in their living room, especially at Hannah and Roberta, waiting to be seated.

"First, meet my Rivka, my wonderful wife," exalts Reuben. "She's the ur-mother of this brood and the ultimate woman of valor. And here are my jewels, and I don't expect you to remember their names. I sometimes call them by the wrong name. My oldest, Shoshanna, and her two boys—Say hello, Shosh. Then Hadar and her husband, Asher, over by the window. And Zechariah, our son. Standing by the door, Tamir and his wife, Tova.

And Tamir's twin, Nehemia, and his wife, Sarah. We've been very busy as you can see, but not to forget our youngest. Come, come," Reuben shouts enthusiastically to his youngest daughter, Batya, her husband, Ari, and his six grandchildren. Standing somewhat removed from the crowd but for a gaggle of children ranging in age from toddler to teenager, a young couple, perhaps in their thirties by Roberta's reckoning, leans against the wall, their eyes riveted on the foreign guests. A *kippah* covers the beginnings of a bald spot on the young man's head; the fringes of his *tzitzit* can be seen peeking from the bottom of his white shirt covered, in part, by an unbuttoned navy blue silk vest. The woman, clad in a long-sleeved black dress that reaches to her ankles, hair tucked beneath a scarf that frames her heart-shaped face, stands close by, holding a sleeping toddler. She is prominently pregnant.

"Come and meet your American cousins. Your great-grandfather, Shmuel Keter, and their grandfather, Mendel Kolopsky, were brothers. You remember I told you Saba changed his name when he moved to Israel. So, Batya, you need to hold up the wall? Look," he says to Hannah and Roberta, pointing to his six grandchildren. "Aren't they gorgeous? Jonah, Elijah, Ilan—the older boys—and Esther and Miriam and the sleeping princess, Rachel—my little granddaughters. Come, *kinderlach*, come sit on Saba's lap." Like feisty puppies released from the confines of a cage, the girls depart their parents' side and scramble helter-skelter onto their grandfather's lap. "I only wish my brother Meir, may he rest, could have been here to see this. And someday, when you go to Paris, you can meet Rebecca and her husband, Jacques." He doesn't mention the absence of Shoshanna's husband, who was killed while sitting in a café drinking coffee several years ago.

Roberta and Hannah spend the next several ten-hour whirlwind days touring Israel—from Safed in the north to the hilltop fortress of Masada and Caesarea in the east, where the sisters marvel over the Roman theater built by Herod; to the south to visit Be'er Sheba, so named for the oath made at the well between the patriarch Abraham and Abimelach (be'er is the Hebrew word for well; schuvu'a, the Hebrew word for oath); and to many sites in between. One day they rent a jeep, just the two of them, and drive to the Judean Desert where they swim in the Dead Sea—known as the lowest point in the world—and squeal in delightful pain when the salt assaults a previously unknown scrape.

Each day they return, exhausted, to their hotel long after the sun sets, with barely the stamina to undress and fall into bed. And, exhausted, they awaken in the morning to greet another day with yet another relative eager to accompany them to another exotic destination.

The hour-long drive from Tel Aviv to Jerusalem becomes as familiar to Roberta as the trip from her home in Santa Monica to Century City, where her law practice is. When there is a respite over tea or coffee or lunch, the conversation inevitably turns to Uncle Samuel's journal—or Shmuel, as their cousins call him—the very journal that brought them on this 7,552-mile quest.

"It's so strange," Hannah comments, "that this man, our uncle, was never ever mentioned growing up. I wonder if Mommy even knew about him." They've raised the topic several times in conversations with Reuben, but with the now familiar gesture of his hand, he waves them away and tells them to have patience. And so they smile and stifle their frustration until, once again, the question resurfaces, only to be rejected with the same admonition for forbearance.

Hannah and Roberta thrill to the pulsating animation of Tel Aviv with its nightlife and its beaches—some gay and, they observe, those nearing Jaffa, predominantly Arab. They exchange condescending glances and raised eyebrows when they pass the Orthodox section with signs specifying the set of rules required for entry to the Separated Beach.

Bathing days for women: Sunday, Tuesday, Thursday.

Bathing days for men: Monday, Wednesday, Friday.

They are pleasantly taken aback to discover countless restaurants catering to "foodies" near and far, with gourmet food that rivals that of Paris or Manhattan or San Francisco. And just as they love Tel Aviv for the diversity of its residents, for its high technology, trendy designer shops, and modernist buildings, they love the composed contrast Jerusalem offers, with its 5,000-year-old history that paints an unforgettable canvas of memories upon their consciousness.

In their first week in Israel, they spend hours in the Old City and the Israel Museum, where they gaze in awe at the Dead Sea Scrolls. They walk the Via Dolorosa and follow Jesus's poignant journey to his crucifixion. And yes, they visit the Wailing Wall, even Roberta giving due respect to the distance required for women. They take three of Reuben's youngest grandchildren to the Biblical Zoo, where they pet the friendly animals, including the pygmy goats. They do not visit Yad Vashem; Roberta claims that after her visit to the Holocaust Memorial Museum in Washington, DC, she's "seen enough of that horror to last a lifetime."

On Saturday, several days before their scheduled departure, they accept Reuben and Rivka's invitation to light the Havdalah candles. Roberta reminds Reuben of his promise to take them to East Jerusalem, the Palestinian section of the city. She wants to see the schools and the hospitals and, particularly, the conditions under which the Palestinians live. She wants, more than anything, to visit the Shuafat refugee camp. She queries him about the Palestinian population of Jerusalem. Reuben tells her that 250,000 Palestinians live within the municipality of Jerusalem and are considered residents, not citizens, of Israel. He claims it was their choice not to accept citizenship as a way of ensuring their identity as Palestinians and because of their belief that the land belongs to them but is only occupied by the Israelis.

Reuben takes a deep breath before speaking. "Look, my dear, dear cousins, what you are asking is not impossible, but only because I am a member of Peace Now would I even consider it— and only because one of my dear friends is a Palestinian who lives at the camp, an important activist at that. Otherwise it would be too dangerous for us to even think of going. You're Americans, remember, and not very popular with the Palestinians."

"Oh, please, Reuben," Roberta pleads. "I've read so much about the situation, and depending upon who or what one reads, there are so many contradictory perspectives. And then I feel so conflicted between my identification as a Jew and my sense of social justice. I need to see for myself."

Hannah interrupts, "I had no idea there was a refugee camp in Jerusalem. But don't you think, in spite of your Palestinian friend, it could be somewhat risky to go there?"

Reuben says that he's not surprised and that even some Israelis have no idea there is a camp in Jerusalem. He informs them it was established between 1965 and 1966 by the Jordanian regime and the United Nations Relief and Works Agency but falls within the Israeli Jerusalem Municipality's borders. At its creation, the population was only 1,500, but now it's approximately 20,000. The statistics vary, he continues, depending upon who has conducted the research. It was built on 203 dunams that Jordan confiscated from their original Palestinian owners, but the Six-Day War intervened, and that put an end to the plan to upgrade the area. He explains that this is only one of many such refugee camps, with others in Jordan, Lebanon, the Gaza Strip and the West Bank with something like 1.4 million people considered refugees.

"Did you know that the Jordanians unilaterally annexed the West Bank and East Jerusalem in 1950?" Reuben asks. Roberta whispers that she didn't know that. He goes on, "The situation is very complicated all the way back to the way the State of Israel came into existence when they confiscated Palestinian land. All I know for sure is that people are hurt and angry on both sides. There are cycles of violence that beget more violence, with the two sides competing to show who is more of a victim and with corrupt leaders on both sides incapable of reframing the situation in a way that could lead to a different outcome. Everyone suffers."

Reuben agrees that the Palestinians—in Gaza, the West Bank, and here in East Jerusalem—have been living like dogs in crowded surroundings without some of the basic amenities, like electricity, schools, hospitals, and roads, and they are understandably resentful because the encroaching settlements deprive them of even more land. He states that even their own people have used them as political pawns, in addition to some Israeli politicians. The settlers, because they are by and large Orthodox Jews, believe they are the rightful inhabitants of the land and are supported by the right-wingers and the Orthodox parties, like Shas or Agudat Yisrael or Degel HaTorah. They accept as fact that the land has been bequeathed to them—by God, no less. "On the other hand," Reuben continues, "where were the Jews to go?"

"As long as you're aware that it's not a tourist destination, not Los Angeles or Tel Aviv, I'll see what I can do," he promises. "I'll call Da'oud and find out if he's disposed to escort us. Otherwise we can't go. I will not permit it! So, no, Hannah-la, to answer your question, it is not one hundred percent safe. But you should see it with your own eyes."

Reuben calls Roberta after they return to the hotel to report that Da'oud agreed to a tour of the camp the following day.

That evening, Roberta pens a letter that she hopes will reach her children before they get home themselves.

My dear children,

Aunt Hannah and I are having an incredible time. I, who

consider myself a fairly articulate woman with typically too many words to express my feelings, am at a loss to describe our experience in Israel so far. I want to commit to memory each and every little detail of our adventure. As you know, I've traveled to many places: Paris, Prague, Costa Rica, Greece, St. Petersburg, Copenhagen, China, Africa, and then some, but there is something about this encounter that leaves me both breathless and wordless.

Not like your Mom, huh? It's beyond this place's ancient history—awesome though it is—and beyond its austere beauty, with its stunning buildings of limestone, called Jerusalem stone. I believe, for me, it has more to do with having found our, if you will, lost tribe, the part of our family that I have been longing to locate—for my "self," consciously and unconsciously, lo these many years.

We are utterly overwhelmed with our relatives' generosity of spirit, their diversity of opinions (some you would hate), and their warm acceptance. They are good people. Now, this may sound bizarre, but I will sometimes look at Cousin Reuben and see a familiar gesture that brings to mind memories of my old Zaide Mendel, or even of one of your great uncles, especially Uncle Stewart. Or I see a gesticulation that speaks to me of my mother, your grandmother, Dora—a raised eyebrow or the way she wiggled her foot when she was upset. It was always a dead giveaway and still sends shivers down my spine. This is all unsettling, mysterious, and awe-inspiring at the same time.

Oh, my darling children, there is so much more to tell, but I'll leave the rest of the travelogue for my return. Reuben has invited us to their place the night before we leave, and Aunt Hannah and I want to make sure, since time is growing short, that we entertain them when we can squeeze it in. He says he has something precious to give to us. It has to be the journal that he wrote about. (About time, I'd say.) Precious indeed. I've been waiting impatiently to

*get my hands on it since our arrival. No, actually before. I think
I mentioned that it was originally in Yiddish but that Reuben had
it translated into Hebrew for his own comprehension, then into
English after he made contact with us. How incredible can this be?*

*I so look forward to seeing you and the children again (our
numbers are paltry in comparison with theirs) and to hug you
and to tell you all about every detail of our trip. About your new
cousins, the country. Its politics. All. You must put Israel on your
travel agenda. Yes, I know you can't do it now, what with all the
expenses of raising children, but still, if there's any way to arrange
it, I'd be happy to help a little. Love to my precious grandchildren.
I miss all of you.*

> *Hugs,*
> *Mom*

*P.S. Tomorrow I visit the Shuafat refugee camp. A bit anxious and
eager. Both!!*

Chapter 16

THE CAMP

Early the following morning, Roberta paces outside of her hotel, waiting for Da'oud and Reuben to arrive. She eats a hard-boiled egg and a cucumber that she picked up from the hotel buffet. Within two minutes of their appointed time, Da'oud and Reuben arrive, obliging Roberta to quickly down the rest of the snack.

Furious that Roberta has broken her promise not to get into Palestinian-Israeli politics, or any politics for that matter, and just a little worried about the dangers of such an adventure, Hannah decides not to join them. She claims that she needs to begin to pack, to write some postcards, but mostly to recover from the hectic pace of their adventure-packed days.

Da'oud bears a striking resemblance to Reuben, sans red hair. He is a strongly built man who, at first glance, appears a bit intimidating because of his enormous size. He has curly black hair and a somewhat tousled beard that sheathes his face, a bear of a man. Following Reuben's introductions, Roberta cordially declines Da'oud's invitation to sit in the front seat. She prefers the anonymity and freedom of the back seat, where she can observe the surroundings while listening to their conversation—not that she can fully comprehend it. The men speak in basic English scattered with Hebrew and Arabic words, which to Roberta's ears sound strangely similar. Da'oud explains that the root of both languages is Aramaic, so to the unpracticed ear, they sound the same.

Because Da'oud holds a Jerusalem ID, the route to the camp consists of driving on Nablus Road, the main thoroughfare connecting Ramallah to Jerusalem. As they come nearer to the camp, Roberta sees signs—in English, Arabic, and Hebrew—announcing Beit Hanina and Shuafat and the Pisgat Ze'ev settlement, named for Ze'ev Jabotinsky, the early Zionist leader. There is no sign, however, for the camp. At a snail's pace, they follow a meandering route, passing through a short tunnel and then across the central highway that leads to Jerusalem.

Da'oud passes a building encircled by barbed wire fencing—a small girls' school, he informs them—and then points to a turquoise UNRWA sign with white writing pronouncing their arrival at the Shuafat refugee camp. When they reach the camp's military checkpoint, three Israeli security guards, barely older than Roberta's youngest child, who is twenty-five, greet them frostily. They confer briefly with Da'oud and then wave the car on after he presents his residency card.

The road into the camp opens onto an uncared-for square. As Roberta peers out the rear view window, the scene is one of a grimy main road clogged with traffic heading out of the checkpoint—the one and only gateway to and from the camp, where the residents show their blue Israeli ID to leave for work. The unpaved roads of the camp, the lack of sidewalks, the noise, the garbage and waste that is strewn everywhere distress her. A fowl stench pervades the air, most likely, Da'oud explains, from the exposed sewage. He tells her that the camp is run by the United Nations Relief and Works Agency under the jurisdiction of the Jerusalem

Municipality and jokingly refers to it as "Chicago," because, he explains, of the organized crime and drug trafficking.

"Have you ever been to Chicago?" asks Roberta, just a little miffed at the comparison.

"No, why should I go there when I live here and am witness to it daily?" Da'oud responds. "Look over there at those kids exchanging drugs in broad daylight. It's routine. Like Chicago, no?" He makes the justification that an infrastructure is all but absent, which leads to shortages of water and electricity and inadequate health care, education, and transportation. "And no employment for these young kids to make a living."

With growing agitation, he explains that even the local school is located next to a factory that pollutes. He stresses that these conditions pertain not only to the Palestinians living in this camp but to Gaza, as well as the West Bank. He slams his hand down on the dashboard and exhales noisily.

"But all is not darkness here," he carries on, trying to compose himself. "You'd be interested to know that they built a Women's Center, founded last year as part of a Community Development Center built, by the way, by the German government. The Germans, not the Americans. And there's a nursery school and kindergarten and library and some vocational training going on and a summer camp. There are also literacy programs, and, can you believe, they are in the process of building a fitness center for women and a battered women's shelter?"

Roberta asks about the incidence of family violence in the camp.

"It is a major issue. You've got to understand that Palestinian men feel so hopeless about their situation, having no future. This is all they've known, so they take out their frustrations on the women and children."

"So what else is new?" responds Roberta. "I know that very

well. We have the same problem confronting us in the States, where there's poverty and crime, but it doesn't only happen in pockets of poverty. And not only in Chicago, my friend. You do know that we have shelters for battered women too?"

She questions Da'oud about the nearby luxury structures she notices nestled upon the nearby hillside. He tells her that it is the Pisgat Ze'ev settlement built in 1982. "After the Six-Day War," he continues, "Israel annexed that land in violation of the Fourth Geneva Convention, and it's against international law."

"Well," Reuben interjects, "some might not agree with that perspective."

After Da'oud insists, once again, that it violates international law, a stony silence fills the interior of the car.

Roberta asks Da'oud if it's safe to walk. He says it is, and after parking the car, they walk on the main road with its narrow alleyways. Roberta glimpses families living in recently built but crumbling structures that appear to have been abandoned in the middle of construction, with stairways, doors, and passageways strewn with wreckage and fallen rocks and bricks. Da'oud shoots Roberta a perplexed glance when she asks how people can live this way. Rather than answer her question, he describes the way in which the Israel government's discrimination against the residents of East Jerusalem was to encourage them to move out of Jerusalem and into the West Bank. "They don't want to make life too comfortable for us so they can have it to themselves," he snarls. "If we leave, they can build even more settlements like Pisgat."

As they make their way through the dilapidated, narrow alleyways with their falling-apart two-story buildings—consisting of two-room apartments—small dark shops, and motorcycles maneuvering the rock-strewn streets, a middle-aged man gets off of his motorcycle and falls into an impassioned conversation with Da'oud. Da'oud later translates that the man thought the two visitors might be inspectors from the Jerusalem Municipality and wanted them to know how unhealthy the living conditions were. He wanted to take them to his two-room apartment where three families now lived. Where no one had a place to sleep. Where his children caught disease from one another. After calming the intruder and assuring him that no one was a representative of any authority, Da'oud informs them that those who live in the camp can tell under which jurisdiction it falls, that of UNRWA or the Muslim Waqf or the JM, with the Jerusalem site the most underserved. He continues, "But regardless of which authority, all neighborhoods endure horrendous living conditions, filled to capacity dwellings, and substandard basic services."

Roberta wonders if it's diplomatic to ask how this refugee camp compares with those in Gaza or the West Bank. Finally, she gets her courage up and is surprised to learn that there are other camps, not only here in East Jerusalem, the West Bank, and the Gaza Strip but in Syria, Lebanon, and Jordan as well.

"Let me educate you, Roberta," Da'oud states. "First of all, there are over seven million Palestinian refugees worldwide. My numbers may not be exact, but they are close enough. Check them out. There are more than one million refugees living in camps in Gaza, well over two million on the West Bank." He tells her he is uncertain about the numbers in Jordan, Lebanon, and Syria, but he does know there are nine camps in Syria, twelve in Lebanon, and in Jordan, ten. "I do know," he continues, "that the West Bank has the largest number of recognized refugees, and that in all camps, these people suffer from unemployment, depression, post-traumatic stress, illness . . ." He stops midsentence and abruptly turns and walks toward the car.

On the ride back to her hotel, Roberta thinks about Palestinian terrorism and their despotic leaders; she thinks about the aborted peace efforts, and then her mind turns to the Jewish ghettoes in

Europe——the Pale of Settlement, for example, that she read about as she pursued her family's history——and wonders how this differs from that. Groups of people isolated in ghettoes because of their religion, or the blacks living in their ghetto because of the color of their skin, or so many others because of their political affiliation or ethnicity or sexual identity. She considers whether one must always avenge history by repeating the trauma to another group further down the pecking order. She wonders how this situation can possibly be resolved or how peace can ever be achieved given this sordid account. She is quiet, even sullen, overcome by a sense of futility and sadness.

Chapter 17

THE MEANING OF NAMES

The evening following the camp tour, Roberta and Hannah treat Reuben and Rivka to dinner at a spot recommended by the concierge at their hotel. The restaurant is housed in an Ottoman-era villa in Tel Aviv's Neve Tzedek district. One discerns from Rivka's expression of surprise that this is not an eating place they would have come to on their own. No one talks about Roberta's camp experience.

Not wanting to appear like rich, ugly Americans—which they are neither—Hannah and Roberta pass by the bottle of Dom Pérignon listed on the menu for $159 USD and settle on a more reasonable but "not too shabby" Veuve Clicquot. Hannah toasts the cousins, affirming her admiration for them, and expresses her gratitude for finding *mishpucha.* After a round of toasts, Roberta orders a slow-cooked lamb dish, as does Reuben. Hannah and Rivka both order mozzarella-filled veal meatballs in a chicken-and-sage sauce. Afterward, although they complain that they couldn't possibly put another morsel of food in their mouths, the quartet somehow manages to scarf down the house specialty, an Arabian filigree pastry stuffed with cheese and served with sage ice-cream topped with honey.

Over coffee—black and thick as mud—Rivka talks about her children. "What can I say? They are all so very different. I swear, sometimes I think that each one came from a different set of parents. From the moment she came out, my youngest was observant. She just took on the injunctions and rituals of Judaism—and believe me, she didn't get it from me. I'm what you call an ethnic Jew, not at all observant but proud to be a Jew nevertheless. Yes, every so often I light Shabbos candles, and we do have Passover but with no mention of God, but that's it. We're both atheists, you know. So who knew when we named her Batya—that's Hebrew for *daughter of God*—that she would grow up Orthodox?"

"Names have meanings," interjects Reuben. "There's a not-so-subtle message conveyed when one names a child, perhaps subconsciously. Don't you agree, Hannah? We even have a naming ceremony, for God's sake."

"She's so good, so sweet, so passive. But about her religion, she's a warrior," continues Rivka, paying no attention to Reuben's comment. "I worry for her health though. Pregnant with her seventh child and she's only thirty-three. No contraception. How much can her little body stand?" She sighs.

"She's stronger than you think," asserts Reuben. She must take after her great-grandfather, Shmuel, which reminds me, Robbie and Hannahla, remember you're having dinner with us on your final night in Israel. Don't forget! I have something I want you to have. Yes, I know. I know you've been *hocking* me the whole time you've been here. Anyhow, don't think I didn't notice. So come early, we have a lot to talk about."

"So, how would you translate Shmuel into English?" Hannah asks.

"Samuel," Rivka responds.

Rivka turns the conversation back to the children. "My oldest son is progressive, wouldn't you say, Reuben? Typically, his opinions are the same as ours, more or less. It's just what I would have expected from a child raised in our home with our strong convictions about diversity and treating others as you would have them treat you." She pauses and then adds, "He's also gay."

"But you didn't tell us what Zechariah means?" observes Hannah, not knowing whether to pursue that theme.

"It means *remembering God*," smiles Reuben. "So I guess it doesn't always work that way since Zech is not religious at all. Not at all. And, by the way, we accept him and love him for who he is, in case you're wondering."

"Okay, that he is liberal is easy to understand," Rivka moves on. "But I cannot understand how our Tamir became so conservative. Yes, you heard right," she affirms as she notes Hannah's stunned expression. "As liberal as we are, our son Tamir is the opposite. He even voted for Netanyahu as prime minister. That's the closest Reuben ever came to having a fistfight with a child. He didn't, but it was dreadful. Every night, an argument at the dinner table. Words and names thrown around. We finally agreed not to talk politics anymore, except between the two of us. We're very political people, you know. We belong to the Histadrut."

"I'm not familiar with that name," remarks Roberta. "I know Likud and Labor and—actually, now that I think of it, that's all I know."

"There's the Green Party," chimes in Hannah, delighted to contribute to the discussion.

"True, Hannah," adds Reuben, "and Histadrut means *the Union*, which is shorthand for the General Union of Workers and is made up of many labor unions. I have some books about it that I could give you, Robbie, if you're interested, that is. And you too, Hannah."

"I'd like that, thanks," Roberta responds.

"So how did Tamir become so conservative?" Roberta wonders out loud.

"I swear," Reuben asserts, his voice now raised an octave, "I believe it was in reaction to me and to his place in the family, the middle child. And yet his twin holds a different point of view. Batya was the baby and beautiful, and by the time she came along, all we wanted was another girl. If we were praying people, we would have prayed for a girl. Everyone pampered her and treated her like a doll. She was always, as Rivka said, spiritual. Loved nature. Planted flowers. Wrote poetry. Somehow it was safe for her to express herself; I don't think it was a rebellious act at all. It came from her heart. And Zechariah—well, he was the first son and a wanted and adored son. You know—a prince, a Jewish prince. He knew from the beginning he was wanted and loved and that we thought him special, so he could identify with us—with me —and had no need to rebel or prove anything to anyone. He knew who he was."

Reuben goes on to talk of the time he spent with the older children clamoring for attention, especially at the dinner table with every word that fell from Zech's precocious mouth treated like gold.

"Then when Tamir came along," he continues, looking for agreement from Rivka, "he couldn't compete with our beautiful girls with all their words, so he had a lot to prove. Sitting on a lot of anger too, most likely against me. I think I was harder on him than the others."

"What does his name mean?" asks Hannah, trying to change the subject.

"*Tall*," answers Reuben. "And that he is, the tallest of the lot. Over six feet. Except for his brother. I keep thinking I did something wrong. That it was my fault. That he had to rebel against me, to retaliate against my harshness."

"Well, my husband," Rivka says, "who knew you were a psychoanalyst? For me, I am convinced our children came out the way they came out, with their philosophy intact. You weren't around that much and I, their mother, saw it. A mother knows. But I'd like to call your attention to how you just now put Tamir's point of view down, like it's a disease. I don't like his perspective any more than do you, but you can't just explain it away by his place in the family or as rebellion against you. It's demeaning. Could he not come to his viewpoint on his own, despite the difference with you? He's not exactly stupid—he's quite intelligent. In fact, he just may be the smartest of the bunch." Following an awkward silence, Roberta and Hannah simultaneously call for the bill.

The sisters arrive at Reuben and Rivka's by cab the night prior to their departure, insisting that Reuben not make the trek to their hotel for the hundredth time. Before leaving, they stop at the hotel's gift shop to purchase an orchid plant, a parting gift to the Keters. This time it's Hannah who says, "Damn the expense. They've been so good to us, and orchids are so rare in Israel. Let's do it."

After a typical Israeli dinner of grilled lamb on pita bread with a salad of tomatoes, cucumbers, and green and red peppers followed by ice cream for dessert, Rivka, with the help of Hannah and Roberta, begins to clear the dishes from the table. After they are finished, Reuben opens the closet door in the entryway to retrieve a package wrapped in layers of linen cloth. Gently, and with starched ceremony, he unpeels the fabric and then unfolds layers of tissue paper to reveal a sheaf of brown-edged lined paper. The lettering, written in Yiddish hieroglyphs, is unreadable to Roberta's eyes. Reuben's eyes fill with tears. "Here it is, my dear cousins—like a good woman, more precious than diamonds and rubies."

In silence, as if they have entered a sacred temple, the group of four sit staring at one another, appearing like a medieval tableau, frozen in time and space. "Nu, so isn't this what you've been wait-ing for?" asks Reuben. "So I'm showing it to you, but we can't touch it. It will fall apart. When I copied it myself—I wouldn't trust anyone else to handle it—some of the pages began to dis-integrate. But I want you to at least see the original. I've made translated copies for both of you." He explains that he wanted this time with his cousins for Rivka and himself. "The children will come by later to say goodbye."

Slowly, Hannah and Roberta begin to move and then talk—the tableau thawing. "I feel as if I've been socked in my stomach. I mean, I knew that was why we came and that you were going to show it to us, but the reality is different from my fantasy. I thought I'd grab it and pour through it immediately. Now it's almost like I'm afraid of what I'm going to find," Roberta says. "Who is this man? And if he was Grandpa Mendel's brother, how come we didn't know about him? Is there some secret that our parents were hiding? Did he murder someone?" Hannah nods her head in agreement.

Reuben's response is a knowing smile. "It's okay. Be at peace."

The evening ends when the children arrive to say farewell with long embraces, kisses on both cheeks, tears, and many promises to stay in touch, to telephone, to e-mail, to visit again, and, for Reuben and Rivka, to make a trip to America. Hannah murmurs, "*Shalom, l'hitraot*," and Roberta adds, "Next year not in Jerusalem but in Los Angeles." As they walk to the cab that will carry them to their hotel for their final night in Israel, each carries a manila envelope containing their very own copy of Uncle Shimshon's journal.

"Oh, my God," whispers Hannah, "I have goose bumps."

~

The hotel clerk calls with a wakeup message. He speaks in flaw-less, albeit accented, English. "Good morning. It's five a.m.

The weather is predicted to be sunny, with temperatures in the nineties. I would be happy to call for you a cab."

Roberta and Hannah slip into the jeans and T-shirts they set out the previous evening. Their bags are packed and stand by the door in anticipation of their early departure.

"I'm dying for coffee," exclaims Roberta.

"There are thermoses of coffee and paper cups in the lobby for early birds. We can grab some and drink it in the cab on the way to the airport. Come on, let's go. I'm kinda sad. You?"

They make a last-minute inspection of the room, searching for overlooked items; they open and close drawers, check out the bathroom counter, and peer into the medicine cabinet. At the final moment, Hannah places four twenty dollar bills on the bedside table for the housekeepers. And then they shut the door to their Israeli adventure and to the space—inner and outer—they shared for the past two weeks and a day.

As if by previous agreement, the taxi ride to the airport proceeds in circumspect silence, with Roberta and Hannah both gazing out the window, absorbing the final sights and sounds of the city as it comes alive in the morning's first light. A sigh escapes the lips of one, then the other. Even the striking new terminal at Ben Gurion Airport, with its gold Jerusalem stone façade, does not disrupt the subdued stillness. Dedicated to their thoughtful quietude, they roll their bulging baggage down passageways that seem unending until they reach the security checkpoint, where the silence ends. Abruptly.

Unlike security agents in the States with their tight-lipped, surly approach, the young examiners give lie to the gravity of their interrogation by their pleasant banter. But as they query each passenger, one discerns the way they scrutinize the traveler's facial expression, their pattern of speech, and their body language as they look for signs of edginess, apprehension, or controlled fear.

Does he fidget? Does she touch her chin? Or nose? Does he avert his gaze or look slightly to the right when asked a question, in seeming pursuit of the correct answer? Those signs, they've been taught, indicate deception.

The eyes are dead giveaways—the gateway to the soul. And so the inspectors carefully peruse the passengers' eyes to see if pupils are contracted or dilated or if they dart spastically from side to side, like the palsied hand of a Parkinson's patient. The El Al security guards have been educated to rely on their sixth sense—to pay close attention to the human factor rather than to the contents of luggage or to whether a tourist carries liquids in four-, six-, or eight-ounce containers. They do not, for example, require that passengers remove their shoes.

"Eh, where have you been? So what was your business in Israel? So you came to meet relatives? Nice! Please to give me their names. Where are the receipts for your hotel room? Who is this woman that you are traveling with? Sisters? You don't look alike. Why different last names? Why did you stay for two week in Tel Aviv?" All solicited with a laid-back, affable bearing that contradicts their goal: to weed out terrorists.

"Gee, do you think we look like terrorists?" Roberta whispers, a little too loudly, to Hannah. "Wouldn't you think they'd have better things to do with their time than to interrogate middle-aged women? Like we're out to blow up the airplane or the terminal. Jeez, I mean, do we look like fanatics or something?"

"Oh, for God's sake, Rob, will you kindly shut your mouth. It's not funny. And don't give me that look. You want to end up in jail? I don't!"

"Oops, sorry, you're right," Roberta replies.

Once installed in their side-by-side aisle seats—suitcases placed securely in the overhead bin, seatbelts fastened firmly across laps—they simultaneously open the packet that holds copies of the journal of Shimshon (Samson) Kolopsky, Shmuel (Samuel) Keter. They wave away the steward's offering of a beverage prior to takeoff, wanting nothing to stain the manuscript or to disturb their concentration.

Chapter 18

SHIMSHON'S CHRONICLE

October 21, 1961

To those who might be interested in one very old man's journey from Odessa to Israel—and foreign places in between—I write this account from memory. Everything I write comes from my heart and, I swear on my blessed mother's grave, is true. If it is out of sequence or a bit inaccurate, blame it on the passage of time, with its erasure of recall, and the weariness of a man who has lived too long. Mostly, I will pass over what is hazy (because maybe I have embellished it over the years so that I now believe it to be true) and write only what is clearly etched on my mind, what I know to be true—as much as anyone can really know what is accurate and true. It is not to cover up any bad deeds, believe me, because there is abundance, and I will write about some. I'm writing for many reasons.

First, to look squarely at the life I have lived—the good and the bad of it—and to set the record straight as I know it. Second, because I want my children and grandchildren and great-grandchildren to know who I am, who I was, and that I existed and made some small difference. And third, I write for my own selfish purpose: to keep my ninety-nine-plus-year-old brain active and to reassure myself that the path I took, with its many twists and turns—turns that deprived me of mother, father, brothers, language, country, and more—was the course I had to take. Forgive me if I meander at times, but I must follow the dictates of my mind. So because of these aims, and probably more that I am unaware of, and despite my failing eyesight and ears that turn everyone's words into mumbles, I begin.

My name is Shmuel Keter. I began life as Shimshon Kolopsky, or Samson, in Odessa in 1862, which makes me ninety-nine years old—soon to be one hundred. Whoever thought, like Moses, I would live so long? I, however, have no beard. Ha! Ha! I used to answer to the name of Shimshon, but when I moved to Israel, such a long time ago, I took the name Shmuel, or Samuel. Those few who know me from old times sometimes call me Shimshon, or Samson. Confusing! I repudiated the name given me by my father—he who discarded me like a piece of drek because I could not, would not, accept his way of life—and so, I discarded him and the name he gave me. Still, I sometimes dream in that name, so it's confusing even for me. I named myself, which makes me my own father. What a strange thought.

In my journey from Odessa to foreign ports, which I'll tell you about, I read many things—whatever I could get my hands or eyes on. Histories, books on law, a few novels, newspapers, and even, you may be surprised to learn, the Bible. Even the Qur'an, which, by the way, I found of great interest. I read Rumi, a Persian philosopher-poet who was born in 1207. Whatever came my way and in whatever language (not to brag but I know five because I had to survive and had to understand what people were saying), be it something I found or something that was given me by a comrade or stranger or, I'm sorry to admit, something I may have stolen, for example, Rumi. Be aware that I didn't read the Hebrew Bible for religious reasons (although I was drawn to it more than to other religious tracts)— oh no—but because I liked the stories. They are tales about mothers and fathers, husbands and wives, sisters and brothers, daughters, fathers and sons, betrayals, wars, pestilence, plagues, and morals, both good and not so good. Some very bad. Evil. And a little sex thrown in for spice. I applied these stories to my own life. I tried to learn and live from them. Was I successful? No, but they served as road signs.

What I didn't like? I did not like, for example, the portrait of a wrathful God—one who destroyed villages, like in the account of Sodom and Gomorrah, or one who annihilated a people to teach a lesson, like in the story of Noah and his Ark. Imagine a God who drowns everyone in a flood and warns his favorite to build an Ark. That kind of God is neither a God I respect nor would pray to even if I believed. And what kind of a God tests one of his beloved children by commanding him to sacrifice his son? And what kind of a son goes along submitting to a father who would order such a sacrifice—asking no questions about what's in store for him? That story about Abraham and Isaac, I shall never understand, and I reject it because it takes me back to my father's sacrifice of me. Yes, he too sacrificed me by choosing his God over me. But, unlike Isaac, I did not go along. Neither did the God of my father restrain his hand to spare me, the way he did with Abraham.

But, as I said, I learned from those myths, just as I learned from the Greek or Roman myths. I learned and took solace from the way some of the characters acted, especially those who resisted oppression and authority and operated upon some inner principle, or who disobeyed society's standards when they were wrong. Take the story of Yael, the wife of Heber, who, with spike in hand, stole into the tent of General Sisera, the sworn enemy of the Jews, and after he fell into a deep sleep because of the milk she'd fed him, she drove the spike deep into his temple and killed him. She said no to the rule of the host protecting a guest and yes to some deep internal principle she had to obey. And there was Judith, who killed Holofernes and saved the Jewish people. No sweet little flower, she. And Ruth, who followed her mother-in-law after her husband died. Such bravery and loyalty from women.

The Bible talks of courageous women—women of valor—which brings to mind my Miriam, who, at fourteen, proved herself to be just such a woman, because when the Cossacks arrived one day, she ran from her home to distract the vermin away from her parents' home and away from her baby brother. She was raped by the bastards and then killed. She died to save her family's lives. That is valor! How lucky she was not to live to know that the disgrace she endured was in vain. How thankful I am that we "knew" each other before she was ravaged so, at least, she could know true love and devotion. I would gladly have given my life to save her. She was the only woman I truly, wholly loved. Thinking of her now brings tears to my aged eyes and rage to my wilting heart.

Oh, I had so much rage in my heart because of that and for many other reasons: because of Miriam, as I said, because of my father's denunciation of me, for the way we Jews were treated worse than rodents—denied education, moved from big cities to the Pale, unless we were useful to the landowners—for the moneyed classes who fomented the peasants to violent acts against the Jews—all as a cover for their own greed and debauchery. Yes, they used the serfs as pawns, drawing their attention to the Jews and away from the poverty of their existence and the bondage under which they were held. I suppose there were some semi-decent rulers, like Czar Alexander, who tried to reform his father's restrictive and tyrannical rule that protected the big shots—God forbid they should have to till their own soil or give up a small parcel of their land or the fruit of their peasants' labor so that others could live a decent life—but that's the serfs' story; they never stood up for the Jews. There were thousands and thousands of serfs starving and unemployed, and the powers that be used the Jews as scapegoats. So what else is new, I ask?

All the way back to ancient times when Simon bar Kokhba led a revolt against the Romans in 132 CE because Jews were exiled from Roman Palestine, and again when the Crusaders killed most of the Jews of Palestine, and again in 1903 when the Kishinev peasants were incited to rampage against Jews because the Russians lost the war with the Japanese—it was our fault? Did they ever consider, how could a tribe so abused and abject be so powerful? They used the murder of two kids to dredge up the libelous story of how Jews use Christian blood to make matzos and to blame us for the killings to inflame them.

I had seen so much, more than any human should have to endure. I witnessed the rape and murder of women and children, not only my Mir-iam's. I saw the murder and torture of old men dragged by their beards. I saw infants thrown onto pitchforks. I saw homes and synagogues burned. Books destroyed. Animals killed, with their blood spread over the Jews' doorposts by those very same peasants, and on Easter. So I should feel sorry for them? For whatever reason, they were monsters, and I retaliated. But in the process of murdering monsters, I became one myself. I came to realize that I was enjoying the power—no, more than that, if I am honest, the very act of brutalizing another human being, I turned them into animals, into nothings, to do what I did. I found myself enjoying the smell of spilled blood. I liked watching the blood seep into the ground, making beautiful patterns in the soil. I took pleasure in watching them die in agony, gasping for breath, pleading for help, their eyes full of dread. It's too horrible to remember, but I must face the truth about myself no matter how repulsive. But unless one lives through it, unless one is a witness to such atrocities, it's hard to comprehend, so I beg you not to judge too harshly—I do that to myself—unless you've been there yourself.

Oh, yes, I could excuse myself for aiming my righteous rage against our enemies: the bullies, the evildoers, the Cossacks, the upper classes. And I do not regret it for one moment—it had to be done. But sometimes I went too far. Sometimes I killed just because I had an urge to kill. To feel the knife go in. The hammer crack a skull. There! I said it. Woe to anyone who looked cross-eyed at me when I had that impulse. Down deep I knew it had so much to do with the stone of hate lodged in my craw—the loathing caused by my father, who had murdered my soul. You see, unlike Abraham, he didn't open his mind to hear the voice of God or, as I would say, his own conscience. What is God if not our own sense of right and wrong—our own moral code of behavior, of justice? But we have to be available to hear it. For so long, I couldn't hear it. Well, the stone grew with each twist of the blade, with each blow of the hammer. Each act helped assuage the hatred, but only for the moment. Like when one takes medicine to reduce a fever, soon, very soon, the medicine wears off, and the fever spikes again with the need for more, always more. For me, my medicine was more blood. More violence. More killing. There was no quelling the feverish rage or staunching the need for blood. For years, I couldn't sleep. I would see visions, the doctors called them delusions, of the faces of those I killed or mangled intermingled with memories from the pogroms—and Miriam's mutilated body lying bleeding and dismembered. And then when finally my sleep was restored, the dreams began—recurring nightmares with images of the brutality. It didn't stop. I went insane. I was not fit company for anyone, and so, like Moses, I wandered in the wilderness—not in the actual desert but in the wilderness of my mind. I walked the streets for miles each day. I spent nights under the stars or in alleyways, unprotected. I took menial jobs wanting to soil myself—collecting garbage, sweeping streets, cleaning toilets in public places, shoveling snow, anything that would bring shame on me. It was my self-inflicted punishment. I looked like a beggar, but slowly, slowly, I began to recover.

I first had to learn to trust, but before I could do that, I had to learn to forgive myself for becoming a fiend. I think of King Lear, who had to go mad before he could understand the suffering of others. There was no " fool" to show me the way or to protect me. I needed to take the blows that came as retribution for my bad deeds. My rage could explode, like a bomb, without warning. My misery left me feeling empty. Dead. So, as you can imagine, along the way, I made many enemies and lost many friends, including my wife, Ruchele, who, in due course, divorced me. Who could blame her? I hurt her and others who tried to love me. I could not love in return; I could only hate. How can you love anyone who loves you when you detest yourself? To love me meant that they were bad or stupid or fraudulent. But let me tell you: what saved me were my children, who loved me throughout this ordeal. And I loved them in spite of their coming from my putrid loins. How could I continue to hate myself if these prized beings loved me and forgave me? They were my saviors—the ones who repaired my damaged heart and soul, the ones who restored me to the human race. I had three boys, but one boy stood out, the one I named after my brother, Mendel—the one who *became a rabbi. He would seek me out wherever I was hiding. He would clean me up, make certain I had food, and find lodgings for me. He tried to reason with me, tried to understand what I was going through without judgment. To him I owe my life.*

On the other hand, I'm thankful to say that I never got over my hatred of the ruling class. And, as far as government—any government—is concerned, as far as politicians go, to this very day, I curse them. They are all a bunch of corrupt ganefs and murderers looking out only for themselves. Unlike me, however, they get others to do their dirty work so as not to befoul their own rotten hands. But no matter; there is blood on them. Like Abraham, they sacrifice our innocent youths to fight their wars, to maintain their power, to live in their palaces, to sail on their yachts, to adorn their wives in silks and diamonds and rubies.

But I stray from my story, as I warned you I might. Back to the question of why I chose the name Shmuel, or Samuel. I wrote in my journal a quote taken from the Bible—I think, if my memory doesn't betray me, someone was describing Samuel: "He raiseth up the poor out of the dust, and lifteth up the beggar from the dunghill, to set them among princes, and to make them inherit the throne of glory . . ."

Now that impressed me. I believe in justice and equality and freedom for all, in sharing the earth's bounty, in the need to care for the poor. No one should have to go without food or clothing or medicine or a roof over his or her head, nor should they have to work until their hands bleed, the way my poor mama did. People must have the opportunity to do worthwhile work, whether it is the work of the heart, the hand, or the mind. In my book, the artist is an equal to the farmer; the farmer, to those who do manual labor. I have lived my life holding to those values as best I can. Even before my father betrayed me, I felt hatred toward those who selfishly hoarded all the material possessions—the crowned heads, the landowners, and even some in the shtetl who had more than others and didn't share. My mother, Adina, was my model; she was gentle as her name translates. Why should others die of starvation when my cupboard is full—when my land grows

with an overabundance of vegetables and grapes and olives, while others'
land is barren? And why should others shiver from cold, without warmth
and a cover to their name, when I have the heat of fire and two blankets?

So, a little about Samuel—that's English for Shmuel, my adopted
namesake. He lived in the eleventh century before the Christian Messiah was
born. He was a fighter, and that's like me in my younger days before I got
kicked out of my father's house. I had organized a group of men—actually
we were just boys, barely fourteen, fifteen, and sixteen, some younger—to
fight the Cossacks. I would sneak out of the house at night after everyone
was asleep to meet my comrades (there was one girl, as well, who fought
alongside us and was, in fact, caught and shot). We had collected tools over
the months, some removed from those who came to beat us up—shovels,
picks, rakes, and the like—and when the killers came, we would spring
forth from our hiding place and thrash them. Some got away, but others,
barely breathing, lay spilling their guts on the earth. And while I think
back on that with mixed feelings, I am proud to say that I became the leader
of our group, not only because of my strength but because I was shrewd and
knew no fear. Unlike the biblical Samson, I had brains and brawn—a born
leader, some said. So like Samuel, who stood up to authority by opposing
Saul as king, I opposed the czar and his cronies and did what I could, in
my minor way, to overthrow them.

But to tell the truth, the most important thing in my regard for Samuel
was that he, like me, had been dumped as a child. Not by his father, no, but
by his mother, Chanah. Oh, yes, you'll say her motive was different from my
father's, more noble, and that may be true, but the fact remains, she gave
him up because of her promise to God that if he filled her infertile womb,
she would grant him the fruit of it. So, as the Bible says, she "loaned" Sam-
uel to God for the rest of his life. Loaned him! She didn't own him. What
right did she have to loan him—mother or no—to God? Or to anyone?
No matter what you call it, she deserted him. And what right did my father
have to demand that I believe as he did and to declare me dead—to sit
shiva for me—when I wouldn't? So there it is: my kinship with Samuel

and why I took his name and why I renounced my father and repudiated the name he gave me. Don't think I don't know that my own mother did not stand up to my father for me, but that is too painful for me to explore.

Over the years, especially after I had my own children, I tried very hard to reflect upon it from my father's point of view, thinking that as a father I could be more compassionate, to forgive him, so I could talk to my children about their grandfather, but I couldn't. It would have felt like yet another betrayal but by me this time. It would have been like swallowing poison. I never talked about my parents—not even my mother or my brother Mendel. He, though, I could forgive.

As far back as I can remember, I felt like an outsider in my family. You may ask why. I asked myself the same question. First, I was taller and bigger than my father by the time I was twelve. I could wear his boots and shirts—not his pants because I was already taller than him. I didn't look like the rest of the family, me with my red curly hair and blue eyes and hairy arms and legs, them with their black hair and brown cow eyes and barely able to grow a beard. I was strong, like a bull, and liked to run and play games. When given a chance, I preferred to be with friends, and, yes, I liked to talk but about important things—real things like how to change the world, how to revolt against unfair conditions, how to fight the god-damned murderers, Cossacks, serfs, and landowners alike. My father and brothers always had their faces in the holy book, going along with whatever fate came their way—saying, "It is God's will and not for us to question." I say one makes one's own destiny. I refused to read and study Torah. Not so Mendel. And yet, he was just a kid wanting his father's love—just like me, only I couldn't yield.

My father and I had many fights. Worse than fights. They got so bad, at times I came close to striking him. My mother—I told you her name was Adina—would get in between. She was a good woman but passive, though not when it came to her children. She deferred to my father's whims and demands because she didn't want arguments, and I think, although it was an arranged marriage, she'd grown to love and respect him. She wanted peace. She was observant, but she was more practically so and less rigid about the rules. She prayed; she lit Shabbos candles—all that—but she'd reason, "Well, if this means such and such, then perhaps God would want us to do thus and such." I think being a mother and in touch with life and death makes you more compassionate, more accommodating. But when it came to my father, for her, his word was law. I don't blame her; she was a woman of her time.

I was the oldest son of three. Moishe, the middle son, was the first to leave the shtetl—I learned that by word of mouth after I was disowned. He was a little like me, but he did what he had to do, quietly, and didn't have to announce it the way I did. I never learned to do that; it felt degrading. I also heard that he had two boys who became doctors, supposedly classy ones in Boston. They even have a chapel at some fancy college named after them. Imagine, from shtetl to palace.

So there was Mendel, known as the scholar—unlike me who was labeled the firebrand, the revolutionary. But in my opinion, he was a sycophant and the bane of my existence at that time. Always the golden boy—religious and pleading to sit by my father's side to read Torah. Because of that, as you can imagine, he was my father's favorite, while I was my mother's favorite. She must have known I needed her to balance the pain I experienced because of my father's partiality for Mendel. But I was also the one to collect wood for her, carry water for her to boil, or dig up the potatoes in the little plot she kept outside of our little house. I needed her love the way a newborn needs sustenance. Beneath it all, as I now understand, much of what happened between Mendel and me had to do with rivalry for my father's love and approval.

It was a little like the biblical story of Abel and Cain. They too were brothers who couldn't get along. Cain, the oldest—like me—was the farmer tilling the soil, which is what I became after moving to a kibbutz in Israel. But unlike me, Cain killed his younger brother. I shudder to think what might have happened had I stayed. Then again, maybe it was destiny that I left, to spare me that act of murder. I can't help but feel that instead *of my killing someone, I was killed, so to speak; my soul was killed.*

After my father sat shiva for me and after I left home for good, I would return, surreptitiously, when I was needed, like when the thugs were set to attack. We had scouts out and about who would report back to me. I quickly became their leader, as I told you—not bragging, but it was a fact. My gang and I would vault out of the woods with our "weapons" to beat them to a bloody pulp, to defend the shtetl and our families. Did Papa know of what I did? Would he have been proud of me? Of that I will never know. He was so mulish, he would never have been able to withdraw his "death sentence" or even own up to being proud of me. And yet, he too was a man of his time. For a while, Mama would get word to me to meet her someplace. She would look so sad and old and small wearing her black dress with a black babushka wrapped around her head—always bringing me some thick black bread or a potato or a piece of meat or some clean clothes. After a while, she stopped coming, maybe because she felt disloyal to my father, or maybe she feared causing trouble for me if someone ever followed her. Or maybe it was just too painful for her to see me in the condition I was in—skin and bones—and she had to put me out of her mind. Who knows? What I know now is that I took after my father in many ways—we were both strong-minded, angry men—so maybe she was afraid of him, although, to my knowledge, he never laid a hand on her. I'd have killed him. His great temper and loud voice, like mine, could be frightening. I did my share of scaring others. So although hard to admit, we had things in common.

After a time, with a few friends, I began to spread out farther and farther beyond the woods surrounding our shtetl. We ventured out to the countryside and became fascinated with rumblings of a revolt building, an uprising that would make a better life for one and all and, most importantly, make a safe haven for the Jews—to know what it was not to fear opening the door, or be called kikes, or have to silently watch some Ukrainian hood knock a Jew's kippah off his head or demand that he step off the road to make room for him.

My activities brought me to Vilna—I believe the year was 1897—yes,

I was thirty-five. I hooked up with a group of like-minded men, and a few women, who set out to bring the Jewish workers in the Russian Empire together. We were socialists from geographical names that, at the time, were only words on a map: Poland, Latvia, the Ukraine, and Lithuania. We called ourselves the Algemeyner Yidisher Arbeter, or the General Jewish Labor Bund. I began to study men like Marx and, later, Trotsky. What I understood of their writings, I liked. I didn't want to hear, nor was I truly interested in, some of Marx's technical economic terms, like "use value" or "commodity" or "non-alienated labor." I was tired of hearing words—only words—and wanted something practical that would lead to action. I especially liked his idea that "religion is the opiate of the people." That summed up the way I felt. A poem that he wrote, I don't know when, still speaks worlds to me:

I am caught in endless strife,
Endless ferment, endless dreams;
I cannot conform to life,
Will not travel with the stream.

But when I came across a piece he wrote when he was young, I didn't like what he said about "the Jewish question." By the way, he was a Jew whose father converted him to Protestantism when he was six. In the piece I just referred to, he wrote that Jews were "money-minded." He wrote that the Jewish problem would disappear when we defeated Capitalism and when the Jews became assimilated. Ha! How would he think of Communist Russia knowing about the crimes perpetrated by Stalin and his faction? No one lets the Jews forget they are Jews. So I shouldn't hold his youthful writings against him—certainly I had ideas that I'm not proud of, and I can excuse him for that—but I think he spoke out of both sides of his mouth when, in spite of his vehemently speaking out against anti-Semitism, he did nothing to oppose the persecution of the Zionists and the suppression of the Jewish religion by the authorities. I still don't get it. How does one stand for freedom and emancipation—political or human freedom—and then not speak out when one group's freedom is obstructed, even if one vehemently disagrees with its viewpoint?

I like this poem written by a German pastor—not a Jew—who regretted his own indifference during the Nazi era:

First they came for the communists, and I did not speak out—
because I was not a communist;
Then they came for the socialists, and I did not speak out—
because I was not a socialist;
Then they came for the trade unionists, and I did not speak out—
because I was not a trade unionist;
Then they came for the Jews, and I did not speak out—
because I was not a Jew;
Then they came for me—
and there was no one left to speak out for me

So, back to my experience in the Bund. Originally, we fought to establish a legitimate, if only a minority, role as members of the Russian Social Democratic Labor Party, or the RSDLP, but we were turned down. You see, unlike the Zionist movement, the Bund did not want to live in Palestine, nor did we want to speak Hebrew. What we wanted was to speak in our own Jewish national tongue—Yiddish—and so demanded rightful status as a secular minority—a "nation," you could say, without borders. That was not to happen—in part because Comrade Lenin opposed those demands—and so we parted ways with great resentment. Later, because of political urgencies, we mended our fences but remained a splinter group due to factors too complex to go into here. And, to be honest, it's one of the things that is somewhat fuzzy in my memory.

By the way, I have a picture of me taken in 1905 when I was forty-three, in Odessa, with the Bundist self-defense group. I look so young and full of hope, but I see traces of the man I would become, even the alte kacker I am today, minus the wrinkles. There is a very young woman in that picture who would become my wife and the mother of my children, but that's for later.

While in the Bund movement, I met people like Mikhail Liber. Don't get me wrong; that doesn't mean I was one of the big shots—not even a little shot. Once, I saw Lenin speaking at a meeting of the Second All-Russian Congress of Soviets. I don't remember the year, but what I do remember is what he said: that government should not keep secrets and that they should always be under the supervision of public opinion. He said that a government is strong when people know everything. That sounded good to me—even now it's a lesson to be learned—and for a while I was taken in and believed that the new Russian government would liberate the masses, including the Jews. I read that, like me, Lenin had a Jewish grandfather, and, like me, he changed his name from Vladimir Ilyich Ulyanov, but who knows why. Anyway, during the Russian Civil War I came to see that we could not stop the anti-Semitic pogroms nor the restrictions constantly imposed on the "kikes." Nor could we change the way we were always the fall guys for everything—like it was in their blood.

You notice, I say the "Russian" Civil war because it was no longer my war. I could no longer believe there would ever be a secure place for Jews in Russia—Soviet or otherwise—or in any other place. Around that time, in France for example, I learned about a French captain named Dreyfus—a wealthy Jew—who had been falsely accused of treason and sentenced to life imprisonment, even after the authorities learned that the evidence was fake. Mobs took to the streets shouting, "Death to the Jews." How couldn't I believe that Jews would always be running from hatred and murder and guilt and blame? And I was right, because we know now—so many years later—that former Bundists were murdered during Stalin's era, may the devil roast in Hell. And we know too that thousands of Jews were sent to work camps or murdered outright in Siberia. It was not my wish to leave Russia, but I knew that it was only a matter of time before they would "come for me," as that German pastor said.

So again, the pattern of betrayal repeated itself—first my father and now Mother Russia. From events that I've read about, I know that had I remained in Odessa, I would have perished a long time ago. I read recently that some five thousand Jews from Odessa were killed in a concentration camp near Gvozdavka. Now, don't you think I was perceptive to have determined to immigrate to Palestine? Just think, my precious children, you would not have been born had I not made this decision.

This leads me to wonder what happened to my parents and to my brother, Mendel. Were they one of the five thousand—left to disintegrate in a mass grave? Did they die of starvation in Russia? Were they shipped off to the labor camps in Siberia or to a concentration camp in Germany? Or maybe they joined Moishe in America—just maybe they left before all of this happened? So many questions and so few answers. I'll never know, and that's my tragedy. My one consolation has been my children and, for a while, my wife.

I'll tell you about that now. You recall that I mentioned the woman in the picture—her name was Ruchele. That was in 1905. I was forty-three and not too bad looking. She and I became friends in spite of a seventeen-year age difference; we spent a lot of time together talking about what to do and what the future held for us. We consoled each other about our losses, for she too had lost her entire family. Eventually, as these things go, we became more than friends. I can't say it was love, but we had things in common: our socialism, our political passion for changing the life of the working class by agitating the masses to rebellion, creating self-defense groups to fight the pogroms, and, finally, leaving Russia. In 1909, when I was forty-seven, Ruchele discovered she was pregnant and insisted on marriage. For my part, I held no need to get either state or religious sanction for our relationship, but since it was important to her, we got married. And Meir was born, a beautiful boy.

Why we left: We were gravely disappointed, as I said, that in 1903 the Russian Socialist Democratic Party rejected the Jewish Bund's demand for a self-governing arrangement, which led to our walking out. And we were disappointed once again, in 1904, when we discovered that members of the Bund had been shipped to Siberia. Added to that, when a fresh wave of anti-Semitic pogroms took place in "Mother Russia," it forced us to see the *writing on the wall—one had to be a numbskull not to. And that's when we knew, despite my initial antagonism toward Zionism, that we had to immigrate to Palestine.*

I had been reading about a socialist-Zionist movement led by Ber Borochov dedicated to the very same ideals that I believed in. Borochov was encouraging the intelligentsia, the landowners, and the capitalists to return to what he called "productive labor." By that he meant a return to the soil—something I dreamed about, most likely due to my need to rid my hands of the blood that stained them. I also think it had to do with the garden my mother planted and the loving memories it held. When I think of it now, I can almost smell the ground, moist with fresh rain. Where else could we do that but in Palestine? There had been some short-lived talk for Jews to immigrate to Argentina and Uganda. It didn't happen, so, after two years, taking all that we had saved (which wasn't very much), we immigrated to Palestine in 1911. I was forty-nine. We had one child, who was two, and another boy, Daniel, was born onboard the ship. Those two children were unplanned, unlike the next—yet another son born in 1913. He, a sabra, I named after my brother Mendel. We dreamed about living on one of the collective farms and cultivating the land and forming socialist parties there. We heard of others who had had similar dreams but had to return home with their dreams devastated. With no water and the soil packed full of rocks, confronting starvation, they just gave up. We took that into account but were determined to succeed.

From the moment we resolved to leave, both Ruchele and I never uttered another word of the Russian language—we spoke Yiddish—and believe it or not, I can barely call up a word of it now if my life depended on it. Speaking Yiddish, as I've said, conformed to the Bund's philosophy to maintain it as a national language. But when we got to Palestine, it was a different story. To survive, we had to know the language of the land, and so we studied Hebrew in every spare moment in between planting crops, digging up the soil, building homes and schools and hospitals. Of all those tasks, for me, in spite of my having learned five other tongues (I was much younger), learning Hebrew was the hardest. Ruchele was much better at it than I was, but I never got beyond a simple level of speaking. When my kids got older, they would make fun of the way I spoke. They would mimic me and laugh among themselves. They never said it outright, but I know they were ashamed to bring their friends home because of it. Most of the time, they refused to speak Yiddish, except when they needed something. So a lot of our conversation was done with hand gestures and pointing, with a few words of Hebrew and Yiddish thrown in. But when they got older, they scolded us for not knowing Yiddish better. Kids! Huh!

Life on the kibbutz was tough, but we took to it like ducks take to water. Dressed in blue work shirts and khaki shorts, at first we slept in tents, got up early, ate in the communal kitchen once it was built, cultivated the land, planted almond and olive trees, and, added to that, cleaned the kitchen or shower or toilets. There were community meetings in the evening after we visited the children in the "baby houses." We went to bed early, weary from the long day's work, but were exhilarated from what we were achieving. It was a good life. Until, as I mentioned, my nightmares began and until I had to remove myself from my family. Until my mind began to wander. Until I began to abuse my wife. I'm so ashamed of that, even though, before she died, I begged for forgiveness. Ruchele was a good wife and didn't deserve my cruelty.

January 13, 1962

It has been three months since my last entry. It seems I've had a heart attack, and then when I was recuperating in the hospital, I suffered a stroke that has paralyzed my left arm and hand—my writing hand. Writing now, as you may imagine, is impossible, so I've asked my great-grandson, Yaa'kov—Meir's son, may he rest in peace—to take down the remainder of what I have to say. There is much I had planned to write, but because I must conserve my energy, I will have to skip. I want to finish my story, but I fear there is little time left for that. I am, after all, one hundred, since I had a birthday when I was in the hospital, and so very tired. Yaa'kov suggests that I tell you a little about my sons and my grandchildren before returning to my story. So here goes: my oldest child, Meir, was born in Russia. He would have been fifty-three had he not died of lung cancer last year. He smoked himself to death. And Daniel, as I've said, was born on the ship as we traveled to Palestine. He is fifty-one and moved to the United States to go to college—in California—and never returned but for annual visits. He married a Catholic woman, Diane, and converted. And then there is my son Mendel, our sabra, who, believe it or not, became a rabbi. My children's mother wanted all our children to have Hebrew names so they would fit in, but I insisted this one be named Mendel. He's married to Chanah. And, by the way, I should mention that I not only changed my name to Samuel, in Hebrew that's Shmuel, but also changed my last name to Keter. That was also Ruchele's idea. I took particular pleasure in changing it to Keter, the Hebrew word for crown—*my way of thumbing my nose to the czar because now I, not he, was wearing the crown, while his head was naked.*

Now for my grandchildren. Meir had Yaa'kov, who now writes for me. He is twenty; his brother, Benjamin, is nineteen, and his sister, Eliana, is seventeen. Reuben, my youngest grandson, had six children. But I must leave off for now. Suddenly my eyes are closing with sleep. I feel so tired. And possibly Yaa'kov needs a rest, although he'd never say. As for the remainder of my grandchildren and great-grandchildren, my mind is too muddled. Yaa'kov will help me to remember all their names tomorrow. Until tomorrow.

January 14, 1962

I am Yaa'kov, Meir's son. My beloved great-grandfather died this morning at 10:31 a.m. He was sleeping when I arrived at 9 a.m., and I waited until he awoke to pick up where we'd left off yesterday. At one point he opened his eyes, looked at me as if he wanted to say something but couldn't, and then he closed his eyes, squeezed my hand, whispered, I think, "Miriam" and "chazak v'ematz," and died peacefully, as they say.

He lived a full, long, meaningful—but difficult—life, as you can read from his journal. He kept so much to himself. I knew nothing of his days in Russia or Poland or wherever else he roamed and nothing of his early days in Israel or what he called his breakdown or his early political activities. He was a complex man, at times depressed and sullen, but, for me, always loving and interested in what I and my siblings and cousins had to say. He was not the kind to say, "I love you," but we knew from his actions and the looks he gave us that he loved us. He always had time for us, except when he went on his walks. Although a flawed individual, I loved and respected him as much as I could any human being. I was most like him, with my curly red mop of hair and my size, and so I believe we had a special connection, but perhaps my brothers would say the same thing. He also looked a great deal like my Uncle Reuben.

He arose at six every morning, working in the fields side by side with his coworkers almost until the end. He never complained and always shared the work equally. He would, at times, disappear for days, or weeks, without an explanation other than that he just needed to think. We knew not to question him, but I had the sense that he was trying to escape from a demon or something from the past. He would get a panic-stricken look on his face, and we knew that a walk was about to happen. And when he returned, his tranquil demeanor returned with him.

He spoke only of his mother, never his father, and of her only in the most loving terms. According to him, she was a saint. Well, not a saint. Nor did he speak of his brothers; in fact, I didn't know he had any until I read this memoir. Only once, when we stayed up late one evening and he'd had a bit too much to drink, he revealed the love he once had for a woman in his youth—a woman he claimed to be the only woman he loved. I did not know her name, not until minutes before his death as I sat with him by his bedside. I had a premonition when he said he was tired that he would be leaving us soon. We always had this special way of communicating without words. I only hope he somehow understood. I must confess that I spoke to him as I sat waiting for him to awaken this morning, telling him of my dreams, my fears, my longings. I told him I loved him. I believe, somehow, he heard, and that's what enabled him to let go. In spite of the fact that my great-grandparents were divorced, he never spoke ill of my great-grandmother, nor she of him. I never knew why they divorced, only that they both decided it was best for them to separate. That's what they both said. Actually, I don't know if they ever divorced. They remained friends until she died of cancer ten years ago when she was seventy-three. He was by her side when she took her final breath. I think my great-grandmother loved my great-grandfather until her dying day and was really distraught when they separated. She never said, but I knew from the way she looked at him that the profound love remained. She once told me that he was father, husband, and best friend to her. After her funeral, he disappeared for a full week and returned looking like some homeless person.

Here's what I know about him: he hated the ruling class, politics, governments, and authority. He hated what had, for him, begun as an agrarian utopian dream of equality for all men and women, Arab and Jew alike, and ended as a place of intolerance, bigotry, violence, and war. He was heartbroken, and yet he continued to believe that the young people would find a way to move past the prejudice of their elders.

When he first arrived in what was then called Palestine, his kibbutz bordered on an Arab village, and he befriended many Arabs, and they him. They helped him plant and pick the crops when he and his kibbutzniks needed help, and he lent a hand to build a water tower for them. He always gave them what the kibbutz didn't need after they gathered the crops. His best friend was an Arab, Mahmoud. Saba would visit Mahmoud, and his friend would visit him. They spent many an evening together, sharing a pipe—talking throughout the night about the events of the day. He died an atheist, but he never judged those who believed, although I think he had no truck with orthodoxy of any kind. Saba adhered to the principle of nonviolent resistance. He liked Gandhi. He also believed that a national consciousness had to be established whereby identities would blend, where neither Jew nor Arab would hold privilege, where religion would be irrelevant, that is, it would make no difference if one believed or didn't believe. He thought that one didn't need religion to be a moral person and that one could be moral or not, with or without religion. He wanted to believe that it would be best for both Arab and Jew to identify as Israelis. On that, I don't agree, because I believe that both Arab and Jew need their own land, their own identities—to esteem their own histories. But this is about him, not me. He looked forward to a time when military service would be nonexistent but when citizens—Arab and Jew—would be required to perform some national service, whether that meant building roads and hospitals, teaching children, caring for the elderly, or helping to build municipal services for what he called his "Arab brothers and sisters." He said over and over that we all came from the same DNA. He was a socialist from the top of his head to the tip of his toes—but it was his brand of socialism. He claimed to dislike any "ism" or "ist," especially communism. Idealistic? Unrealistic? Sure, but that's who he was, my great-grandfather, my saba, my zaide. He died whispering the name Miriam and chazak v'ematz. Imagine, his final words were in Hebrew.

I, Yaakov, have nothing more to say except chazak v'ematz, Saba.

EPILOGUE

Roberta and Hannah close the journal as the plane makes its final approach to the Los Angeles Airport. The passengers scurry to stretch their legs and retrieve their personal belongings after the arduous flight. Roberta and Hannah remain in place, as though fixed in their seats with Krazy Glue. Struggling to contain their sorrow, they keep their eyes straight ahead, knowing that if their gaze connected, they would lose it. As the cleanup crew enters the plane and the flight crew hurriedly departs, with no other option but to get to their feet, they appear for all the world like they have just lost one of their most beloved relatives. And they have.

GLOSSARY OF
YIDDISH TERMS

Afikomen	Last bit of matzah, eaten at end of Seder
Aishet chayil	A woman of valor
Alte kacker	A mildly pejorative term for old man
A shaynem dank	Thank you very much
Balabosta	A Jewish mistress of the house
Bar Kokhba	A revolt of the Jews led by Simon bar Kokhba against the Roman Empire 132–136 CE
Benching	Performing the blessing after the meal
Bimah	Torah-reading table in synagogue
Bissel	Little
Boychick	Yiddish meaning boy, endearing
Bubbe	Grandmother
Bubkes	Nothing; something worthless
Cheder	Religious lesson or school
Chuppah	A canopy under which a Jewish couple stand during their wedding ceremony
Daven	To pray
Drek	Junk; rubbish
Eli, Eli	The opening words of the Psalm 22
Elohim	One of the names of God in the Hebrew Bible
Farbissener	An embittered fool

Fermisht	Confused; mixed up
Fershtays	Understand
Fleishig	Made of, prepared with, or used for meat
Gabbai	Rabbi's synagogue assistant
Ganef	Thief
Gantze macher	Bigwig
Gelt	Money
Goldene medina	The Golden Land
Gottenyu	Dear G-d
Halacha	The laws of the Jewish faith
HaShem	The name (in place of G-d's actual name)
Haskala	Nineteenth-century European Jewish "Enlightenment"
Havdalah	Prayer bidding farewell to Shabbos
Hock	To bother incessantly
Hock mir nicht kein chinik	Don't knock a teakettle at me
Ikh hob dir in drerd	Go to hell
Kaddish	Mourning prayer
Kaki	Shit
Kenahora	A magical phrase to ward off the evil eye
Ketubah	Traditional marriage contract
Kike	Racist epithet for Jew
Kinder (lach)	Small children
Kippah	A brimless cap worn by Orthodox Jewish men (Hebrew)
Kishka	Guts
Kohanim	Descendant of Aaron; member of priest class
Kvetching	Complaining

Lamed Vavniks	Thirty-six righteous people
Lamden	A scholar
Landsman	Fellow native (of the old country)
Latkes	Potato pancakes
Litvak	A Jew from Lithuania
Machi	A made-up form of Machatonim (plural) which denotes the parents of the people your children marry. The male parent is your mechuten, and the female, your machatonister. I believe there is no equivalent in any language except Hebrew/Yiddish.
Maven	Expert
Mazel tov	Good luck; congratulations
Mechaya	Relief; joy
Mechitza	Partition between men and women in shul
Mein kinde	My child
Mensch	An honorable, decent person
Meshuga	Crazy
Midrash	Ancient commentary on part of the Hebrew Scriptures attached to the biblical text
Mieskeit punnum	Ugly face
Mikvah	A bath used for ritual immersion and cleansing
Milchig	Made of or derived from milk or dairy products
Minyan	A quorum of ten Jewish men required for traditional Jewish worship
Mishpucha	Family
Mitzvoth	Religious commandments
Moshiach	The Messiah
Nafka	A whore

Nisht duggehdacht	May it never happen
Nu	So?
Nudnik	Pest
Oy! Gevalt	A cry of fear or help
Pale of Settlement	A geographical area of Imperial Russia in which Jews were ordered to live
Paskudnyak	A lout; a scoundrel
Pish	To pee
Plotz	Explode (meaning, die)
Pupik	Navel; belly button
Rebbe	Rabbi
Rebbetzin	Rabbi's wife
Saba	Grandfather (Hebrew)
Schlep	To haul or carry something awkward
Schmalz	Rendered chicken fat
Schmateh	A rag; a cheap piece of clothing
Schmutz	Dirt
Schnapps	Liquor
Schtup	To have sexual intercourse
Shabbos	Saturday, the Jewish day of rest
Shalom, l' hitraot	Goodbye, see you soon (Hebrew)
Shayna meydeleh	Beautiful girl
Sheitel	Wig, especially for married women
Shema	A prayer in Judaism
Shiksa	A non-Jewish girl or woman
Shtarker	Strong; "big shot"; asinine
Shtetl	Eastern European Jewish village
Shul	Synagogue

Siddur	Daily prayer book
Tallit	Prayer shawl
Talmud	The authoritative body of Jewish tradition comprising the Mishnah and Gemara
Tante	Aunt
Taschlich	Jewish atonement ritual to case away one's sins, performed on first day of Rosh Hashanah
Teiglach	Small, fruit- or nut-filled pastries dipped in honey
Todah robah	Thank you very much (Hebrew)
Toomel	Noise; commotion; disorder
Torah	The written Jewish law
Traif	Foods forbidden by Jewish dietary laws
Tsuris	Pains; troubles; problems; distress
Tuchta	Daughter
Tzaddik	Righteous person, especially a rabbi
Tzimmes	A sweet stew made with yams and other root vegetables, dried prunes; part of the Rosh Hashanah meal
Tzitzit	Fringes worn on corners of four-cornered garment
Ushanka	A Russian fur cap with ear flaps
Vas machst du?	How are you?
Vey iz mir	Woe is me
Yarmulke	Skullcap worn by Jewish men, especially during prayer and religious study
Yarzeit	Anniversary of a death
Yehudah	Hebrew name for Judah, the fourth son of Jacob (Israel)

Yenta	A gossip
Yid	A pejorative term for a Jew
Zaide	Grandfather
Zol zein guzunt	May you go in health

ACKNOWLEDGMENTS

I am deeply grateful to Richard Lichtman, who supplied courage when mine faltered and who listened with a kind but keen critical ear. It is due to his belief in me and his love and continued insistence that this book has seen the light of day. Good night, sweet prince, and flights of angels sing thee to thy rest.

I am indebted to the many who read, inspired, and commented on my manuscript with intelligence and insight. My heartfelt thanks goes to my son Rabbi Brad Artson, my in-house scholar and historian of all things Jewish; my daughter, Tracy Artson, a talented psychologist who read my manuscript with loving sensitivity to nuance; my dear friend Jackie Hackel, who prodded and poked me to publish; and to Linda Tucker for her careful reading and enthusiasm.

For their unwavering support and faith in me, I am grateful to my daughters-in-law, Elana Artson and Dawn Osterweil; my "other-daughter," Julie Criss-Haggerty; my sister Harriet; and my grandchildren, Jacob and Shira Artson and Sydney and Benjamin Osterweil-Artson. I am proud to be their grandmother.

For their friendship and generosity, I thank Carolyn Angelo, Bob Carrere, Anya Lane, Shira Levy, Andy Pesce, Margaret Sjostrand, Melanie Sperling, Billie Lee Violette, Merti Walker, and June Katz my devoted *machi*.

I am so thankful to my editor, and now friend, Jane Cavolina, who helped smooth an awkward word or phrase into narrative prose.

My special thanks to the team at She Writes Press for believing in my multigenerational story about an immigrant Jewish family—my gratitude for bringing the book to publication.

ABOUT THE AUTHOR

Barbara Artson is a retired psychoanalyst who calls San Francisco her home. She regularly contributes essays and reviews of films and books to professional journals. In addition to a PhD in psychology, she holds both BA and MA degrees in English literature and taught Shakespeare as a graduate student while also completing the unfinished Dickens novel *The Mystery of Edwin Drood,* years before the musical production on Broadway. Like Dora in *Odessa, Odessa*, Artson's mother stitched elastic to the waistbands of women's bloomers.

SELECTED TITLES FROM SHE WRITES PRESS

She Writes Press is an independent publishing company
founded to serve women writers everywhere.
Visit us at **www.shewritespress.com**.

The Belief in Angels by J. Dylan Yates. $16.95, 978-1-938314-64-3. From
the Majdonek death camp to a volatile hippie household on the East
Coast, this narrative of tragedy, survival, and hope spans more than
fifty years, from the 1920s to the 1970s.

Portrait of a Woman in White by Susan Winkler. $16.95, 978-1-938314-
83-4. When the Nazis steal a Matisse portrait from the eccentric,
art-loving Rosenswigs, the Parisian family is thrust into the tumult of
war and separation, their fates intertwined with that of their beloved
portrait.

An Address in Amsterdam by Mary Dingee Fillmore. $16.95, 978-1-63152-
133-1. After facing relentless danger and escalating raids for 18 months,
Rachel Klein—a well-behaved young Jewish woman who transformed
herself into a courier for the underground when the Nazis invaded her
country—persuades her parents to hide with her in a dank basement,
where much is revealed.

Even in Darkness by Barbara Stark-Nemon. $16.95, 978-1-63152-956-6.
From privileged young German-Jewish woman to concentration camp
refugee, Kläre Kohler navigates the horrors of war and—through
unlikely sources—finds the strength, hope, and love she needs to
survive.

The Sweetness by Sande Boritz Berger. $16.95, 978-1-63152-907-8. A
compelling and powerful story of two girls—cousins living on separate
continents—whose strikingly different lives are forever changed when
the Nazis invade Vilna, Lithuania.

Tasa's Song by Linda Kass. $16.95, 978-1-63152-064-8. From a peace-
ful village in eastern Poland to a partitioned post-war Vienna, from a
promising childhood to a year living underground, *Tasa's Song* celebrates
the bonds of love, the power of memory, the solace of music, and the
enduring strength of the human spirit.